Where the Road Leads Us

ALSO BY ROBIN REUL

My Kind of Crazy

Where the Road Leads Us

ROBIN REUL

sourcebooks
fire

Published by Sourcebooks Fire, an imprint of Sourcebooks
P.O. Box 4410, Naperville, Illinois 60567-4410
(630) 961-3900
sourcebooks.com

[Library of Congress Cataloging-in-Publication Data]

Printed and bound in [XXXX].
XX 10 9 8 7 6 5 4 3 2 1

This one's for you, Dad

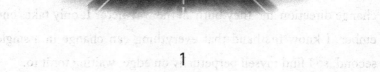

1
JACK

FRIDAY, JUNE 4, 6:42 A.M.

The simultaneous occurrence of my eighteenth birthday and my last day of high school arrives with zero fanfare. I should be excited on both counts, but instead I'm lying awake in bed, staring at the ceiling like I've been doing since four a.m., fighting off a panic attack. I feel as if I'm held together with off-brand masking tape.

The rising sun pierces through a slat in my shutters directly into my eyes. I have to get up soon anyway, so I drag myself out of bed to open the window. I'm greeted by a brown mushroom cloud of smoke rising from the horizon. The hazards of living in Southern California; if it's not earthquakes, it's wildfires. This one looks pretty bad. And naturally, my mother isn't even here. If my high school graduation and eighteenth birthday weren't important enough to make her leave her book tour and come home, wildfires burning out of control with zero percent containment sure aren't going to.

The winds haven't stopped blowing for three straight days. A grayish-brown haze permeates everything. I'm anxious about leaving for New York tomorrow while this is going on. Big fires like this never get put out that quickly. Often, they jump highways and weave through canyons until they burn all the way down to the ocean, destroying everything in their path. What if the winds change direction and they burn all the way here? It only takes one ember. I know firsthand that everything can change in a single second, so I find myself perpetually on edge, waiting for it to.

"The Imperial Death March"—my mother's ringtone— pierces the early morning silence, jarring me out of my thought spiral. I'm tempted to let it roll to voicemail, but I pick it up at the last possible second.

"Hey, Mom." I lie back down and rub at my eyes.

"Hi, babe! I wanted to make sure I got to wish you a happy birthday and happy graduation because my schedule is so packed today." Bingo. Less than three seconds to make it all about her. That might be a record. She barely takes a breath before she launches into her litany. "I have *Good Morning America* and then that *Vanity Fair* thing in the afternoon, and then my agent is meeting me for drinks to talk about the next two books. Trust me, I'd *much* rather be there to celebrate and see you get your diploma, but I know you understand. I'll make it up to you when I see you on Monday in New York, I promise. I'll take you to Jean-Gorges for dinner."

And then to someone in the room she says, "Jesus, what does

a girl have to do to get a latte around here?" It's followed by her lilting laugh. It's fake. I've actually heard her practicing it.

"No worries. It's only a once-in-a-lifetime opportunity," I say, half joking.

"Exactly." She thinks I'm talking about her and the press tour she's on, when I'm actually talking about me. My mother, gotta love her, is completely self-absorbed. "How are you holding up otherwise? The news makes it look like the whole city is on fire. Is it smoky where we live? Make sure you don't leave any windows open. I dread what the pool is going to look like from the ash."

I want to tell her how much it sucks that Dad isn't here, or my brother Alex, and that most of the time, it seems like she doesn't want to be here either. Or that sometimes I hold my breath until it feels like my lungs will burst and that some days, I wish they would.

But we don't have those sorts of conversations. We never have. She pays my therapist Carole to listen to that stuff. And her question was rhetorical. So I stick to my standard response. "Fine." It's easier that way.

"Good. Jesus, my kid is graduating, and he can vote now. I feel so old. It seems like I should impart some parental wisdom or something."

I sigh and watch my ceiling fan spin in slow circles. This is more for her benefit than it is for mine. "Imparting wisdom seems reasonable given the circumstances."

She's ready. I can almost picture her scrawling it on her hotel bar napkin last night in anticipation. "Life is always going to have highs and lows, so don't focus on the parts you can't change.

Today is the beginning of the next chapter of your life. It's a blank page, and you've got the pen."

"You sound like you're reading the Google search results for self-empowerment memes. Or the conclusion of a keynote."

She laughs. "It's actually from Chapter Sixteen in my latest book, but it's good, right? It's a hundred percent applicable for you."

It's not though. I have never felt less like I was holding the pen.

"People pay twenty-eight dollars a pop for that knowledge because they know it's the truth. How lucky are you that you get this sage wisdom for free?"

I roll on to my side and close my eyes. "So lucky."

Someone talks in the background, and I can tell Mom is distracted because she misses the sarcasm in my voice. "Anyway, you all packed for tomorrow?"

No.

"Almost."

My stomach tightens. I landed a paid summer internship in New York before I start at Columbia this fall. I'm booked to leave on a red-eye tomorrow night. I've gotten as far as putting the empty suitcases in my room.

"Great. I'm busy all weekend with a million events, so I'll see you Monday. The hotel is prepaid, so order some room service and check out the city—have an adventure—and I'll probably be there around four or five on Monday after the signing, unless I get held up."

She always gets held up. She won't be there until at least seven thirty because she'll end up going out for drinks afterward, and we both know it.

"Sounds good."

A production assistant tells Mom she is needed on set now, which is fine because I need to hop in the shower and get ready. Natasha and Ajay should be here soon.

I tense up and sigh deeply, thinking about Natasha. Ever since college decisions were released and I got into Columbia University—Natasha's dream school—and she didn't, the vibe has been off between us, and it's been amplifying my stress about leaving. She'll only be a few hours away at Tufts just outside Boston, so at least our relationship won't be too long distance. I'm hopeful once we get through the summer and settle into our new routines at college, we'll be fine.

When Natasha's fire-engine-red Kia Soul pulls up in front of my house, I put on a smile. I try to take a deep breath to recalibrate myself, but the air smells like every ashtray in every casino in Vegas combined.

Ajay is already in the front seat, so I climb into the back. This morning he's dressed like a cross between a frat boy and the manager of a Best Buy, with his royal blue polo, black, belted pants, omnipresent flip-flops, and black hair gelled to perfection underneath a backward Stanford ball cap. He puts his bare feet up on the dashboard that I helped Natasha sticker bomb two years ago when she got the car.

"I hope they don't run out of hash browns," Ajay says, his brows forming a V.

"Hey!" She swats his feet down. "What is your obsession with these hash browns?"

"Seriously, that happened to me once there. How do you

- - 5 - -

run out of potatoes at a breakfast restaurant? I felt like I was in nineteenth-century Ireland."

Neither of them wishes me a happy birthday. I wonder if they've forgotten.

"I need some coffee on an IV drip," I say and yawn, hoping there is enough caffeine for this day.

It only takes one loose thread to unravel an entire sweater. Every object—animate or inanimate—has a saturation level, a boiling point, a limit to its physical or mental capacity or capability. As I press my head into the seat back, I consider that this may be what it feels like to be approaching mine.

My eyes snag on the constellation of freckles on Natasha's right arm shaped like an upside-down heart. A month ago—on the same day as the spring concert—she was bored and drew on herself, connecting the dots with a black Sharpie. Outlined like that, the end result looked like a poorly inked tattoo of a nutsack. Naturally, it wouldn't wash off, and our band director was super pissed, because the concert dresses are short-sleeved. I can't help but smile thinking about it.

"Did I tell you that Nikul's friend ate an entire bowl of cannabis gummies at a party and they found him asleep in a tree at the center of campus?" Ajay's older brother Nikul goes to Stanford, where Ajay's heading too. He often regales us with wild tales from his brother's college life. Ajay will take ten minutes to tell a two-second story if you let him, so I pretend like I'm listening, but in actuality I'm stealing glances at Natasha as she drives.

She looks very "signature Natasha" today, with her heart-shaped mirrored sunglasses, bright-red lipstick, and mismatched patterned socks peeking out of her beloved, silver, thrift store Doc Martens that, legend has it, were donated by Frances Bean Cobain, as in the late Kurt's daughter. I'm pretty sure the thrift store dude was bullshitting her, but this *is* LA, so you never know. Her copper curls are pulled into a high ponytail, and small, silver earrings in the shape of arrows dangle from her ears.

Natasha catches me looking at her in the rearview mirror, and we exchange tight-lipped smiles. She drives over a pothole, and the car suddenly dips down to the right. The force of it smacks my head sideways against the window. I cry out in surprise and pain.

Natasha pulls the car over and whirls around, apologetic, frantic, and wide-eyed. "Oh, jeez, Jack, you're bleeding. Try not to get it on the seat," she says and reaches for a crumpled fast food napkin stuffed in the cup holder. Crumbs tumble to the car floor as she holds it out to me. "Wow, that's a lot of blood. I am *so* sorry."

She looks pretty worried. Something warm and wet cascades down my cheek. I touch my face, and my finger comes away red.

"No worries. You can't help failing infrastructure," I say, pressing the napkin against the source. I unbuckle myself, scoot to the center seat, and lean forward to look at the damage in the rearview mirror. "It's superficial. Facial injuries can sometimes bleed a lot because there are so many blood vessels close to the skin."

"You're going to have to Photoshop your wound out of your graduation picture," she says and covers her mouth with her hand.

"I'm pretty sure I'll live, though I might need a second napkin."

"Tell people you got in a knife fight or something," Ajay jokes as he digs out his wallet and hands me a Band-Aid. He is the kind of the guy who carries one around just in case because you never know, which only adds to his charm. My dad always admired his preparedness. "Girls dig a guy with a scar and a story."

"That'll last about five seconds," she says and grabs her purse from the floor and digs through it then extracts a tampon. She rips the plastic wrapper with her teeth and hands it to me by the string. "Here, hold this to your head with pressure. It's super absorbency."

To her credit, it makes perfect sense, which is how I end up holding a tampon against my head for the rest of the drive to the restaurant.

Fifteen minutes later, the three of us are crammed into a booth at the Pancake Shack—the gold standard by which all other pancake restaurants should be judged; if you can imagine it, they can put it on a pancake, whether it belongs there or not. We discovered it last year, and we've come here a few times, though never during the week. It's fairly empty compared to the weekends, when there's a line out the door.

Ajay holds up his mug of coffee to make a toast. "Happy birthday to Jack and happy get-the-hell-out-of-high-school day to us all."

"Cheers to that," Natasha says as we clink our mugs together. So she does remember, though she hasn't made a big deal about it being my birthday like she has in the past. It might as well be any other day. I chalk it up to the fact that she's focused on graduation happening and her speech, which I know she's nervous about delivering. She's rewritten it six times.

"And to Subliminal Sunrise, which will always remain the greatest '80s cover band in history," Ajay adds.

"Yessss," I say. We clink mugs again.

Subliminal Sunrise was the unfortunate byproduct of a truly terrible idea we had a couple of years ago to form an '80s cover band for the school talent show. We had T-shirts made. I still wear mine all the time. We played a kickass version of Duran Duran's "Hungry Like the Wolf" and immediately disbanded after taking third place.

I order the Happy Face—a birthday-cake-flavored pancake stack with extra whipped cream and a triple side of hash browns. At Pancake Shack, there's a silent understanding that aging is mandatory, but maturity is optional.

"Are you guys excited for Carly Ginsburg's party tonight?" Natasha asks, adding another creamer to her coffee.

"Isn't it basically going to be a bunch of wasted, half-naked, entitled assholes playing loud music, hooking up, and grinding against each other in the dark?" I ask.

"Exactly," Ajay says with a grin.

Confession: none of us have ever been to a "real" high school party. Not the kind Carly Ginsburg throws, the kind involving red cups and bad decisions. I want to go, mostly out of curiosity, but I also don't really care. I unfold my napkin and lay it across my lap. "We could do something else. I mean—I'm also fine with kicking back and watching a movie and ordering some food or something," I suggest, half hoping they'll take me up on it.

Natasha immediately dismisses the idea. "Are you *kidding*? I am *not* going to spend grad night holed up watching Netflix and eating pizza like every other weekend of my high school existence."

The way she says it makes it sound like a bad thing. I don't let myself get worked up. Regardless that it's my birthday and last night in LA, she's entitled to want to go to the party. It's not like we're never going to see each other again; we'll be alternating weekend visits. It's just crappy timing that this is all happening at once.

Ajay's eyes light up with excitement. "I've heard Carly's house is off the hook. All the rooms have themes, and there are hidden passageways."

"I once heard her dad has an actual Batmobile," Natasha says as I turn my head and glance toward the back of the restaurant.

There's a girl sitting by herself in the far booth near the bathrooms. Her nose is buried in a well-worn copy of *Hitchhiker's Guide to The Galaxy*, which happens to be my absolute favorite book of all time. I've seriously read it a dozen times. It's the book that made me want to be a writer. The idea of making shit up and getting paid for it always seemed like the ultimate dream job to me, but my parents were not behind creative writing as a college major, let alone a career. They're all about practicality, job security, and the ability to pay rent.

The girl's hair is short and purple and spiky, which makes her ice-blue eyes stand out even from this distance, and she's wearing a chunky, light-gray sweater despite it being nearly eighty degrees outside. Her ears have multiple piercings from lobe to helix. Her face is familiar, in the same way that a person you've seen a million times but don't actually know can look familiar. As if sensing my gaze, she looks up and locks eyes with me. I quickly turn away.

"We're going together, right?" Ajay asks. "I can pick everyone up."

I don't want to be tied to anyone else's schedule. I make up some excuse about needing to finish packing and having to be up early and how I'll meet them there. I purposely don't look at Natasha for fear I might see she's visibly relieved.

After draining two cups of coffee in record time, Ajay excuses himself to use the bathroom, and Natasha and I are finally alone. Something seems off about her, more so than usual.

"Are you okay?" I ask.

She finally looks at me. "Yeah. Why wouldn't I be okay?"

"I don't know. You're acting kind of weird."

"Why? Because I don't want to stay home and watch movies instead of go to a party?"

"No." I sigh. "Never mind. It's fine."

"Well, obviously it's not fine, or you wouldn't be saying that," she huffs.

I angle myself toward her slightly. "I feel like I'm missing something here. Did I do something?"

"I don't want to get into this right now."

"Into what? So obviously there *is* something."

She raises her eyebrows. "Can we talk about this later please?"

"Why can't we talk about it now?" I ask.

"Because."

"Because why?" She doesn't answer me and closes her eyes. "What is going on, Natasha?"

"Please stop."

I know I'm poking the bear at this point, but I can't help it. "No. I want to know what's up."

She sighs deeply and opens her eyes, then looks directly into mine. "I want to break up, Jack."

"What?"

"I've been thinking, Jack and—I think we should go back to being just friends."

I shouldn't be surprised. Things haven't felt the same between us for a while now. The reality is she probably would have done it a lot sooner, but she probably felt like she couldn't because I've been struggling with my dad's death since he passed away a little over a year ago. At least she cared enough to recognize the poor timing, but her obvious distance has in some ways been worse. I know my grief has been difficult for her to navigate. It never dawned on me that she might actually opt to let go.

"Wow," is all I can muster. I feel slightly shell-shocked.

She shakes her head, defensive. "See—this is why I didn't want to say anything. It wasn't supposed to be like this."

"Oh, so you've been planning this for a while then?"

Ajay is on his way back to the table from the bathroom. "I don't want to get into this now with Ajay here. We can talk later at school while we're setting up."

"Yeah, no sense in ruining breakfast, right?"

She ignores my obvious sarcasm and fakes a smile as Ajay returns to the table. Our server follows him with the pancakes, complete with a lit, rainbow-swirl candle shoved in the strawberry nose. Ajay sings "Happy Birthday" off-key and loud enough to attract the attention of some of the other patrons who smile and join in.

The collective noise becomes a muffled roar, as if I'm underwater. I pinch the fleshy part of my left palm below my thumb—something my therapist taught me to help ground myself when my anxiety builds—and try to act normal, whatever that is anymore.

I pretend to make a wish and blow, so as not to keep everyone waiting. But the truth is, I feel like it deserves some proper thought this year. I lick the whipped cream off the base of the candle and shove it in my pocket for later.

"Oh! I almost forgot!" Natasha roots in her purse and pulls out a small, red box tied with a silver bow. She puts it on the table in front of me.

"You didn't need to get me anything." She just broke up with me, but now she's giving me a birthday present?

"I got it a long time ago, actually. I couldn't return it." Her face is expressionless, her mouth a straight line. What a heartfelt gesture. I slide off the bow and open the lid of the box. Inside is a winking red-chili-pepper bottle cap opener that reads BITE ME. Natasha says, "It reminded me of my favorite dinner and movie night. And it's also a practical kitchen utensil."

Natasha, Ajay, and I did this thing where we'd watch a movie and eat food that reflected the cuisine of the city where the film took place. New Mexico Night was a standout, mostly because Ajay had some mock trial practice and couldn't be there. Natasha and I ordered in these amazing chicken burritos and marathoned all three *High School Musical* movies, which are set in Albuquerque, New Mexico, even though they were actually shot in Utah. It's also the night we first hooked up. The fact that her gift happens to reference that particular moment is ironic in light of recent events.

"In keeping with the practical theme," Ajay says as he slides an envelope across the table toward me and grins.

"What's this?" I am genuinely curious, because Ajay has never given me an actual present in our eight years of friendship.

"Best I could do with short notice," he says.

I tear off the end and give it a shake, dropping the contents into my palm—a single condom. But this one is special—its white packaging has a Pokémon ball on it and lettering that reads "Don't Catch 'Em All." I feel my cheeks flush red. It's not at all awkward or embarrassing to be sitting next to my suddenly ex-girlfriend holding a condom that I definitely won't be using with her. "And we wonder why Ajay is terminally single."

Ajay swigs the last of his coffee in one gulp and says, "Don't laugh. A condom is like a Swiss Army knife; it has multiple uses that don't involve sex. You can use it as a fishing lure, an ice pack, a jar opener, a water container. You can cut it up to make rubber bands, hair ties, make things waterproof, *and* it protects against STDs. It's my way of saying: may you be ready for anything life might throw your way."

I can't imagine what more life could throw my way at this point, but I thank him for it nonetheless. As I'm tucking it inside my wallet, Purple Hair Girl walks by our table. She totally sees me do it, and an amused smile flickers on her face as she passes. Even though I will never see her again, it bothers me that she's going to walk around thinking I'm one of those douchey guys who carries a condom around in his wallet desperately hoping for action.

2
HALLIE

FRIDAY, JUNE 4, 7:37 A.M.

My break is over. I dog-ear the page in my book and take one last sip of my coffee before heading back toward the kitchen. I'm über-self-conscious as I pass the front booth with the three teenagers seated in it. I recognize them from when I used to go to Madison High—two clean-cut guys and a girl with fiery red hair and a pinched expression, like someone who's lactose intolerant and discovered halfway through her soy pumpkin spice latte that it was mistakenly made with whole milk. Smart kids from the right zip code with ironclad futures who will probably never have to sacrifice anything or suffer a day in their entitled lives. I wonder if they even appreciate how lucky they've got it.

I'm pretty sure the guy on the end was in my creative writing class, although he looks taller, less pubescent, which makes sense since it's been a couple of years. What was his name? Jack? Jake? Definitely a monosyllabic name with a J. He seemed sort of interesting. Quiet. Cute. Nerdy in a cool way. His stories were funny. We weren't friends or anything; I doubt he'd even remember me. I look different now too.

I steal a glance as I pass their table and can't suppress a smile. Monosyllabic J is holding a condom package in his hand. He looks right at me and grins sheepishly, not so much with recognition as with embarrassment.

As soon as I set foot in the kitchen, Mom beelines toward me. She wipes whipped cream from her fingers on the front of her rust-colored apron. "Hallie, could you please prep the sandwich toppings for lunch and brew a fresh pot of decaf?"

She looks exhausted. The circles under her eyes are deep and purple. Her roots are white and in need of a touch-up, but she hasn't had time because she's been at the restaurant almost nonstop, especially since Dad had to take on a side job in the evenings to help keep things afloat. I've had to fill in more often.

In the kitchen, I dump the old coffee filter and add a new one, spooning the grounds from the industrial-size can of instant decaf into it. Through the pass window, I see Mom smiling at a guest as she takes his order, blissfully unaware of everything I'm dealing with. A wave of guilt washes over me. When she asked how things had gone at my appointment yesterday, I'd said *fine*. She didn't press for details because it was a routine follow-up. I've never been dishonest with her. I've never had a reason to be, but I reason with myself that I'm gifting us both another seventy-two hours of status quo before it's dismantled.

After the call came late yesterday afternoon, I went straight to my room, jammed my earbuds in, and cranked up my music. I logged on to the board to see if Owen was hanging out in the chat room. He always knows what to say to keep me from sinking too deep into the shadows. But then I saw his post, and it felt wrong to tell him. He has enough to think about right now without needing to hear my bullshit.

Owen Wilder has talked me off countless ledges. We've never met in real life, but our friendship is genuine. In some ways, it's *more* genuine. Friendships in real life tend to be way more complicated. But this one's complicated too because Owen is dying.

This weekend, specifically.

I've never actually known someone who died, unless you count my goldfish, Max. I won him at a carnival, and he lived for three years. He was like the Energizer Bunny of goldfish, and then one day, without warning, he leapt from his bowl and landed on the counter, where I found him the next morning—bone-dry, mouth wide open. Owen dying is way more intense, obviously, but at least he's had time to prepare—as much as anyone can for such a thing.

I pull out a head of romaine lettuce, a half dozen tomatoes, an onion, and a jar of pickles and lay them on the counter beside the cutting board. As I rinse and pat the lettuce and tomatoes dry, I think how despite his diagnosis, deep down, I believed Owen would be okay. And as long as he was okay, I would be okay too.

He's one of those people who are larger than life—so positive, able to find the good in anything and anyone to the point of being annoying. He likes to make people laugh, always trying to boost morale. He knows how his story ends, and yet he still talks about wanting to become a Broadway star and live in a brownstone adjacent to Central Park with his future husband and half a dozen French bulldog rescues.

Owen never stopped allowing himself to dream and make long-range plans, and that's something I still can't bring myself to do. And with good reason.

Last night Owen posted in the Updates thread that his health has taken a downturn, and he's decided it is time. He wants a celebration of his life that he can be part of, so he's throwing a party tomorrow and invited anyone who can make it.

I want to be there, of course, but there are some hiccups: (a) He lives in Oregon, and I'm in Los Angeles, and (b) the odds of my parents being down with me traveling by myself to another state to meet a dying boy I've befriended on the internet before he ends his life is less than zero. That blows way past their collective comfort zones.

And they don't even know about the call I received yesterday. Now that I'm eighteen, the doctors talk directly to me. That call has only pushed me to want to go. I'm tired of feeling like I have to ask permission from my parents or my doctors or the freaking universe to live my life. If my doctor can treat me like an adult, it seems like my parents should too. I don't have the luxury of time to make them comfortable with the idea of my going to Oregon.

By the time I'm done prepping and get everything into chilled metal bins for the lunch crowd, the three teenagers in the front booth are gone. Most likely on their way to graduation practice. I passed the digital signboard at the high school on my way in, and it said that was today. I already got my GED a few months ago, so I won't be there.

I also won't be spending my summer taking selfies at the beach with half a dozen of my closest friends or loading up a cart with cute dorm essentials; I won't be heading off to college in the fall. My parents long since burned through those savings.

I can accept it for myself, but it's the worst thing in the world knowing I robbed my little brother, Dylan, of that. He's such a smart kid. He doesn't deserve any of this.

Another server arrives, so Mom tells me I can leave. I take the bus home because I still don't have my license. Unheard of for most eighteen-year-olds, but I don't actually mind. I like the bus. I can be anybody on my way to anywhere, the same as everyone else. We're all background extras in each other's stories as we move collectively from one space to the next. It's a different experience every time.

At home, I anxiously check the message board for an update on Owen. I was nervous to look again while I was out in the world in case something had happened and I needed to fall apart. As I scan the recent posts, I realize I'm holding my breath.

Nothing.

Okay, that's actually a good sign. No news is good news.

My phone chirps with a text, and I nearly jump out of my seat. It's Lainie, this girl I know from a jewelry-making class and hang out with sometimes. She's going to her dad's beach house this weekend and wants to know if I'd like to come.

Lainie's cool. She doesn't ask a lot of questions. We mostly make jewelry, talk about movies we've seen lately—surface stuff like that. Before I got sick, I used to dream of becoming a professional jewelry designer, a true artisan who travels the world collecting precious stones that I handcraft into beautiful pieces to sell. After my diagnosis, I lost my passion for it. It seemed point-less to think about the future when I didn't even know if I'd have a place in it. Lainie's been trying to encourage me to get back into it. I've only recently made my first piece of jewelry—a brace-let—in nearly six months.

My parents would absolutely encourage me to go. It could be the *perfect* cover story. If they think I'm spending the weekend at Lainie's, I could go to Oregon and be back without them ever knowing I'd been gone.

I break it down in the most general terms to Lainie. I tell her I'm going to visit a friend but that my parents might not be cool with it because they can be overprotective. As usual, she doesn't ask for details, which I appreciate, and she agrees to cover for me on the off chance my parents call. We spend the next few minutes working out a plan, and then I'm online checking bus times because this is actually happening.

I'm really doing this.

There's a bus leaving at ten thirty this evening with open seats. If I travel overnight, I don't need a hotel. But I *do* need a credit card to buy a ticket. Fortunately, there are ways to navigate around that.

I tear around at the back of my closet until I unearth the Hello Kitty suitcase from Target that my grandmother sent me for Christmas three years ago. It still has the clearance tags on it. She's always sending me fun cat things because she knows I love them even though I can't have one because Dylan is allergic. I never imagined I'd actually have a use for it.

I don't need much, really. I'll only be gone for two days. I pull together an extra T-shirt, a hairbrush, clean socks, and underwear.

My eyes snag on the bottle of pills sitting on my desk. I hate the way the drug makes me feel, but I'm supposed to keep taking it every day. I pop open the cap, empty one into my hand and am about to swallow it down when I hear a noise in the other room.

Dylan's home. He calls out, "Hello?"

"Yeah—I'm here!" I yell. I quickly shove my half-packed suitcase in the closet and shut the door.

I find him in the kitchen pouring a glass of milk to go with a large stack of Chips Ahoy! cookies. He's at that totally awkward stage of being a thirteen-year-old boy where his voice cracks and his feet, arms, legs, and hands seem to be growing faster than the rest of his body. His sandy-colored hair hasn't seen a comb in a while, but it doesn't seem to bother him.

"Hey! How come you're home? No end-of-school pool party blowout bash where everyone gets hammered on Capri-Sun?" I kid.

He dunks a wedge of cookie in the milk. "Nope. They were going to Raging Waters."

I can hear the downward lilt in his tone that lets me know he's disappointed but isn't dwelling on it, because what's the point? He doesn't get to do a lot of the expensive stuff his friends do. He had to give up extracurriculars like karate and piano lessons, but he takes it all in stride and doesn't complain. I wish I could be more like him.

The thing is: he deserves to be celebrating with his friends at

Raging Waters, getting sunburned and eating overpriced food that gives them stomachaches, enjoying being a kid.

"You wanna play some Super Smash Bros.?" I offer. He'll totally kick my ass, and we both know it.

He bounds across the room to turn on the console and grabs the remotes.

"Challenge accepted. I'm Ike. And you're *not* playing as Kirby again."

"No fair. Kirby's my jam," I tell him as a grin spreads across his face. Kirby's defense mechanism is jumping high in the air, which allows him to avoid all conflict. He's like a metaphor for my life.

We spend the next hour playing and laughing, and it actually helps me forget about everything for a while. Then Mason, one of Dylan's friends from up the street, calls and asks him if he wants to come over and try some new game he just got for his Xbox, and Dylan's off.

I return to my closet and open the doors, half expecting to find that the suitcase is no longer there and is buried back in its original spot. But there it is, with its hot-pink wheels and handle and Hello Kitty's giant face on the side in a sea of glittery, hot-pink polka dots begging to hit the open road.

Gingerly, I put the suitcase back on my bed, slightly scared of it and all it represents. I pull out the envelope I keep buried at the bottom of my sock drawer where I've been saving up money from work. My intention was to use it for a trip someday, but someday isn't guaranteed, so I'm thinking that time is now. There's enough to cover the last-minute bus fare and a ride to the station but not much else. I tear through the house, digging through drawers and bottoms of purses for spare change, piling the contents on my bed to assess how much cash I have on hand. I'm definitely short of where I need to be. Where else can I find money fast?

That's when I remember the tin in my mom's closet. A few months ago, I went looking in there for a sweater I wanted to borrow, and I discovered a small cookie tin tucked away on the top shelf behind a shoebox. The light layer of dust on the lid indicated it hadn't been opened in some time, so I was curious. There was a wad of cash inside, at least five hundred dollars.

I reason it wouldn't be stealing exactly—more like borrowing it for a spell. And I'd give it all back.

I carefully wrangle the tin out of the closet and pop open the lid. The cash is still curled inside. I should leave some there so it's less noticeable that some of it is missing. I count off a hundred dollars, put the rest back in the tin, and restore it to its hiding place.

I immediately feel horrible for taking it, but I push the guilt aside as I add the money to the stash on my bed. I can't exactly pay for a bus ticket online in rolled nickels, and I'll only call attention to myself walking around with a giant pile of cash, so I opt to transform most of it into a Visa gift card at the 7–11 down the street.

There and back home in a flash, I log back on to the computer and buy the ticket.

In only a few hours, I'm leaving for Oregon to meet Owen and say goodbye.

Holy shiitake, I'm really doing this.

3
JACK

FRIDAY, JUNE 4, 10:12 A.M.

Setting up six hundred chairs in the blazing sun is exactly as unpleasant as it sounds. Even more unpleasant when it's spent listening to Natasha's sermon on why she broke up with me.

She tells me she read an article online that said most high school relationships don't survive the transition to college. "They make up thirty-two point five percent of long-distance relationships with minimal successful outcomes. There's an actual phenomenon called the Turkey Drop where most of them, if they haven't already, break up by Thanksgiving. I'm saving us from being an inevitable statistic."

"Wait—are you being serious right now?" I ask. We joke around in fake statistics like that sometimes. The annoyed expression on her face tells me she is. "Well, if you read it online it *must* be true. Although how do you explain the point five, exactly?"

She reaches for another white wooden chair from the pallet and unfolds it next to the one where I'm standing frozen in disbelief. She rationalizes, "I'm serious. Why risk ruining our friendship or the holidays? We're going to be so far apart anyway. It just makes sense."

"Far?" My eyebrows knit together in confusion. "What are you talking about? New York is like a four-hour train ride from Boston, or around an hour and a half if you fly. You could spend that long going two exits on the 405. It's totally doable."

She sighs deeply, presses her lips together, and then lays it on me. "I'm not going to Tufts, Jack. I'm staying here and going to UCLA."

"Come again?" Surely, I've misheard her. The plan was for us both to go to Columbia University, but then only I got in. Tufts University, just outside Boston, was her second choice. I knew she got into UCLA, but she never said one word about it being an option. In fact, she made a point of saying she wanted to get far away from her parents. For me, moving to New York seemed less overwhelming because I knew she'd be relatively nearby. "Are you seriously telling me this for the first time right now?"

"I decided I want to be in California." She can't even look me in the eye as she says it.

"You said you wanted to go as far away as humanly possible from California."

"I changed my mind."

"Apparently." What the actual fuck? One of the teachers gives me a dirty look for standing here chatting, so I reach for another chair and unfold it with more force than I intend, completing the row. "So basically, you've been lying since April when we committed to schools."

"I figured if I told you sooner, you'd freak out and make a whole big thing."

"Well, to be fair, it is kind of a big thing."

We each grab another chair and walk to place them behind the previous row. "I know, you're right, and I'm sorry. You were a great boyfriend; you didn't do anything wrong. It's just what I want."

Were a great boyfriend. I'm already in the past.

So this is how it ends. I suppose I knew it would eventually. I just didn't think it would be on my birthday while setting up chairs for graduation. She knows I won't make a scene here by reacting. It's obvious she's been waiting to get this off her chest for a while.

"Look," I say. "I know I haven't exactly been the life of the party these last few months, but I'm working on it. And I'm sorry if I've put too much of my shit on you."

She keeps two paces ahead of me back to the chairs. "Please don't apologize. It's not that. You are a wonderful guy, Jack, but—there are a million people we're both about to meet. How can we be naive enough to think that there is no one else out there? Don't we owe it to ourselves to make sure? To have all sorts of different experiences with different people? Allow for the unexpected? We're only in high school. And you can't honestly tell me you haven't felt like we've been drifting apart."

"Are these rhetorical questions, or are you expecting an answer?"

She stops, sighs, and turns to me, then squeezes my hand. "This is for the best. I think we should be real about this and end it before we let it go on too long like my parents did and we grow to hate and resent each other. I love you enough to let you go."

What the hell is that supposed to mean? "Thank you?"

"It actually *is* a compliment. It's just...I know you were—and still are—going through a lot, and I care about you. I didn't want to add to anything. But I also know I can't do this anymore."

So I was right; she didn't do it sooner because she'd felt sorry for me. Poor Jack with his dead father and his estranged, drug-addicted brother. I shouldn't have to convince her to want to be with me. "Wow. I'm sorry it's been such a chore for you."

"That's not what I mean. C'mon, Jack," she says. "I'm sorry. I don't want to hurt you. And I'm serious about wanting us to be friends. I mean—people say that, but I really mean it."

"Maybe we should shake on it." I'm being sarcastic, but she extends her hand and smiles.

And just like that, with a single shake, our five-year friendship and year-and-a-half-long relationship fizzles out like a 99 Cents Only Store firework. We can pretend that our friendship will go back to being what it was before we dated, but I'm sure the odds are slim, and not just because we've seen each other naked. There's undoubtedly some online statistic about that too.

Ajay comes bounding toward us, already finished helping set up. His eyes flick between both of us, reading the somber expressions on our faces.

"Uh-oh, you told him," he says.

"I told him," she replies.

"Wait—you mean—*you* knew?" I ask Ajay in disbelief, and my eyes shoot back to Natasha. "What the hell?"

"I needed someone to talk to, so I talked to Ajay," she says matter-of-factly, as if Ajay is in any way the sort of person she'd normally choose as a confidante, let alone that he's my best friend.

"Seriously? Because I think this seems like the sort of thing maybe *we* should have talked about instead." The fact that Ajay has kept her secret is nothing short of incredible, given who he is. I turn my attention back to him. "You're supposedly my best friend. Why wouldn't you have dropped a hint or something?"

"She told me not to say anything, and frankly, she scares me a little." He smiles sheepishly at Natasha and then says to me, "Hey, I played it completely Switzerland. I was merely a sounding board. Same as I'd be for you. I'm not taking sides. We're all friends here." He looks at us both. "We *are* all friends here, right?"

"Of course," she says. "Right, Jack?"

"We shook on it," I assure him, even though right now, honestly, I don't know what to call what we are. We're rebranding.

As we're leaving, he elbows me and asks quietly, "You okay?"

I shrug it off. "Yeah, of course. Absolutely."

"Cool. It's probably for the best."

I'm sure it probably is, but it only adds to the feeling that I'm slowly losing my grip on reality.

Back home, I take a second shower. As I stand there letting the hot water beat down on my sunburned neck, I think to myself that every decision I've ever made has led to this very minute. Changing a single variable might have changed the outcome, and my life could be completely different right now. Would I make all the same choices I've made if given the ability to go back and do it all over again? Definitely not.

Everything I've done in my life up until this point has been about trying to impress other people or make them happy: my family, my teachers, colleges, friends, Natasha. I needed their approval. But the truth is none of them know the first thing about what's really going on inside my head. Not even my therapist, Carole. I've never felt comfortable being totally honest because I always worried she'd tell my Mom what I was saying, or she'd think less of me if she knew what I was really thinking.

When you're smart, people put all these expectations on you. It's a lot to live up to. What is my obligation to measure up to someone else's definition of succeeding and reaching my potential? What does anyone truly owe anyone else?

While I'm getting dressed after my shower, I steal a glance at the two empty Costco standard-issue black rolling suitcases by the side of my desk waiting to be packed.

What would happen if I didn't go?

Seriously though—would the world end? Or would it be more like Maps when I miss the turn and it automatically recalculates my route?

Would I be making the biggest mistake of my life or the best decision?

I start to feel slightly nauseous and light-headed. My heartbeat quickens, and beads of sweat sprout on my upper lip—the beginnings of a panic attack coming on.

When they first started happening after Dad passed away, I thought I was dying. Now I recognize the early symptoms and start to dial myself back. I take a deep breath like Carole showed me—hold it to the count of five and exhale slowly for five then repeat the cycle four more times. Proper breathing technique is key to keeping calm and in control. Mindful meditative breathing has been proven to trigger physio-biological reactions throughout the body that affect every single cell.

And that's not a bunch of spiritual crap from my mother's *New York Times* bestselling self-help book *Love Your Vagina, Love Yourself* in which she discusses how a woman's relationship with her vagina sets the tone for her self-worth; it's actual science. That shit really helps.

When I'm ready, I grab the first suitcase and open it on my bed. It's like a giant, cavernous pit waiting to be filled. I basically have to fit my life into two bags and a carry-on since I won't be coming back here. I opt not to bring much of anything personal, mostly packing clothes. The posters on my walls and the pictures pinned to the corkboard above my desk already feel like they're from a different life, a different version of me.

As I'm about to zip the first case closed, my eyes snag on the photo by my bed of my dad and me. We were at the beach when I was around eight or so. His eyes are hidden by aviator sunglasses and his navy Columbia University ball cap is askew on his head, damp with surf. He's holding me in his arms, threatening to throw me in the ocean and feed me to the sharks, and we're both laughing. I decide to bring it with me and carefully nestle it inside a sweatshirt.

Dad used to wear that cap all the time. What happened to it? My mother has long since given most of Dad's clothing away, but for some reason, I can't imagine she'd allow that to go. Suddenly, it becomes my mission to find it.

I head to my parents' bedroom and burrow in their walk-in closet. I check drawers and look under the bed and even in the bathroom cabinets, but there's barely any sign my dad was once here. Not even an old toothbrush.

There's one other place it could be.

I wander down the hall to my dad's home office. The door is shut tight like a tomb. Even now, after all this time, entering what was once his private, off-limits space makes me feel as if I'm trespassing. Inside, everything is exactly as he left it.

It makes me sad to come in here. I look around at all his books, framed degrees, and awards, my eyes settling on an ancient family photo propped on the credenza by the window. All four of us in the same place together, something impossible to recreate ever again. I run my finger over the edge of the frame, and a thin layer of gray dust coats the tip of my finger.

I sit down in his high-backed, black leather desk chair and spin around in it once like he used to tell me not to when I was a kid. I shut my eyes and breathe in deeply, hoping to find a hint of his aftershave trapped here after all this time, but it just smells stale, like a place that's been undisturbed for a long while.

My dad will never sit at this desk again. It's surreal. He'll never know what I end up doing with my life, who I end up marrying, or meet his future grandkids. He won't be there to give unsolicited life advice and slip me an extra twenty dollars when I need it or go on a hike with me or grab breakfast at some dive or visit me at college.

I pull open the drawer on the left, anxious to resume my search for the cap and get out of here. It's filled with some pens and a jumble of receipts, the thermal paper so faded, it's impossible to make out where they're from or why he might have saved them. I tug on the drawer to the right, but it's locked. I check the surface of the desk for the key but don't find anything. I walk back to the built-in bookcase and run my hands over the tops of the book spines and then stumble upon it hidden underneath an oversize rook bookend.

I sit back down and hurriedly jam the key in the lock. It easily gives way. There, sitting right on top, is the faded navy-blue ball cap I've been looking for. I'm so relieved to have found it.

As I place it on my head, a surge of grief courses through me, settling like a boulder on my chest. The cap fits perfectly, no adjustment required, almost as if it was waiting for me. I feel like he'd want me to have this, that had he been here, he might have even given it to me as a parting gift before I left.

I return my attention to the open drawer, discovering the rest of the contents are uneventful—more pens, a file folder filled with patient notes and assorted correspondence, a cheap pair of drugstore reading glasses. I reach down deeper toward the bottom, lifting the other papers out of the way until my hand grazes an envelope that catches my eye. I pull it out, and my stomach drops. It's addressed to my brother, Alex, from dad, at a street address in San Francisco that I don't recognize, stamped but unsent.

This means my father obviously lied to me when he said he didn't know where Alex was. Which means there's a strong probability that my mother knew too, and she probably made Alex aware of Dad's death. She must not be aware of the letter though, because if she'd found it as I had, it definitely wouldn't be sealed. Why would they lie to me? Why would he hide the letter from either of us? Dad's the one who kicked Alex out. And why didn't he mail it?

Seeing Alex's name adds to the heaviness in my chest. I miss my brother. When he was around, everything was chaotic and messy and tense, but at least we were a family and I felt like part of something. The five-and-a-half-year age gap between us was like a chasm when I was younger. I didn't understand all that he was going through. He was always real with me and spoke the truth with no filter. For all the horrible things that had happened, he was his own person, and that was something I admired and wished I could emulate.

When Alex left and cut off communication with me, I was angry at first, but then anger gave way to an emptiness I haven't been able to remedy. Grieving someone who is still alive is more confusing than grieving someone who's dead, but it's no less intense. Most days I manage to block it out, but right now it's as if a scab has been ripped off.

I take the letter back to my room and tear it open. It's dated a week before Dad died. When I'm done reading it, it feels like someone has taken my brain and shaken it like a snow globe. It's as if I've intruded on a private conversation. My dad was clearly hurting over everything that happened between them. He apologized for it and told Alex it was the hardest choice he ever had to make and asked his forgiveness. And yet, he never mailed it. Given how bad things were between them, it wasn't entirely a surprise Alex didn't show up for the funeral, though I half expected him to come waltzing in wasted to spite my parents and get the last word. But if he'd gotten this letter—would it have changed things?

I look up and spot the clock on my night table. *Shit!* It's already three fifteen. Graduation starts in forty-five minutes. I stuff the letter into my backpack for safekeeping and then break the sound barrier driving to the high school. I wonder if Natasha has a statistic for how many valedictorians have been late to their graduation.

4
JACK

The faculty does *not* look happy as they usher me toward the sea of white folding chairs I helped place six hours ago on the football field. "Excuse me, pardon me," I say as I hurriedly nudge past the knees of the students in my row.

Ten minutes later, I'm delivering my valedictorian speech to a sea of glazed expressions impatient to get on with the main event. I get through most of it and then, out of nowhere, a red dragonfly buzzes in front of me and lands on the lectern for a second before taking off again. It distracts me.

Ever since my dad died, I see dragonflies all the time. Perhaps I did before, but I never noticed them the way I do now. Every time one appears, I can't help but feel like it's my dad saying hello and letting me know he's still with me. Seeing one today, when I feel so completely alone, takes my breath away.

I clear my throat and try to recalibrate my focus back to finishing my speech, but my mind is suddenly blank. I look around nervously at the crowd, mentally rewinding to the last thing I said, but the words aren't there. It's like looking at an empty screen.

Don't panic, don't panic, don't panic.

The audience must mistake my deafening silence for my having finished speaking, and they erupt into applause. I go with it and exit the stage. I get a few curious looks as I walk back toward my seat. As soon as the next speaker begins, I am forgotten. I look around at my fellow students and wonder how long it will be until we forget each other's names. The likelihood is I will never see 99 percent of them again.

When they start handing out diplomas, I note the cheers from the crowd as each name is called. You can tell who was popular, whose entire family showed up. When it's my turn, a smattering of whoops and applause erupts from the faculty and kids who know me, but otherwise the stands are quiet.

Afterward, I weave through the crowd in search of Ajay. Natasha appears behind him. Ajay shoves his iPhone in our faces. "C'mon, guys, obligatory graduation selfie for posterity."

"If we're all in it, isn't that an us-ie?" I ask.

Ajay snaps the picture, and then shows it to us. Half of Ajay's face is cut off and my eyes are mid-blink and my mouth is open midsentence, making me look drunk, but Natasha is perfect, of course. Her face lights up with delight. "Oh my god, I love it! Post it and tag me," she says.

"Dude, there's Matt Phillips!" Ajay bellows with excitement. Matt turns and lights up when he sees Ajay standing there as well. Ajay turns to us. "I have to give Matty some love." And then he is swallowed into the sea of blue robes, and now it's just Natasha and me standing there.

"My money's on Ajay getting lucky at the party tonight," Natasha says, putting her hand on her brow to shield her eyes from the sun, looking in the general direction Ajay went. "In fact, I predict Ajay gets the prom queen pregnant. In Carly Ginsburg's dad's Batmobile. You're gonna be like 'Natasha totally called that.'"

"That's not even the most impossible part of that scenario. The prom queen is already pregnant," I remind her. It's true.

"Right. I knew that." Natasha turns to me, and we share a laugh. And then it's awkward because neither of us knows what to say. She waves her hand behind her in the general vicinity of the stands. "I should probably go find my parents before there's bloodshed."

I nod. "Right." She hesitates for a second, and I catch an expression in her eyes as she remembers that I don't have anyone to meet up with, and then she takes a step closer and hugs me.

"Congratulations, Jack. I don't know how I would have gotten through these four years without you." She holds on a beat longer than she needs to, and then she pulls away, probably not wanting me to get the wrong idea. "I'll see you later?"

"Indeed."

She points to the cut on my forehead from this morning. "Glad that stopped bleeding. Doesn't look too bad, actually."

"Yes, I think the tampon helped. Sheer genius."

"Just doing my part to make sure you never forget me." She cracks a smile and flashes me the peace sign as she heads toward the stands.

"Like I ever could," I call after her in a playful way, but it's probably the truth because the cut and she are bound to leave a scar.

I have no idea what one wears to a rager. I opt for casual: black jeans, my Subliminal Sunrise tee, and a plain, black hoodie, which I leave unzipped. I slip on a pair of black-on-black Vans high-tops Natasha talked me into buying at the mall a few weeks ago.

"I'm leaving in a minute," I announce to no one, because it's not as if anyone will notice if I decide not to come home tonight. I could literally go anywhere and do anything.

It's grad night, my eighteenth birthday, I'm going to the party of the century on my last night in LA, I have a condom, a bottle opener, and a Target gift card, and I'm accountable to no one. It'd be a shame to waste that opportunity.

Before I go, I turn on the local news and listen for fire updates. It sounds like the wind has picked up and spot fires are starting in all new directions. A fire chief comments that they've not seen a fire this unpredictable since the Woolsey Fire several years ago. He talked about the importance of having a backpack filled with a day or two's worth of essentials ready to go in case you have to leave quickly.

He succeeds in amplifying my worry. Maybe I should pack one just in case and leave it in the car. What if this thing takes off while I'm at the party and I can't get back here for some reason? Or I'm told to evacuate in the middle of the night? What if my house burns down?

I'm letting myself get worked up. I know these are only possible scenarios, not probable ones. Still, like the fire chief says, it's good to be prepared. I grab my blue JanSport backpack where I stashed Dad's letter earlier. I don't bother taking it out. I add the picture of us from my nightstand and stuff the rest of the bag with basic essentials. I throw in my Moleskine writing journal, two pens (in case one runs out), and a pack of gum, and I'm ready to roll.

I shove my backpack in the trunk of my car and plug Carly's address into the GPS. It routes me to one of those giant mansions perched high in the Hollywood Hills. My family is well-off, but Carly's comes from a whole other stratosphere of wealth populated by celebrities, athletes, and heads of movie studios.

I take a cue from the abundance of cars and park on the street out front then walk through the open gates up the very long, steep driveway to Carly's house. There are statues of three Valkyries mounted over the front door. If the loud music spilling forth from inside isn't telltale enough, the condom someone hooked over one of the Valkyrie's wings confirms it's the right house. Her parents are definitely not home.

Natasha and Ajay are already somewhere inside the bowels of the estate, along with everyone from the senior class of my entire high school. The marble entryway is bigger than the entire computer lab at school. As I walk in, I overhear someone say that it's not even fully dark yet and someone has already barfed inside Carly's dad's barbecue.

I carve my way awkwardly through a sea of semifamiliar faces and understand what it must feel like to be a salmon swimming upstream. The crowd moves me along to the back sliding glass doors that lead to a backyard the size of Disneyland. All these different groups of people coexisted in the same place for four years and may never have interacted with the exception of the occasional teacher-chosen lab partnering or group project—until tonight.

Natasha is sitting by the edge of the pool, and by *pool* I mean small lake with a waterfall and center island with bar. Her feet are dipped in up to her ankles. Sitting much closer to her than necessary is Cade Krentzman, this asshat from the baseball team. Natasha's laughing it up at something he's saying, and he scoots even closer to her. He puts his hand on her lower back with a certain familiarity that makes me wonder if it might not be the first time. I hang back on the patio behind a potted palm and watch them for a minute.

Cade reaches behind him and takes a drink from a red cup he has there, his eyes scanning the party before settling back on her like she's prey. She's probably the only girl in our high school he hasn't slept with yet. Would she actually consider hooking up with this jerk?

Reality check: I have no claim on her. She can hook up with anyone she wants to, but it doesn't mean I have to watch.

I go back inside to look for Ajay, but I only get about two inches over the threshold when arms loop around my neck, and I stumble forward as a sloppy, wet kiss is planted on my cheek. I turn my head and there, practically touching noses with me, is Carly Ginsburg.

The way she's slightly swaying betrays that she's definitely indulged in some underage drinking. Her sheer, white top emblazoned with BITCH cuts off right above her navel, and I can see the outline of her black bra underneath.

"Heeeeey, Jake, right? Aren't you like...going to Columbia?" She draws out the *uhh* and because her face is so close, I can smell whatever fruity drink she's had too much of on her breath. She laughs at her own joke. Until the invite, I didn't even know Carly Ginsburg knew my name, let alone my academic plans.

"It's Jack, actually. And guilty as charged," I reply with an awkward smile. It doesn't take a rocket scientist to see that she's totally wasted.

Her eyes get wide as saucers, and she says louder than necessary, "Oh my *god*, wait—isn't your mom *Dr. Suzanne Freeman?* Like as in the famous *sex* therapist to the stars?"

Ugh. "Yeah, she is."

I smile awkwardly as she gives me the once-over like I'm a dessert she's considering from a display case.

"My mother *fucking loves* her. Keeps her book on her nightstand. If you want, I could show you." She smiles suggestively. Honestly, I'd rather see her dad's Batmobile. Someone bumps her as they pass, and it throws her off-balance and straight into my receiving arms.

"Whoa, there. You okay?" I say as Carly steadies herself with one hand on my shoulder.

She leans in close to my ear and whispers, "I think smart guys are hot." She bites at the air as she says the letter *t*. As I struggle to come up with a witty response to that, Drinkerbell's attention is diverted as two other guys walk in the front door. She pounces on them without so much as a goodbye. I turn to look back toward the pool. Natasha and Cade aren't sitting there anymore.

I wander outside and find a quiet vantage point to take in the scene inside a gazebo adorned with little twinkling white lights. People are taking turns going down the waterslide fully clothed, red cups of beer in hand. The music is loud, and everywhere, people are grinding up against each other, dancing and laughing. There's a cutthroat game of beer pong happening on the patio. Not my scene.

I hear Natasha's voice over my shoulder. "This place is a serious dump."

I turn toward her. Thankfully, she's solo. "The worst."

She joins me under the gazebo, her flip-flops in one hand and a red cup in the other. Is she actually drinking beer? "I heard there's a live band coming later, and I don't think it's the kind with a woodwind section. They've headlined at the Viper Room. And... wait for it...she's having real snow delivered at midnight."

"Seriously?"

She shakes her head and surveys the scene. "And get this: Cade Krentzman, who never gave me the time of day until he knew he'd never have to see me again, was totally hitting on me and trying to get me drunk. He kept calling me Kylie."

Is she trying to make me jealous? I mean—why mention that if that's not the endgame? I won't give her the satisfaction. "Yeah, well, Carly Ginsburg just offered me a private tour of her mother's bedroom," I say, and I'm not even lying. "So, where's Cade now? How'd you shake him finally?"

"I told him I had herpes, and it's probably better that I don't share his cup."

I can't help but crack a smile.

"Have you seen Ajay?" I dig my hands in my pockets and look around for him.

"Somebody told him about a free game room downstairs, so that's all he had to hear."

Not gonna lie: that gets my blood pumping too. As if on cue, Ajay comes beelining for me out of nowhere, an all-business expression on his face. He ignores Natasha altogether, looks me right in the eye, and rests both his hands on my shoulders as if he's about to deliver life-changing news. "What if I told you that downstairs, in this very house, there is an actual 1990 Williams Funhouse pinball machine and it is wired for unlimited play?"

"I'd say don't tease." Fun fact: I have always aspired to have my own pinball machine. I have a minor obsession with them. I find them fascinating, from the game play to the physics. My dad introduced me to them. We used to go to arcades and play for hours when I was a kid. In my opinion, the ability to play limitless pinball at will is truly the measure of living one's best life. I've never seen an actual Funhouse machine in person.

"Oh—you know I would never tease about pinball." Ajay loves it almost as much as I do.

"Why have I not befriended Carly Ginsburg sooner?"

"Follow me," he says and disappears into the crush of people clustered at the entrance to the patio.

"Excuse me, I actually have to see this," I explain to Natasha and keep my eyes trained on Ajay's head as I navigate my way through the house and down a flight of gray, shag carpeted stairs.

"Get ready to have your mind blown," Ajay warns as we spill

out into a room the size of a six-car garage lined wall to wall with nothing but video game machines. In the center of the room is a foosball table. It's like a true arcade, filled with an electronic chirping chorus of sound effects and music. It's downright epic. And there in the corner stands the crown jewel—a vintage 1990 Funhouse pinball machine, possibly the creepiest game on the planet.

I walk up to it and run my hand over its surface. Holy shit.

There it is: the score gangway, the trapdoor, the talking Chucky-esque doll head in the upper right-hand corner who heckles players and whose eyes follow the ball when different targets are hit.

Natasha eyes the freaky doll head. "That is truly the stuff of nightmares."

I disagree. "It's beautiful."

I pull back the plunger, set the first ball in motion, and enjoy a solid five minutes of game play before I drain my last one. I keep playing until enough of a crowd forms that I feel bad for monopolizing the machine, and I move on. It did not disappoint.

I spot an empty *Galaga* machine in the corner and smile. My high score of 278,330 is still on the machine at a pizza place off Sunset where Ajay and I like to go sometimes. He's on the other side of the room ensconced midgame, but Natasha is still standing next to me.

"*Galaga?*" I challenge her to a game as she follows me toward the machine.

"I'm not very good. I'll watch." She isn't that into video games.

"That's the beauty of these machines. You don't even have to be good per se—you just have to find out the secret." I press the button, and the familiar theme music starts up before launching into game play.

I teach her how it's done. An hour passes. The party upstairs is raging, and at some point, Ajay disappears upstairs with everyone to check out the band, but Natasha and I opt to stay down here. Now it's just the two of us.

I scan the room for a game I haven't yet played and try to act casual. I'm not sure why she wants to keep hanging out with me down here instead of at the party of the century upstairs. She follows me to the foosball table in the center of the room, and I challenge her to battle. She accepts.

"You don't have to stay down here, you know."

"I know. I want to," she tells me as I set the ball in motion. She sends it careening back at me, and it easily sails through my goal.

I put some shoulder into it, and it gets cutthroat for a minute as we go back and forth. Ultimately, I score.

She smirks. "Lucky shot."

"More like master skill."

Natasha proceeds to kick my ass for the rest of the match. She's laughing, gloating over her victory, and then she elbows me playfully. "I think I found my game."

"I was distracted."

"Face it—I have superior foosball skills. And you hate to lose. But you know you love me too much to stay mad at me," she jokes and bats her eyes.

"That's probably true," I say.

There's an obvious moment here where if she wanted to—if she felt that way about me at all still and had reconsidered—she could take it all back. But she doesn't. Instead, the expression on her face looks somewhere between sadness and cramps, and the words hang in the air between us like a piñata waiting to be cracked open.

"It's going to be weird driving by your house knowing you're not there," she says.

I can't take it anymore. I take my hands off the yellow, plastic foosball handles and look her in the eye across the table. "What are we doing?"

"What do you mean?"

"This." I motion with my hands between us. "This whole back and forth sort of flirting but not flirting even though we're broken up, hanging out with me instead of being upstairs at the party. It's really confusing."

"I still care about you too, Jack. I just don't want to be your girlfriend anymore."

Ouch.

It's suddenly claustrophobic being alone in this room with her, like she's hogging all the oxygen. I pull my phone out of my pocket and make a show of checking the time.

"*Holy* shit! I didn't realize how late it is."

Her brow forms a V. "It's like—barely nine-something at the most."

"I should go." I make my way toward the stairs. Natasha follows me up to the main floor and outside to the fresh air where I can breathe. I need to get in my car and drive away from here as soon as humanly possible.

"It's not even midnight. You can't leave before the snow," she reasons.

"I'll get plenty of snow in New York. I have to finish packing and get up early." It's a weak, transparent excuse because it's grad night and my birthday and no one would ever say *Screw this party in favor of packing and getting a good night's sleep.* But I really don't care if she's buying it.

"If you're leaving because of what just happened, please don't."

"I'm not."

I totally am, and we both know it.

"Okay, well can I walk you to your car at least?" she asks.

"Why?"

She looks at me incredulously. "Because you're leaving, and I'm not going to see you for a really long time." She says it more like a question.

We don't speak a single word all the way down the long, treelined driveway until we reach my car and discover that the assclowns parked on either end of my vehicle have left a scant two inches between our bumpers. Plus, we're on a hill, which makes it next to impossible to navigate out of the spot.

Are you fucking kidding me right now?

"No bueno." Natasha frowns, eyeing my predicament. "I can give you a ride home...let me text Ajay and let him know. I could take you to pick up your car in the morning before you go."

I hold up both my hands in surrender. "Just—stop, okay?"

"Stop what?"

"This. Being so nice to me like we didn't just break up."

"Okay. I'm only trying to help." She looks hurt, and naturally I feel guilty because this is what I do.

Every neuron in my brain starts firing at once. I don't want Natasha to drive me back home. I don't want to sit next to her in the car at this moment and act like everything is fine. I don't even know if I want to *go* home. It's early. But I *do* know I don't want to be here.

"I'm fine. I downloaded an app for a new ride hailing car service today—GoodCarma. I wanted to try them out anyway. I can come back for the car in the morning like you said."

I remember my backpack sitting in the trunk with the letter and my dad's picture and my stuff inside it. I don't want to leave it here, but I don't want her to see me grab it because she'll start asking questions, or worse, make fun of me for having brought it.

"I can totally drive you—it's not a problem," she offers again.

"No, I don't want you to," I say a little more forcefully than I intend, and she backs off at last. I try to smooth things over by adding, "Seriously—I can't have it on my conscience that I made you miss the party. It's the sort of thing where reputations are ruined, legends are born, and rumors are started, and you have a front row seat. One of us should represent."

I pull out my phone and make a show of thumbing through screens until I find the GoodCarma app.

"I can at least wait here with you until your ride comes," she offers and rests her hand on her hip. She cannot take a hint.

"No, I mean it, go back to Cade." I meant to say *the party*, but at that exact moment, a flash of Cade cozying up to her by the pool flits through my brain and the two words transpose themselves on the way out of my mouth. Natasha laughs and looks at me, confused.

"Why would I want to go back to *Cade*?"

"I don't know why I said that." I shake my head and decide if I'm opting for total humiliation, I might as well go all in. "Can I ask you something?"

"Sure."

"Can you can honestly stand in front of me right now and tell me there is absolutely nothing here?"

She breaks eye contact. It's only for a second, but it's enough to know I'm right. "Jack, don't."

I move my face to align with hers, so she has no choice but to look me in the eye.

"Why not? Simple yes or no question."

"It's complicated." She shakes her head and looks away. "You're the best guy I know."

"I'm not quite sure what to do with that."

"I told you. We're going to college. This is the time in our life to experiment and have all these new experiences. I don't want us to hold each other back from that."

"No—what you're saying is you don't want *me* to hold you back from that."

The noise of something crashing and breaking followed by "oh shit!" erupts from the house behind us. Our phones simultaneously buzz with a text from Ajay asking where we are because there's a guy from the swim team who is totally shitfaced and is about to demonstrate the three techniques for shotgunning a beer.

"Well, you definitely don't want to miss that. It sounds downright educational." I pat her once on the back like a coach would to a player after a good play. "Seriously, you should go back to the party. We're cool."

She sighs. "I can't *not* have things be okay with you."

She's used to getting what she wants, but for once, I can't offer that. "That's a double negative. Natasha—you can't drop a bomb like that and expect me to just dial it back to the way things used to be overnight. Give me some time to catch up, you know?"

She nods and gives me a quick hug. I stand there like I'm a freaking statue.

As she backs away from me, she opens and closes her hand like she's catching something in midair and crushing it—my heart maybe—then turns to walk back up the driveway.

So that was a shit show.

I'm grateful actually—she's made this so much easier. At least I leave knowing the truth of it. It's exactly what I should expect from a girl whose name spells Ah Satan backward.

I open the app and punch in Carly's address. It asks for a destination.

Where doesn't even matter right now as long as it's not here or home. I just need a place where I can chill for a few hours and not need to run a tab; the people-watching can keep me entertained, and I'm unlikely to see anyone I know until the party slows down and I can get my car out.

A car passes, and the headlights illuminate two statues of greyhounds on either side of the black, wrought iron gates of the property across the street. It makes me think of the logo on a Greyhound bus.

The bus station would be perfect. It's only about twenty or so minutes away—and *definitely* off the radar for anyone I'd know. I'm glad I thought to bring my journal and a pen at the last minute.

I can find a bench and brainstorm ideas for the choose-your-own-ending novel I've been writing.

What if I actually jumped on a bus and went somewhere?

My mother would freak. I'm so busy enjoying the image of her potential reaction that I accidentally select the GoodCarma pool option, but whatever. It's only a car ride. My phone battery descends a percent and dips into the red as I am informed that my driver, Oscar, will be here in five minutes and is driving a yellow Kia Soul. Natasha's car but in a different color. The universe is basically twisting the knife.

I grab my backpack out of the trunk and lean against my car, waiting. Moments later a sunshine yellow Kia Soul with the image of a giant smiling Buddha and the words *GoodCarma* written on it rolls up alongside me. The *o*'s in *Good* are both yin-yang symbols. The dent in the front bumper does little to instill confidence about my immediate safety.

The driver rolls down his passenger window, and the strains of Survivor's "Eye of the Tiger" spill out. He's in his midtwenties with perfectly tanned skin and a smile straight out of a toothpaste commercial. His dirty-blond hair is slicked back into a man bun, and he peers at me over the brim of his thick, black, plastic-rimmed, Clark Kent glasses. Quintessential aspiring actor who drives a car and is also a bartender at some trendy hole-in-the-wall in Los Feliz hoping to cover all his bases and get discovered. Typical LA. He asks in a thick Australian accent, "Are you Jack Freeman?"

I nod. "Oscar from GoodCarma?"

He smiles and winks at me. "The very same. Any bags, mate?" He jerks his thumb in the direction of the trunk.

"Just the backpack. I can keep it with me," I tell him. I make out the silhouette through the tinted glass of another passenger with short hair in the back. I open the door and duck my head as I climb in. As I'm looking down, I catch sight of my co-passenger's shoes—black flats embroidered with the face of a cat, its two triangle-shaped ears standing up. I look up, curious to see the sort of person over the age of five who would choose this sort of footwear, and my mouth falls open like a fish.

It's the girl—the one from this morning at the Pancake House, with the spiky, purple hair.

5
HALLIE

FRIDAY, JUNE 4, 9:10 P.M.

The car pulls up in front of a fancy house to pick up another passenger. I'm halfway to the bus station, and I'm getting cold feet. Literally, because I'm wearing the wrong shoes, and also because this is beyond irresponsible and a million and one things could go wrong.

And, to be honest, I'm kind of scared to see Owen. Aside from making me think about my own mortality when I'm feeling really vulnerable, can I honestly handle seeing him like that? Is this jumbled feeling in my gut just nerves or coming to my senses? There's only a small window to make a choice here, so I'm hoping the universe will magically deliver an answer.

The driver jumps out to help the person with their bag, and then the passenger door opens, and a guy climbs in. But not just any guy—*it's Monosyllabic J.*

His eyes dart to mine. They're this cool shade of grayish-blue like the ocean after a storm. He smiles and says something, but I can't hear him. I reach up and pull out my earbuds, raising my eyebrows. "Excuse me?"

"I said 'don't panic,'" he repeats with a crooked smile.

I can't say I've ever been greeted that way before. "Okay, I'll do my best."

He huffs a laugh, clarifying, "I was quoting a line from *Hitchhiker's Guide to the Galaxy.* I think I saw you this morning at The Pancake House reading it? I recognize your hair." He gestures to my head.

"Right." So he saw me too, but he doesn't seem to recognize me from school. I narrow my eyes. "Does that line usually work?"

"What?"

"I'm messing with you. You looked terrified there for a minute." I laugh and self-consciously curl a strand of hair behind my ear. "I remember. You're the birthday boy. I didn't recognize you at first without the condom in your hand."

I can see him blush even in this dim light. "It was a gift. And technically it isn't my birthday until eleven forty-seven, though I felt pretty confident the manager of the Pancake Shack wasn't gonna ask to see my birth certificate."

"Unlikely. She's pretty trusting." I smile knowingly. "I'm glad to hear that it's actually your birthday and you weren't just trying to get free pancakes. So many people have no problem lying for free stuff. There's a guy who comes in every week and orders something, eats half of it, sends it back, and orders toast. Of course, it gets taken off the bill, so all he ends up paying for is the toast. They still serve him every time, but of course they *know*."

"You go there every week?" he asks. "Impressive."

"I go there every *day*." I reach into my purse to pull out a stick of gum. I pop it in my mouth, wadding the foil wrapper into a ball and rolling it between my fingers. "My family owns it."

"Wow, that's cool. You must eat a lot of pancakes."

"Actually, I hate pancakes."

I take in the dream catcher hanging down from the rearview mirror along with a pair of red, fuzzy dice and a St. Christopher medallion. The two front cup holders are filled with piles of plastic-wrapped fortune cookies, like the kind they shove in your bag at Panda Express. In fact, I can make out the logo from here, and they *are* from Panda Express.

Oscar pipes up from the front seat as he pulls away from the curb. "Should take us about twenty-five minutes or so to get to the bus station. Traffic is light. I think a lot of people left on holiday early. Are you heading on holiday?"

Great. He's a talker. Monosyllabic J and I look at each other and smile awkwardly and then both start to respond at the same time. "No, go ahead," he apologizes.

I clear my throat. "Not exactly. I'm visiting a friend in Oregon, but it's not actually like a vacation or anything so..."

"I hear they get a lot of rain up there. I have a mate in Portland. He owns a company that makes custom-scented inserts for shoes. They can smell like anything you want—freshly baked cookies, pineapple, roses—I mean they literally extract the scent of roses from the petals and incorporate it into the material of the liner. It's fantastic. It's a Kickstarter thing right now, but it's genius. Who doesn't worry about foot odor, am I right?" Oscar fans his fingers in front of his nose for emphasis.

Aaaaaaand now we're all thinking about foot odor. I'd probably go with s'mores for my custom scent.

Monosyllabic J realizes we are both waiting for him to respond. "Ummmm—" he replies and then stops, either unsure how to answer or not wanting to.

Oscar laughs, shaking his hand in the air like he's erasing his words. "Sorry, sorry, I ask a lot of questions. I'm a Virgo. Virgos tend to be inquisitive. You can tell me to bugger off."

"No, it's okay." He seems to take a beat to consider it and then bobs his head. "I'm going to visit my brother in San Francisco."

"No kidding! I'm heading to San Francisco tomorrow myself," Oscar says with a smile. "Going to a wedding. My ex-girlfriend's, actually. Nikki. I'm about to stop her from making the mistake of her life."

"You're stopping the wedding?" I ask and then look at Monosyllabic J, mouth agape.

"If I play my cards right, there'll still be a wedding—just with a different groom." He smiles and puffs out his chest, clearly proud of his plan.

"You're breaking up her wedding *and* proposing to her? That's very romantic. I didn't think that kind of stuff happened in real life. At least—not to me." Spoken like the true cynic I've become. I used to believe in all that stuff. Funny how someone can be interested, but then they find out I have an incurable disease and quickly disappear.

Oscar looks back at me in the rearview mirror and shrugs. "You can't sit back and let life pass you by. Sometimes you gotta go all in, you know? Otherwise, what's the point? The timing sucks though. The weekends are my busiest time, and I'll miss the money."

"Bummer," Monosyllabic J replies with a nod. It falls quiet except for the sound of an old Katy Perry song turned low on the radio. He turns to me and says, "I once read that Douglas Adams came up with the title for *Hitchhiker's Guide to the Galaxy* while lying drunk in a field."

Color me impressed. The boy knows his Hitchhiker's trivia. "I heard that too. So, you're a fan?"

"It's definitely in my top five favorite books."

"Mine too." I feel a rush of excitement. The only other person I know who has ever read this series is Owen. My face lights up. "Arthur Dent's life is like the perfect metaphor for the human experience. We're *all* exactly like him: constantly traveling, roaming aimlessly about the universe, grappling to find our place in it."

"Except we're not hopping rides on stolen spaceships."

I angle myself toward him slightly. "Do you ever wonder if maybe we're just some alien teenager's science fair project gone rogue?"

"Only all the time." A huge grin spreads across his face. "Seriously, do I *know* you from somewhere? The fact that we've seen each other twice today...pretty weird coincidence, right?"

He doesn't remember. "I don't know...I think that sort of stuff probably happens all the time. Who knows how many times we've both been at the mall simultaneously or in the drive-through at Starbucks? Only today, we both happened to notice." I pull at a loose thread on the ripped knee of my black jeans. "Also, we were in the same creative writing elective sophomore year. With Dawson?"

I watch the recognition register as Oscar chuckles and says, "You two know each other? That's awesome!"

Jack shakes his head, studying me. "Wow. You look really—"

"Different?" I self-consciously run my fingers through my short, spiky, purple hair and wrinkle my nose, smiling.

"Yeah."

His comment shouldn't make me feel overly sensitive, but it does. I've changed so much from the girl I used to be that I've rendered myself nearly unrecognizable. I'm very aware I'm too thin, and I can't freaking wait until my hair grows out. Cutting it all off was a mistake, but I wanted to try something extreme and completely different in the hopes that afterward I would feel different. All it did was leave me with purple dye stains in my bathroom grout and ten inches less of hair. I wonder what he thought of me before and am sure he thinks I look worse now.

I can see he's worried that he's said the wrong thing. He quickly clarifies, "I don't mean that in a bad way or anything. Your hair was longer. Browner. Sorry—is browner even a word? I'm Jack Freeman by the way. I'm not usually this much of a babbling idiot."

Jack! He offers his hand and I shake it. "Hallie Baskin."

"Well, what are the odds of that? *Love* it!" Oscar looks back at us in the rearview mirror and shakes his head incredulously. We make small talk about meaningless stuff, and before we know it, we're turning into the bus station parking lot.

Oscar fishes his hand in his cup holder of fortune cookies and extends two back to us in his palm. "A token of thanks for choosing GoodCarma. Please recommend us to your friends."

I pluck mine from his hand then extract the cookie from the wrapper to read my fortune aloud. "'Accept the next proposition you hear.' Well, that could be dicey, couldn't it?"

Jack tears at his plastic wrapper with his teeth, bites the cookie in half, and pulls out his fortune. "Mine says, 'A ship in harbor is safe, but that's not why ships are built.'"

"Deep. I like it." I nod and pop a piece of cookie in my mouth.

As we get out of the car, Oscar jumps around to the trunk and hands me my Hello Kitty bag. Jack eyes my luggage choice and smiles as he hooks his backpack over his shoulder.

Oscar slams the trunk and then hands us each a business card. "Well, take care, mates. On behalf of GoodCarma, it was a pleasure meeting you both and driving you to your destination this evening. I hope you'll leave me a great review, and if you call me directly the next time you need a ride, I give a ten percent discount." He winks, gets back in his car and drives away.

As I turn to walk toward the terminal, it strikes me that perhaps this is the sign I've asked for: Jack showing up twice in a day and he just happens to be going to the bus station. It's a double coincidence and feels like a call to attention that I'm exactly where I'm supposed to be.

If there's one thing I've learned from reading a million books and streaming countless hours of Netflix over the past two years, it's that feeling scared almost always signals a chance to dig deep and find out what we're capable of.

Time to rise up.

6
JACK

By the time I turn around, Hallie's walking away. She doesn't even look back to see if I'm there.

Not that she should. It's just—the little bit of convo we had in the car seems enough to at least warrant a goodbye. We now exist to each other in a different way. Not exactly friends, but no longer total strangers.

I can't believe it's her.

Hallie Baskin. Two years ago, she had super long, straight brown hair, and her features seemed fuller, less severe and angular than she appears now. Still really pretty though.

I have two random memories of Hallie even though we've never spoken before this evening. The first is her reading a poem she'd written aloud to the class. It was a dark and depressing piece about betrayal and grief, and no one had known quite how to critique it when she'd finished because it was so obviously personal.

The other time was about a week later. She was yelling at some guy in the parking lot of 7–11. His bangs were streaked platinum blond, and he was wearing a red-and-black buffalo plaid jacket with a brown Sherpa collar that reminded me of Paul Bunyan. If he even went to our school, he *definitely* wasn't in AP classes. Hallie was going ballistic, fists clenched, screaming gutturally at him, "Why are you even *here*, Ryan? You're not *real* to me!" The guy stood there expressionless, unfazed by her meltdown.

I remember thinking whatever it was must have been pretty awful. I didn't want to get involved because I had no idea what I'd be getting in the middle of. Instead, I'd grabbed my Blue Raspberry ICEE and a bag of Cool Ranch Doritos and bailed. I thought about it all night long though. I'd decided that the next day in class, I'd check in with her, but I never got the chance.

It was the last time I ever saw her. It was as if she disappeared into thin air.

Until this morning.

I'd always wondered what happened to her in the same way you wonder about a canceled TV series that abruptly ends without resolution. Eventually you make peace with the fact that just because you want answers it doesn't mean you're gonna get them, and after a while you forget about it and move on. Hallie's reappearance is a bit like said series just got re-upped for production two years later by Netflix.

I run and catch up to her, keeping stride. "So, where did you say you're headed again?" I ask, even though I remember.

She turns to me, and her eyebrows shoot up slightly as if she's surprised to find me there. "Oregon. Medford specifically. And you're going to San Francisco, right?"

"Yeah." I hold open the glass doors to the bus terminal for her.

"You should go see the Wave Organ."

"The what?"

"It's a real organ made out of PVC pipes and stone salvaged from a demolished cemetery that plays music when it's high tide. You have to catch it at the exact right time, or you won't hear anything."

"Sounds cool. You've heard it in person?" I ask as we enter the lobby.

She starts walking toward the arrival and departure screens. "No, I saw it on YouTube. I've never been to San Francisco. Always wanted to go though. I've never really been anywhere. My family doesn't travel much."

"Maybe I'll check it out."

"You totally should. I like rando obscure stuff like that."

"Me too. I've only been to San Francisco once when I was little, and it wasn't the best experience."

She looks at me, waiting for the rest of the story. "Well, don't leave me hanging like that."

"I was super scared of bridges when I was small, and apparently the entire time we drove across the Golden Gate Bridge, I screamed at the top of my lungs, certain it was going to collapse from the weight of all the cars. The Golden Gate Bridge is one point seven miles long, so you can imagine my family was pretty pissed off by the time we reached the other side."

She laughs. "That's pretty great."

"I'm sure my parents would disagree."

Three small children dart in front of us, chasing each other between the rows of seats. A heavily tattooed twentysomething couple is making out in the corner. Right next to them, a guy wearing a tuxedo is sprawled across a whole bench, fast asleep. A frowning elderly couple sits in silence, eyeing him over the tops of their bifocals.

I stand side by side with Hallie, pretending to check the info screen. Next to nearly every bus it reads DELAYED.

"What the—" Hallie's jaw drops as her eyes scroll.

"That's a lot of delayed buses." I remind myself that, despite my ongoing story, I'm not scheduled to ride on any of them. It would seriously suck to be any of these other people right now.

Some guy with a major comb-over and a T-shirt that says "World's Okayest Golfer" passes us and says, "The fire jumped the highway, and there's some big chemical accident affecting traffic coming in from the south, causing all sorts of delays. They said those times are an estimate. No one knows how long this will take." He delivers the news with all the dire emotion of a newscaster sharing the latest update on an asteroid set to hit Earth.

This might impact my flight tomorrow. If it's too smoky, can planes safely take off? Wouldn't it affect visibility?

A long line of harried passengers waiting to talk to the lone customer service agent snakes through the terminal. Hallie's expression darkens.

"Great. Well, I guess we might as well get comfortable," she says and moves toward an unoccupied bench by the vending machine and sits down, scooting to the right-hand side to make room for me. It feels like we're in this together—whatever this is.

Until we aren't and she boards her bus and I get a lift back to my car and we never see each other again.

She hoists her suitcase onto the seat between us, resting her elbow against it and sinking her chin into her palm. I rest my feet on my backpack like it's an ottoman.

"Their lack of stellar, on-time performance is disappointing," I joke, trying to lighten the mood. I scan the surroundings and automatically take note of the location of the bathrooms, fire extinguisher, and fastest trajectory to the nearest exit.

"This is *so* typical of my life right now, you have no idea." Hallie puffs out her cheeks and shakes her head, looking visibly distraught. "This could seriously mess everything up. If I don't get to Medford by tomorrow, it could be too late."

Too late for what? "Maybe you could get a flight."

She shakes her head. "Too expensive. I don't have enough cash."

"I could lend you some money."

"You don't even know me. Why would you do that?"

I shrug. "I don't know. You seem like an honest person."

The compliment oddly seems to distress her more. "I couldn't, but thank you. Also, I'm scared of flying. The idea that some big hunk of metal can stay up in the sky will never cease to baffle me. Kind of like you with bridges."

"Fair. You could rent a car," I suggest.

"You have to be twenty-five. Plus, I don't know how to drive."

Who lives in Southern California and doesn't know how to drive? It's nearly impossible to get around without your license.

"Train?"

She shakes her head again. "Nope. Not happening. Seems like there's always some big crash in the news. That Amtrak in Tacoma that came down on the freeway overpass, the Metro-North train in New York..."

"Segway?"

"So far that's looking like my most promising option." She sighs deeply and turns her head to look at the clock on the wall.

My eyes snag on the half dozen earrings arcing from her lobe all the way up to the helix. "Must have hurt like hell getting all those piercings."

She reaches her hand to her ear self-consciously. "Trust me, that's nothing. The cartilage ones hurt the most. Worse than a bee sting but not as intense as say...a stomach resectioning."

"Noted."

I point to a small, indented scar on my left cheek. "See this? To date the most painful thing I ever felt. When I was a kid, I once ran with a lollipop in my mouth, tripped over a sprinkler, and face-planted. The stick went through my cheek." Apparently, I am chock-full of heartwarming stories about my youth today. Maybe next I'll tell her about the time I got diarrhea at Jacob Weitzman's bar mitzvah.

She points to the cut on my head. I'd nearly forgotten it was there. "What happened there?"

"I had a minor altercation with a car window."

"Ouch. You are very accident-prone."

"It would seem so."

She notices my tee. "What's Subliminal Sunrise?"

"A band I was in briefly."

Her face lights up. "You're a musician?"

"Yeah." It's not entirely a lie if you count four years of high school jazz band.

"What do you guys play? Would I have heard of you?"

The very idea makes me emit a short burst of laughter. "Not likely. We broke up a while ago. It was my friend Ajay on drums, I played guitar, and this girl Natasha did vocals and keyboard." Saying her name, I realize it's the first time I've thought about her in nearly an hour. "She's the only one who has any actual talent. She tried out for *The Voice*. She has perfect pitch. That's actually pretty rare. The rest of us totally sucked."

She smiles at the plethora of unnecessary information. "Cool."

"Yeah." The conversation grinds to a halt.

There is a garbled announcement over the loudspeaker. It awakens the sleeping guy in the tux, who then seriously looks like he's going to lose his shit right there and starts yelling, "No! No! *No!*" And then he strings a bunch more denials together at double the volume. "*Nonononono*—are you effing *kidding me*? Seriously, that's *effed up, man! Don't you people have extra buses somewhere?*"

"What did that announcement say?" Hallie asks and squints at the speaker as if that might improve the sound quality.

"I'm guessing—and this is purely speculation based on Tuxedo Guy's nuclear meltdown—that there's another issue with a bus."

The announcement comes again, still garbled. Hallie asks, "Did they say 1446?"

"I'm not sure."

She eyes the small angry mob of travelers forming at the ticket window. "Do you think you could watch my stuff for a sec?" She doesn't even wait for my answer, just walks away and leaves me with her suitcase.

"Uh...sure?"

I watch as she makes her way across the lobby. The change in her appearance is so dramatic from two years ago, and hair color is the least of it. It's hard to know where to focus first when looking at her. Her clothes hang on her body like they're a size too big. From her purple hair down to her cat shoes, it's as if every part of her is demanding to be noticed.

When she returns a few minutes later, she looks like she could stab someone.

"Is everything all right?" I ask her.

"Fine." It doesn't seem fine. Two seconds later she bursts into tears.

I do not know what to do.

The tears lead to coughing, and it escalates quickly. She places one hand to her chest and the other over her mouth. People turn to stare, but no one is concerned enough to get out of their seats.

I run over to the vending machine and feed it bills for a bottle of water. I furiously twist the cap off and hand it to her. She brings it to her lips and takes a big sip then clears her throat.

"Thank you. Sorry. This annoying cough."

Hallie dabs the corners of her eyes with her fist again and bites at her lip, bobbing her knee up and down, looking around the room absently.

"It's none of my business or anything but—you seem a little upset."

She smiles, but the slight wobble in her chin tells me it's the kind of smile someone manages when they are barely holding it together right before they lose it and start crying again. "My bus is still delayed, and they have no idea when it might arrive. I'm now priority status on the wait list for the five a.m. as a backup, but there's no guarantee that will be on time either. The fires have messed everything up. So, I guess that's it then."

She shakes her head in frustration.

It's not my place to ask for details if she's not volunteering them. "Listen, I don't know your situation, but I'm sure if you call your friend in Medford and let her know you'll be delayed, she'll understand. Shit happens, right?"

She sniffles. "It's a guy actually. Owen."

"Oh. I don't know why I assumed it would be a girl. I guess when you said you were visiting a friend..."

She raises an eyebrow. "You don't have friends that are a different gender?"

My mind cycles back to Natasha.

"Of course I do. I think it's a slippery slope though. I mean— once you get close, it's inevitable that one of you will probably develop feelings for the other at some point, even if it's a terrible idea that probably wouldn't work out anyway and could potentially mess up a great friendship."

"Sounds like you've done your research."

"Yes, it's very scientific."

"Still, I don't think that's accurate. I believe you can absolutely be friends with a gender you're attracted to. Otherwise bisexual and pansexual people would never have friends."

"That's a fair point."

"Well, this is the first time Owen and I will meet in real life. We met online in a chat room."

My internal alarm bells go off, but she appears unconcerned.

"Have you never seen an episode of *Law and Order*? Or *Dateline*? It's a classic story—young girl meets guy online who claims to be seventeen but is actually a forty-six-year-old dude with a chronic rash who lives in his parents' basement and collects human hair."

She smirks. "A classic story? Like *Oliver Twist*?"

"More like Oliver Twisted. I'm just trying to look out for you." But it dawns on me that I didn't look out for her that night at the 7-Eleven or after hearing her poem that day in class, and I instantly feel guilty. I didn't know her then, and I barely know her now, but I'd like to think that these days, I'd do things differently. I wonder if she even remembers that I was there.

Some guy, reeking of weed, approaches and starts feeding quarters into the vending machine right next to us. He reads every option out loud before sharing his delight with the entire terminal that the machine has Raisinets. Clearly, he's won stoner vending-machine lotto. He can't even wait until he's back to his seat to tear open the sunshine-yellow box, throwing his head back and gleefully pouring half the contents of the box down the hatch at once, effectively ruining Raisinets for me forever.

"Owen is real. He's definitely not forty-six, although I'm uncertain if he has a basement. To my knowledge the only thing he collects are Pokémon. And there is zero chance of us being more than friends because A, I'm not his type—wrong gender—and B, he could be dead by the time I get there."

At first, I think she's joking. But then she goes on to explain, "He's gay. And he has terminal cancer, and he's ending his life this weekend. Oregon is a right-to-die state, so he has the meds right there for when he's ready."

"I figured out the first part. Didn't see the second part coming though. Wow. Isn't that basically suicide?"

"Suicide is someone who *wants* to die. Assisted suicide is about compassion—not subjecting a terminally ill person and their loved ones to unnecessary pain and suffering in a battle they can't win."

"But it's still taking your own life, right? That's super intense. I guess if the person is suffering and they know there's no cure. But even then—that's a tricky one. What if they make a mistake and say you have six weeks to live and you could have lived another twenty years? How can they know *exactly* how long?"

"But that's just it; it's up to the individual, not doctors or anything else," she explains. "He's decided to take back the only total control over his life he's got—his death. He gets to pick everything out—the music, his clothes, the day and time, who he wants there when it happens. It's all on his terms. Seems to me like the way to go."

"I guess." I think about how my dad went. On an operating table, splayed open—all the technology and modern medicine couldn't save him. Definitely not on his terms.

"Owen said he'd keep going until it got too intense. He doesn't want to put himself or his family and friends through that, which I respect. His family is super supportive." Her brow furrows, and she sighs deeply. "You probably think it's weird if I tell you that the one person who completely gets me is someone I've never actually met."

"Not at all."

"And it's looking like it's going to stay that way." She looks so disappointed. "I really wanted to meet him."

"Sure." I know what that is to be denied closure with someone—not only with my dad but Alex too—and how it messes you up a little bit every single day of your life, like some app perpetually running in the background. I sincerely hope she gets to Medford in time to see him.

"Well, anyway, fingers crossed there's no issues with your bus too." She adds and smiles, but her sadness seeps through like water in a paper bag. It's a look I recognize because I see it on my face in the mirror every day.

For a second, I allow myself to imagine that I am on my way to go see Alex. It unearths a roller coaster of emotions. I've loved him and hated him at the same time for so long now. What would that be like? When we were younger, we used to be close, but then things started to change when he went to high school. He started acting out, getting into trouble, partying hard. I was scared he would die, furious that he wouldn't stop. It was hard for me to understand addiction when I was younger, how it lives under the skin, waiting for the opportunity to once again hijack your brain. Things seemed to spiral out of control whenever he was around, but now that I'm older, I realize it wasn't entirely his fault.

I didn't get to have closure with my dad, but it's still achievable to have it with Alex. Maybe the timing of my discovering that letter is because Dad is trying to give that to us both. I'm supposed to leave tomorrow, but Alex deserves to know how Dad felt. And it could be my chance to talk with him about everything that's happened, to finally uncover the truth and move forward feeling a sense of resolution one way or another.

My car key digs into my thigh. I reach into my front pocket to adjust it, and as I extract my hand, my fortune from earlier spirals to the floor, settling faceup next to my shoe.

"A ship in harbor is safe, but that's not why ships are built."

I lean down and pick it up, turning the paper over and over between my fingers.

Honestly—I would give anything to get lost for a while, to burn the map. Sad but true: in eighteen years, my ship has yet to leave the freaking harbor unless you count the literal cruise I went on to Mexico with my family when I was nine. In fact, the most spontaneous and outrageous thing I've done in years was this one time I tried sushi from a gas station.

That exact moment, an older woman walks by wearing a sweatshirt with a glittery, red dragonfly on the front. It feels like an unmistakable sign from Dad, as if he's somehow weighing in and validating what I'm thinking.

I glance at the clock on the wall. I have less than twenty-four hours until my flight. Technically, I don't need to be in New York until Monday morning when I start my internship and meet my mother for dinner. Nothing is stopping me from actually going.

Alex, who always forged his own path, might be the one person able to help me make sense of the chatter and static in my brain. The more I think on it, the more I realize how much I need to see him before I leave for good.

I might also be able to help Hallie get a little farther down the road safely, upping the chance she gets to see her friend. It's an opportunity to clear my past karma and help change her story.

Mine too, maybe.

I covertly pull up the Greyhound website on my phone and with a few keystrokes discover there's a bus leaving from San Francisco to Medford, Oregon tomorrow morning at eleven thirty.

Perfect.

One minor glitch: my car is currently completely blocked in at a party that won't end for at least another four hours, and there's a ticking clock here. There's no time to waste waiting for my car to be freed, and Hallie is apparently scared of every other form of transportation except buses. So how do we get there?

Then a light bulb goes on over my head. *Karma.*

"Wait here," I say to her even as I'm on my feet moving toward the exit. Halfway out the door, I realize I've left my backpack inside with Hallie. Having entrusted me with her bag, I have equal faith that she won't bolt with mine. Right now, every second counts.

Normally, I'm not a big risk taker. If playing it safe were an Olympic sport, I'd be a gold medalist. My therapist, Carole, says I need to do what scares me so I can prove to myself that things rarely go as badly as I spin them in my brain. I'm about to test-drive that theory.

Outside the terminal, I walk briskly down the line of cars parked in the taxi zone on the off chance Oscar's miraculously still here.

He's not.

But he gave me his business card. I dig in my back pocket for it then whip out my phone and punch in his number. My heart is racing. It's a long shot he'd even go for the idea, but I'm thinking on my feet here.

He answers on the third ring. I can hear the strains of the late George Michael's song "Freedom" at full volume, and then quickly he turns it down and says, "Hello, this is Oscar. What's the word, bird?"

His voice catches me off guard because suddenly there's not a trace of the outback in it. He sounds more like he's a mobster from New Jersey.

"Oscar the GoodCarma driver, right?"

"The very same."

"I didn't recognize your voice. You had a thick Australian accent. This is Jack Freeman. You drove me to the bus station about a half hour ago?"

He laughs. This time when he speaks his voice is void of any regional dialects whatsoever, just straight-up California. "Yeah...I'm not really from Australia. I'm originally from the Valley. North Hollywood born and raised. I was working on my accent earlier. I'm an actor. I'm up for a small part in this commercial and thought it might kick it up a notch if I played it Australian, you know? They'll see my range. You completely bought it, right?"

"A hundred percent." A little flattery can't hurt, and he had me fooled.

"Excellent. I watched every Hugh Jackman movie in existence twice until I nailed it. You forget something, my friend?"

"Wow, that is commitment to craft. Actually—I'm calling because I have a business proposition for you."

"You have my full attention," he says. I silently cross my fingers and hold them up.

"You mentioned that you're headed to San Francisco to stop your ex's wedding *and* you have to give up a weekend of pay, which sucks. Here's the thing, Oscar: all the buses are delayed coming into and out of LA from the south right now, and I need to get to San Francisco too. I know a win-win solution to our misfortune."

He shuts off his stereo entirely. "Go on."

I quickly pull out my wallet and inventory the contents. "I am offering a high-denomination Target gift card, eighty-six dollars cash, a coupon for a delicious high-quality burger from In-N-Out plus all your gas and caffeine in exchange for your services if you'll consider leaving slightly ahead of schedule and driving me to San Francisco tonight instead. It's like getting money to do something you were going to do anyhow. And also, I'm going to ask the girl from earlier if she'll come with me."

After a long pause, he says, "Give me ten minutes to stop by my apartment on the way to get my stuff and we're good to go."

"Seriously?"

He chuckles. "Yeah, sure, why not?"

I exhale, relieved. "You, Oscar, are a fantastic human. We'll meet you in front of the bus station as soon as you can get here." I turn on my heel, fist pumping the air as I hurry back to the terminal.

I'm hopeful I can convince Hallie to come with me, but even if I can't, I am now fully committed to making this journey. If she doesn't want to join me, I won't need Oscar's help to get to San

Francisco. He can just take me back to Carly's house instead. I can wait until my car is freed, and then I'll drive myself.

I've been moving through my life on autopilot, trying to please everyone else. But everything is different now. Dad isn't here anymore, Natasha and I are done, and Mom is three thousand miles away, literally and figuratively. I can't lose Alex too, not when there's still any chance to make things right.

I make a beeline for the bench by the vending machine where we'd been sitting. Hallie's not there. And neither is my backpack. Instead, there's an older Latina woman in her spot. A little girl with pigtails is resting her head on her lap. The woman looks up at me.

"Excuse me, did you happen to see a girl who was here just a minute ago? Purple hair, lots of ear piercings, shoes with cats on them?" I ask her, trying not to sound too panicked since I've literally been gone less than five minutes. If even. *What the actual hell?*

The woman nods and speaks low so as not to wake the little girl. "Yes, she was here. She gave me her seat so my granddaughter could sleep. I think she left."

"She *left?*" My stomach lurches with panic. Where could she possibly have gone in that short an amount of time? I frantically scan the room for purple hair and a Hello Kitty suitcase.

Nothing.

It's possible she was put on another bus after all.

Or she could be in the bathroom.

On the chance it's the latter, I sit down on a bench facing the bathrooms and decide to wait it out for a few minutes just in case. After four people come and go, it sinks in that she's not in there either, and people are starting to look at me funny like I'm some perv.

I must have read her completely wrong. Perhaps she saw my leaving as an opportunity to shake me off and she snuck out, taking my backpack with her. The backpack and clothes I can replace, but my heart lurches thinking about losing Dad's letter to Alex.

Sadly, this was the most excited I've felt about anything in a long time, which I suppose only underscores my need to take more risks.

I stand up, defeated, ready to leave and put all thoughts of Hallie Baskin back on the shelf when I spy a pair of shoes with embroidered cat faces poking out from a bench toward the back corner of the waiting area, partially obscured by a large, fake potted palm.

My adrenaline surges as I cross the room toward her, and she comes into full view. She's leaning against her suitcase reading. My backpack is propped carefully on the other side of her. She looks up at my hasty approach and quickly snaps the book shut.

"Where the heck did you go?" she asks, her tone part annoyance, part worry.

"Where the heck did *you* go?" I shoot back.

She bobs her head in the direction of this scary-looking guy who looks like he jumped out of an America's Most Wanted poster. "That dude was freaking me out. I didn't want him staring at me all night. And then this other lady needed a place where her kid could lie down so—"

I cut her off and smile. "What if I told you I might have a solution to the current lack of transportation situation?"

"Have you commandeered a bus?"

"Better. I'm driving with Oscar to San Francisco, and I think you should come with us."

7
HALLIE

FRIDAY, JUNE 4, 10:16 P.M.

I emit a single laugh and look at him like he's just suggested we fly on a spaceship to the moon. "Drive to San Francisco? With you and Oscar the GoodCarma driver we met less than an hour ago? And you were worried about me going to visit some boy I'd met online because I might end up on *Dateline*?"

"Yes." He moves his backpack aside and sits down on the bench, angling toward me. "Hear me out. San Francisco is more or less halfway to Medford. Since we're both heading north, we might as well keep each other company. You could get your ticket changed to leave from there on a morning bus to Portland which would still probably get you there before this one would, and you'll have a story to tell."

He's actually serious. I don't even know how to respond. Aside from the fact that he and Oscar are basically strangers, most of my money is wrapped up in my bus ticket, which I'll still need, and my funds are limited. I can't risk taking on more.

I tell him, "I could barely afford my ticket as it was. I didn't budget for any extra expenses."

"There wouldn't be any," he assures me. "Like I said, I'm already going there. You're basically just freeloading. Besides, your fortune *did* say something about accepting the next proposition you hear, right?"

I laugh. It's a generous offer, and it definitely increases the odds I will get to see Owen before it's too late, which is not a guarantee otherwise at this point. "So, if I go and you turn out to be a serial killer and they find my bits in a shallow ditch on the side of I-5, I can sue Panda Express."

"Exactly. Well, maybe not *you*, because you'd be dead."

"Right." I study him for a minute then say, "Can I ask you a question? And you can be totally honest with me. I won't say anything."

"Yes, I have never missed a single day of school since kindergarten. I'm that guy. The rumors are true."

"Impressive, though not quite where I was headed."

"Not sure what else it could possibly be," he jokes.

I tilt my head and narrow my eyes, trying to figure him out. I've noticed little details that on their own look like nothing, but together they add up enough that I have questions, if not theories. Normally, I'd say it's none of my business, but if I'm going to consider keeping company with him for the next six hours, it seems reasonable to know what I'm getting myself into.

I ask him, "Truth: Does anyone know where you are right this minute?"

He laughs, but I can see the question catches him off guard. It's obvious my gut was correct and I'm on target. "Why would you think that?"

I shrug. "Just a vibe. I'm pretty good at reading people. You're sitting in a bus terminal alone on grad night. You've checked your phone about a million times. And you're wearing your hoodie inside out, which, unless it's a fashion statement, means you're distracted. I think there's more to your story."

He bites back a smile. "You've really Scooby-Doo'd this, Velma. *You're* here. So, does that mean there's more to *your* story?"

"Of course."

He reaches back, feeling for the exposed tag and blushes as he casually rights his sweatshirt. "You're right. Nobody knows where I am right now, but that's because *I* didn't even know I was going to be here."

"I see."

"I'm supposed to be leaving for New York tomorrow to start this internship and then college in the fall, but a lot has changed since I made those plans. I'm hopeful that seeing my brother may be the key to making sense of it all. I didn't even realize how important it is to me to go visit him until I saw you tonight. Since we both need to get from A to B, I thought it would be cool if maybe we went together. I mean—to San Francisco. Not to see my brother, obviously."

"Oh. Wow. That sounds intense." He seems harmless, but I still sense there's more he's probably not telling me. Of course, there's plenty I haven't told him.

He looks at me encouragingly. "Whaddya say?"

Everything in me wants to, but my brain starts coming up with all the logical and obvious reasons why I shouldn't. I can't simply jump in a car with two guys I've basically just met, although technically it's not all that different than hopping on a bus with fifty complete strangers. He actually looks a little surprised, if not disappointed, when I reply, "I'm sorry. I can't. But thank you."

"Oh. Sure. I understand," he says. He grabs his sideburns and pulls them straight on either side of his head and smiles. "It's my hair isn't it? I know—it's way too long and does this flippy thing over my ears."

"That's it, you got me." I laugh. "Plus, I never trust a guy with a side part."

"I knew it."

"It's nothing personal."

"Sure, I get it." He stands and reaches for his backpack, sliding his arms through the straps. "Well, Oscar should be here any minute, so I should probably go wait for him out front."

"It was nice seeing you again, Jack. Safe travels and good luck."

He smiles and gives me a little salute before he turns on his heel to leave. "Yeah, you too."

I open my book again, trying to focus on the words, but I steal another glance at him, his back to me as he pushes open the door a little harder than necessary and exits the terminal. Just like that, Jack Freeman disappears all over again.

As the minutes pass, I start second-guessing my decision. I may not know Jack, but there's a familiarity about him that makes me feel safer traveling with him versus being alone. And if seeing

Owen is important to me, this could be my best, if not only, shot at making that happen. From the sound of it, I'm not going to be on a bus anytime soon.

I'm tired of factoring in what everyone else might think, playing it safe, and letting fear control me. I want to make my own decisions and not have to answer to anyone else for them. On the heels of all this upsetting news, I have never needed to feel more alive and in control. I can't let fear win.

I think about what my fortune cookie from earlier said about accepting the next proposition I hear. Maybe it's a sign.

Before I can talk myself out of it again, I'm up out of my seat, hoping I'm not too late.

He's leaning against the wall outside the terminal, checking his phone while he waits for Oscar. I yell, "Hey!" as he, along with everyone else in the vicinity, looks my way. He breaks out into a smile.

I drag my Hello Kitty suitcase noisily behind me as I catch up with him. I blow my bangs out of my eyes and tell him, "I hear messing with a fortune cookie fortune is like seven years bad luck or something."

"I've heard that too," he replies as he shoves his phone in his pocket. "Does this mean what I think it means?"

"I think it does." I smile and add, "In fairness, I believe I should provide full disclosure. No one knows where I am at this moment either, and I'm guessing we both have our reasons for wanting to keep it that way. Therefore, I've changed my mind, and I'd like to take you up on your offer if you're still offering."

"I am."

I tip the handle of my suitcase toward him, an act of trust. "Watch my bag for a sec so I can change my ticket."

The conversation flows from the minute we get into Oscar's car. I have to say: in all the scenarios I'd run through my mind about what this night would be like, spending it driving to San Francisco and baring souls with Jack Freeman from creative writing class was definitely never one of them. Life is full of surprises. Perhaps not all of them bad.

Despite the rumored traffic snarl because of the fires, the freeway out of Downtown LA moves surprisingly well at this hour. As we change lanes to merge onto the 101, Jack turns to me and asks, "So do you still write poems?"

"No. I haven't written poetry in a long time. I wasn't very good at it anyway."

"Don't say that—I remember your poetry was—"

"Depressing as hell?" I laugh, and he joins because we both know they were pretty dark.

"I was going to say intense."

"Right." I grin and tuck one leg underneath myself to get comfortable. "You are too kind."

"I thought they were really good."

"Thanks. How about you? Are you still writing?"

"Yeah, I'm working on something that could turn out to be pretty cool. We'll see."

"Is it a novel or short story or...?"

"It's an idea I've been playing around with for a while. It's—um, a choose-your-own-ending novel." He seems to brace himself for my reaction—a laugh, a look, some indication that I think it's a silly idea.

"You write for kids? Nice."

"Actually, it's for adults. I think it's an untapped market. A story doesn't have one de facto ending. That's not realistic. The outcome hinges on the series of decisions that preceded it. You alter one thing and everything that follows changes. The reader is in total control of the story at all times. There are multiple stories within every story, so it has the ability to span every genre. It's limitless."

"I'd read that," Oscar says.

I nod in agreement. "I like it. So, what's it about?"

"It's about this guy and girl who meet at this Coachella-esque music festival. She gives him this package to hold and says she'll be right back, but then she disappears. Then there're all these mishaps, and all these other people want what's in the box, and they have to figure out how to find each other again."

"So, depending on the choices you make, they find each other, or they don't?" I ask.

"Exactly."

"I can see the tagline now: 'Happily ever after rests in *your* hands,'" Oscar says in a dramatic announcer voice, and we all laugh.

"That sounds really cool," I tell him. "So, what's in the box?"

"If I tell you that, what would be the point of reading it?" he jokes, raising his eyebrows. "There's some details to still work out, but yeah, we'll see what comes of it."

"Are you going to be a writing major, then?"

He shakes his head. "Biological sciences."

I nod. Not surprising it's something brainy. "Where are you going to college?"

"Columbia University."

"That makes sense."

He laughs. "Why is that?"

"I remember you. You were the kind of guy who filled your free periods with extra science and AP classes, joined all the right clubs, and were on a first-name basis with the entire faculty including the janitors. I'd even go so far as to bet you probably had your entire high school schedule figured out before you even went to freshman orientation."

"On behalf of all supersmart kids who take extra science and AP classes everywhere, I'm pretty sure I should be offended," he tells me. "Also, Phil was not just a janitor, he was a mentor."

I smile and tuck a strand of hair behind my ear. "It's not a bad thing. I'm just saying it was unusual to see someone like you in a throwaway elective like that when you could be building a satellite or learning Mandarin for fun."

He winces. "Ouch."

"It's a compliment?" As if that wasn't obvious.

"Oh." He smiles. "I didn't actually look at it as a throwaway elective. In fact, it was probably my favorite class."

"Mine too. Well, Columbia sounds exciting."

He nods. "I guess. My dad went there, and the idea of my going there meant a lot to him. It means a lot to me too, but...I don't know. I've been working toward going to Columbia and doing this internship this summer for so long, and now that it's happening, there's a part of me that wonders if it's what I even truly want. Columbia represents everything my dad was and who everyone expects me to be, and I want a chance to define myself on my own terms. I don't know that I can do that there without feeling like I'm being measured against him. It's a lot of pressure. So it's got me thinking, is all."

I nod. "Basically, you're in a real-life choose-your-own-ending novel featuring you as the protagonist."

"Ballsy," Oscar pipes up.

I draw invisible spirals on my thigh with the edge of my thumbnail. I'm sure whatever Jack's grappling with is very real for him, but our lives are so different. His is filled with opportunity and options. Jack is waffling about having to go to one of the finest universities in this country, and meanwhile I'd kill to go to *any* college.

It bothers me when people who have everything don't realize how they sound to someone who has nothing. Normally I would tell him to check his privilege, but he seems like a genuinely nice guy; I know he's not consciously trying to be an entitled jerk. I don't know the whole story.

"So, are you considering not going, then?"

"I don't know." He shakes his head. "I don't expect you to feel sorry for me."

"I don't."

He huffs a laugh. "How about you? Are you headed to college too?"

"No, maybe someday. For now, I have work, and it's just too hard with my schedule. It can be hectic sometimes," I tell him without getting into the details. I change the subject and bring it back to him. "So, if you didn't go to Columbia, what would you do?"

He shakes his head side to side, as if weighing his options. "At the moment I am plan-lite. I have no idea. This is all sort of developing minute-by-minute."

"And when you think about it, isn't that the way it should be? Whatever you want to do should be based on who you are and what you're vibing with in that moment."

"Totally."

I root in my purse and pull out the water bottle he bought me earlier. As I raise it to my mouth to take a sip, my engraved, silver chain bracelet edges out from underneath the cuff of my flannel shirt.

He squints, trying to read the three words etched on the metal band joined to the chain.

"*Alis volat popriis.* She flies with her own wings," he says. "Nice."

"You actually understand that?" This impresses me more than his getting into Columbia University.

"I self-studied for the Latin AP."

Of course he did.

He smiles, and he gets this cute little dimple right where he showed me the lollipop stick impaled him. Hs earnest nerdiness is disarming. I always felt inadequate by comparison to kids like Jack who consistently went above and beyond while I was simply trying to get through. I worked my ass off for my grades, and it all seemed to come so effortlessly for them. I'm plenty smart, though it was never reflected in my grades, and then at some point, I stopped caring because it didn't matter the same way. College wasn't on the radar anytime soon. I often wonder what I might have done differently, how my life might have been if I hadn't gotten sick.

"I could try to impress you with saying that's how I know this phrase too, but the true story is I actually found it on a Pinterest board, and it resonated with me," I tell him.

"In my defense, Latin, along with Greek, is the language of medical terminology, which is why I learned it. My parents figured it would be helpful," Jack tells me.

I rub the metal strip on my bracelet between my thumb and index finger. "I made this. I like making jewelry. This is my mantra right now. It's kind of like saying I want to live my life on my own terms. I think you just have to reach that point where the alternative is unacceptable."

He leans in closer, inspecting my handiwork. He points to the two wire-wrapped stones on either side of the band. "It's pretty. What kind of stone is that?"

"Tourmaline. For protection from negative energy and spiritual grounding," I tell him. "I'm a big believer in the energy of stones."

I wonder if he'll think that's way too crunch-granola New-Agey, but he actually seems interested, and we end up having a long discussion about the meanings and healing properties of different stones. We continue talking until we're way out in the country, well past Santa Barbara. The headlight beams from passing cars are the solitary source of light slicing through the darkness.

The song "Dancing Queen" by ABBA comes on the radio, and I ask Oscar to turn it up a little. It's one of those tunes that I can't help but sing along with when it comes on. It always puts me in a good mood.

Oscar starts belting out the lyrics, and then Jack and I join in.

The three of us are singing at the top of our lungs and laughing because all of us are slightly off-key, which only makes it more awesome.

When it's over, Jack says, "My friend Natasha loves that song." He pulls out his phone, checks for texts, and clicks it off again with a smirk as Oscar and I discuss what current musicians will stand the test of time and one-hit wonders of the last decade. Jack leans his head against the glass, looking out the window, lost in thought. I can tell by the look on his face that he's definitely reacting to not hearing from someone. He reminds me of how I was after my ex-boyfriend Ryan and I broke up.

"So is Natasha the girl?" I ask.

Hearing me say Natasha's name seems to take him by surprise. "What girl?"

"The one who has you staring all melancholy out the window and checking your phone every five minutes." I grin. His cheeks flush. *Busted.* "I notice small details. C'mon—it's a long car ride. We have to talk about something. I'll tell you my deep, dark secrets if you tell me yours. Who can I tell that would even care?"

"With an offer like that, how can I refuse?" He tucks his phone back in his pocket. "She's my ex-girlfriend. As of today, actually. We were friends first, and then we dated for around a year and a half, but it didn't work out."

"Unless she's the one and you're letting her get away," Oscar interjects. "And then you spend the rest of your life comparing everyone to her and realize you should have fought harder for her to stay."

"That's actually not making me feel better," Jack replies.

"It's hard to go back to being friends once you've crossed that line," I tell him. Thinking about Ryan stings a little even though we broke up two years ago. Not because I still care about him, but because it still bothers me how I gave my heart so freely to someone who didn't deserve it. "Sometimes severing ties is the best thing."

"Did you know that love has similar effects on the brain as cocaine?" Jack offers. "And a breakup, on a chemical level, has a lot of the same side effects as drug withdrawal."

"That makes total sense," Oscar says. "Love is science. I was never any good at science. Always a drama kid."

A patch of lights crops up in the distance, and I realize how badly I need to pee, stretch my legs, and find caffeine. The feeling is unanimous. Oscar tells a funny story about the time he played a barista in a TV spot for urinary incontinence. Laughing while talking about peeing only makes me have to pee more.

I make out a CHEVRON sign as it comes into view on the horizon, and Oscar accelerates the car ever so slightly. By the time we pull into the gas station and Oscar rolls up to the pump, I'm gripping the door handle, ready to jump out.

The lights around the perimeter of the buildings cast everything in a soft, tangerine glow. The air is brisker than I anticipated. Jack and Oscar trail right behind me to the mini-mart where we obtain the restroom keys and then divide and conquer.

When I'm finished, I wait for them inside the warmth and fluorescence of the mini-mart. I pour myself a cup of coffee that the attendant assures me is fresh despite how it looks and the fact it tastes like the bottom of the La Brea Tar Pits. After I doctor it with enough creamer to make it semipalatable, I peruse the snack aisle, assessing my mood: Bugles or Pringles, Mike and Ikes, or M&M's.

Jack comes up alongside me and reaches for a Kit Kat. Always a good choice. He glances at the clock on the wall and says, "It's well past midnight, which means my birthday is officially over. I'd always felt ripped off as a kid because my actual time of birth was eleven forty-seven, so it was only my actual birthday for thirteen minutes before it was an entirely different day."

"Happy belated birthday," I tell him as I settle on M&M's. Plain. No, wait—peanut. No—plain.

He reaches into his pocket and fishes out a candle. It's broken in half, held together by the wick. It looks familiar.

"Is that the candle from our restaurant?" I ask as I swap the M&M's for a Milky Way.

"Yeah."

"I thought so. I picked those out. I liked the rainbow stripes."

"They're very festive."

"Your candle has seen better days."

"It still works though. I'm thinking I could cut the wick at the broken part and get two wishes out of it."

"This is exactly the sort of out-of-the-box thinking that got you into Columbia, no doubt," I kid as I toss the subpar coffee and grab a fresh bottle of Evian water out of the adjacent cooler. "Did you ever notice that Evian spells naive backward? Which explains why they get away with charging like, two bucks for a bottle of this stuff."

"Do you think a birthday wish can still come true if it's not actually your birthday?"

"I'm sure there's some sort of grace period," I assure him.

He spots a two-pack of Hostess chocolate cupcakes on the shelf and reaches for it then holds the package up in one hand while dangling the broken candle in the other. "Then we should celebrate. I have two cupcakes and an extra wish. Plus, it's my birthday, so it would be bad form to say no."

We make our way to the register with our bounty. The twenty-something, scruffy-looking guy behind the counter looks annoyed at having to drag himself away from watching closed-captioned ongoing fire coverage on the TV hanging on the wall long enough to ring us up.

"Any update? Are they any closer to putting this thing out?" Jack asks him.

He shakes his head as he punches at the register keys. "Still zero percent containment. It's already destroyed two hundred structures and is threatening more, jumping ridgelines."

The network shows a graphic of a map of the fire's path, and it has definitely edged closer in the direction of home since I left. It's still miles and miles away, but with these powerful, unpredictable wind gusts, you never know. It only takes one ember.

Jack buys everything, including my bottle of water and candy and a black lighter with a picture of a green alien head on it. He holds up the candle and asks the attendant if he has anything that can help us cut the wick. Wordlessly the guy pulls out a Swiss Army knife, places the blade against the exposed ropy center and gives it one swift tug. It splits in two, and he immediately returns his attention to the television. I imagine there are a lot of people besides us who aren't going to be getting much sleep tonight.

Outside, Jack tears off the plastic wrapper, shoves a half of the candle into the chocolate frosting of each cupcake, and hands one to me.

"I've got it on good authority that making a wish on a birthday candle when it's not your birthday results in the same likelihood of said wish coming true," he says.

"Happy birthday!" We clink cupcakes.

"Happy unbirthday. You ready?" He holds up the lighter. "You gotta be all systems go because there's a very small margin of time and space between lit candle and lit cupcake."

I laugh, brushing away a mosquito, and then nod. "Yep, ready."

"One-two-three-go!"

I close my eyes tightly, concentrating hard on my wish. *I wish that everything will be all right.* It's sort of broad and general, but it covers a multitude of things. I blow out the candle and then look at Jack as he blows his out too.

Oscar emerges from the mini-mart with a sixty-four-ounce fountain drink in one hand and a hot dog that's probably been spinning on the roller grill since six thirty yesterday morning in the other.

"No." Jack shakes his head. "Everything about this visual indicates we won't be getting far down the road before Oscar may need to stop again for a different sort of gas."

"Let's hit the road, comrades," he says in a thick cockney accent. "That guy in there asked me if I was from the UK. I gave him some story about how I'm on a US tour with my band, and we got into a whole thing about how Brits lose their accents when they sing. Never really thought about it, but he's right."

"Phonetics," Jack tells him, and Oscar and I look at him like he's spoken in a foreign language. "It's about the way the words and syllables are more drawn out when someone is singing versus speaking, plus the air pressure used to make sounds is stronger when you sing."

"You should be on...Jeopardy or something," I shake my head in amazement. "No joke, you're like...Human Google."

He laughs. "I can honestly say I have been called many things but never 'Human Google.'"

Oscar takes a bite of his hot dog and washes it down with a sip from his drink, barely slowing down enough to chew as he starts recounting a list of British recording artists that sound completely American. "Rod Stewart, Elton John, Eric Clapton, Sting—"

We follow him around the corner toward the gas pump where he left his car, and he stops abruptly. I nearly bump into him, and then I realize what he's looking at. Or rather—*isn't* looking at.

Oscar's car is gone.

And all our stuff is in it.

8
JACK

SATURDAY, JUNE 5, 1:30 A.M.

"What the——" Oscar says in an agitated tone devoid of any accent whatsoever.

"How could someone take the car?" I ask Oscar. "We were gone for like five minutes, and you had the keys, right?"

He shakes his head in disbelief. "I can't believe this happened again."

"Did he just say 'again'?" Hallie asks me.

Oscar pats his pockets and comes up empty. "I must have left the key fob in the car."

"Who would want to steal a Kia? No offense," I say to Oscar.

"None taken," he assures me. He looks slightly more panicked as he adds, "If you leave a review on Yelp or anything, please don't hold it against the company. It's entirely my fault."

Actually, it's my fault. None of us would be here right now if it weren't for me and my half-baked idea.

"Well, they can't get far," Hallie reasons. "I mean—it's a car with a giant Buddha head on the sides. Pretty easy to spot, which probably also shows you the level of intelligence we're dealing with. I'm sure it won't take the police long to find it. It's like a beacon."

"Statistically your best chance of recovery is within seventy-two hours of when a car is stolen," I tell him. It's as if all the useless trivia in my head has found its purpose tonight.

Hallie goes white as a ghost and shakes her head. She reaches into her purse, moving the contents around in search of something. "Well, I don't know about you two, but I can't wait around here for seventy-two hours. I *have* to be on that bus to Medford tomorrow."

I correct her. "It's after midnight, so tomorrow is now today."

She comes up empty-handed and visibly stressed. "Great. My phone is in my suitcase, which is in the car."

Oscar pats at his pockets again. "Shit, mine too."

The muscles across the back of my shoulders stiffen. We're barely out of LA, and already things are not going according to plan. Of course, there *is* no plan...but if there were, this would not be part of it.

I'm good at thinking fast on my feet in high-pressure situations. Every problem has a solution. Another one of the reasons Dad said I'd make a great doctor. I pull my phone out of my pocket and click it on. My battery is down to 15 percent, but it's enough to make a call anyway.

"First thing is to report it to the cops," I advise Oscar. "And probably your insurance company too."

Oscar shakes his head. "Hmmm. Not sure that's a good idea."

Hallie narrows her eyes and a V forms on her forehead. "Why not?"

He sighs deeply and then adjusts his glasses on the brim of his nose. "The short version? If I call the police and they find the car, they'll need to inspect it to file a report, and if they do, there's a solid chance they'll find my weed stash in the middle of Terrapin's ashes, and there's probably at least a good two ounces. So that could be problematic. And the unpaid parking ticket is bound to come up, which, for the record, was *not* entirely my fault. And if GoodCarma gets wind of any of it, they'll probably let me go because they already think I'm a liability after the falafel incident. Not to mention, if I end up in jail, I'll miss breaking up the wedding."

So many questions right now.

"Okay, who or what is Terrapin?" Hallie asks, putting her hand on her hip. Interesting she focused on that first.

"Nikki's dog. Or was."

"At least two ounces? Wow," I say. My heart thumps in my chest. We could have been pulled over at any time. I find that simultaneously infuriating and thrilling.

My dad once went ballistic because he found half a joint in the ashtray of Alex's car. Two ounces would have probably made him pop a vein.

"You ride around with your weed stashed in the ashes of your ex-girlfriend's dead dog?" Hallie asks, stringing it together. It's admittedly not the sort of thing one hears every day.

"It's a pretty foolproof hiding spot. Not too many people are going to go digging around in there." Oscar smiles, impressed with his own logic, and then realizes anew that his weed and the dog are gone. "He was a stray we took in, and he was already pretty old, so we ended up having to put him down. I got the ashes when we split up. I was bringing him with me because I thought seeing him might remind Nikki of how happy we were together."

"That's weird. But sort of heartwarming, in a way." Hallie grins. "Isn't marijuana legal in California? What's the big deal if you were caught with it?"

"You can have up to an ounce," I tell her, "but anything over that is a misdemeanor unless you have a license to sell it. Do you have a license?"

Oscar winces. "Not exactly."

"Hmmm, then transporting it could be a separate offense. On a scale of one to *Pineapple Express*, this is definitely small-time but still not ideal." I could stop there, but I feel the need to clarify how I'm so knowledgeable on the subject. "I was on the debate team and legalization of marijuana was always a hot topic. And my brother is a recovering drug addict."

Actually, I have no idea if Alex is sober these days. I don't know the first thing about him anymore.

I notice a black, glass orb hanging from the metal overhang above the gas pumps. I redirect the focus back to the situation at hand. "Okay, gas stations have surveillance cameras. Ask the guy inside to rewind the video, and you might be able to get a look at who did it or see what direction they went."

"Yeah, but what if he's required to call the cops?" Oscar points out. "If it happens on their property, I bet they have to get involved somehow."

"Possibly. But maybe he'll be cool. Less hassle for him, right?" I say.

Oscar plops down on the curb by the pump and holds his hands against his temples as if doing so will keep his brain from exploding. I know the feeling. He shakes his head. "They have cameras inside too that would record my conversation with him. I don't know if I can chance it."

"Look, I think two ounces is not gonna be a big deal. They may not even find it."

"It may actually be slightly more."

"Like how much more?"

"Maybe closer to three ounces. No more than half a pound."

Hallie's eyes widen. "Are you a drug dealer?"

"I think of myself as more of a mobile-operated, unlicensed dispensary. This is LA! Rent is expensive here. People are always asking if I know where they could go to buy weed, so I decided to cut out the middleman and provide the service myself. On holidays I also sell roses. You have to be one step ahead of your customer—to know what they want before they do—or you can't make it in this town."

It's scary how that almost makes sense.

Hallie puts her hands on her hips. "So—you're not willing to call the cops or look at the security tapes. How exactly do you expect to find your car? And what about poor Terrapin? Do you want him tossed in some dumpster like he's nothing? You've only left one solution. We have to take matters into our own hands."

We?

I realize she's serious, so I tell her, "This isn't *Return of the Jedi.*

I hardly think we're qualified to go after these guys on our own. We have no idea who we'd be up against. What if they have guns or nunchucks or something?"

"Good point," Oscar says. "So, what do we do?"

My dad used to track my brother's every move through his phone. He knew where he was 24–7, could easily catch him in a lie if he was somewhere other than where he claimed to be—at least, until Alex figured out ways to get around it.

"You said both your phones are in the car, right? We can use the Find My Phone app or log into iCloud. We should be able to track where the car is, assuming the phones are still inside it."

Of course, that raises the inevitable question: *Then what?* I have trouble confronting the people at the counter at In-N-Out when they mess up my order and forget the grilled onions, let alone a ring of car thieves.

Oscar's face lights up like a Christmas tree as I power up my phone. "Brilliant! Could that actually work?"

"It's pretty straightforward." I power it on and sit down next to him.

Hallie shakes her head. "I turned my phone off. It'll just show the last known location. It's useless."

"Use mine," Oscar says leaning in, anxiously waiting to get the process started.

Time passes agonizingly slowly as we wait for my phone to boot up. With every passing second, the gap between us and the car grows, as does the likelihood they've pitched the contents. Hallie peers over my shoulder as my home screen finally lights up and I search for the Find My Phone app. My battery indicator glows ominously red and dips to 13 percent. Hopefully it's still got enough juice to let us locate Oscar's phone. I silently chastise myself for not charging it in the car earlier.

The cell service here is terrible, and it takes forever for the screen to load. Once I get the app open, I pass my phone to Oscar, who punches in his ID and password with the texting speed of a ninety-year-old. We wait for the app to get a reading and load the map.

"C'mon, c'mon, c'mon," I say under my breath as if it might speed up the process any.

Finally, an animated map appears showing a web of streets and highway with a moving royal-blue dot. *Bingo!* Oscar's phone appears to be alive and well and travelling north a few miles ahead of us on the 101.

"Holy shit! That's them!" Oscar shouts excitedly, watching the dot on the screen as it appears to exit the highway and head east. "They're getting off the highway."

The dot moves another space and then seemingly comes to a stop. My phone battery diminishes further still to 12 percent. It could power down at any moment. Oscar looks to me for the next move as if I've done this before and have all the answers. "Now what?"

Before I can answer Hallie says, "Now we go get it."

She adjusts her purse on her shoulder and starts walking away from us toward a silver, older-model Toyota pickup truck that pulled in alongside one of the pumps one island over.

Oscar and I exchange glances. "Wait, Hallie! Where are you going?" I yell after her. She doesn't answer—doesn't even so much as look back.

Even from here I can see the naked ladies on the mud flaps

and a bumper sticker in the same font as the Subway logo that says "Zombies: Eat Flesh." Below it is another that says "Horn broke, watch for finger." The only thing that gives me any hope he's not a total asshole is the decal on the back window in the shape of Yoda that says "Toyoda." The driver is a heavyset older man with white hair and a ZZ Top–esque long beard wearing an oversized, button-down Hawaiian-print shirt. He eyes Hallie cautiously as she approaches.

She starts chatting the guy up, but we can't hear them. She turns around and points in our direction. He looks us over. There's no arguing that, visually, we're like three pieces of a puzzle that don't quite fit together—Hallie with her purple pixie haircut, Oscar with his man bun and Clark Kent glasses, and me looking like a walking Target ad in my nondescript black hoodie and matching brand-new Vans high-tops. The guy strokes his long beard contemplatively and nods with a smile. Hallie turns around excitedly, gesturing to us to come over.

We scramble to our feet and begin walking toward them. Pickup Truck Driver Dude grins as we approach. His cheeks and nose are rosy in the light. Up close he looks like an edgy, off-season Santa Claus.

"Guys, this is Dale. I explained our situation, and Dale has kindly offered to give us a ride to help us try and find our car," Hallie explains and introduces Oscar and me.

Dale extends his beefy hand and pumps each of our hands in turn like we're conducting a business transaction. "Nice to meet you. So y'all got your vehicle stolen, huh? That's a bitch. Happens around here quite a bit. We get a lot of bored teens jacked up on drugs looking to joyride. They usually just drive 'em around for a while and then abandon them when they hit something or get bored, whichever comes first."

"We really appreciate it," Oscar tells him. "It looks like they're only a few miles away up the highway here. We've been tracking them on Jack's phone."

"No trouble. Happy to help. I'm heading that direction anyway. Glad for the entertainment and the company. Did two tours in Vietnam...I'll be damned if I'm scared of some two-bit, teenage car thieves." He chuckles, and his eyes twinkle. "Let me finish up here, and we'll go hunt down those scumbags."

I ignore the fact that the bed of his truck is loaded with tied-off green garbage bags that could be filled with anything from yard waste to human body parts, and we open the passenger door to climb into the cab of his truck. There are only two seats up front, making for a tight squeeze...and there's also a gun rack attached to the ceiling that holds a wooden baseball bat wrapped in what appears to be barbed wire. Hallie sees it too because she grabs my arm and squeezes it like she's a human blood pressure cuff. I swallow hard.

Dale registers the expression on our faces and chuckles. "That's Lucille. I take it you're not big *Walking Dead* fans."

All three of us shake our heads as Dale goes on to explain, "I'm not much for guns, but if anyone messes with me, pulling that out seems to do the trick just fine. Go on and touch it if you want. It's a plastic replica. Got it at Comic-Con a few years ago. Looks real though, right?"

I touch a spike gingerly, and it gives and bends ever so slightly.

I have a replica of Luke Skywalker's lightsaber. It has real die cast metal parts and motion sensor–controlled sound effects. I'm guessing it probably wouldn't make anybody crap their pants with fear, but it's still pretty cool.

Dale jerks his head toward the rear of the truck. "Two of you can sit in the back there. Just keep your heads down so highway patrol won't see ya, and one of you can sit up here and navigate. Trust me, I'm harmless as a kitten."

He winks and removes the nozzle from his gas tank and screws on the gas cap. Then he walks around to the driver's side of the truck and climbs in.

"You should sit up front so you can be on the lookout for it," Hallie tells Oscar. Also, everyone knows that whoever sits up front is the first to go if this guy is some sort of serial killer. We'd have a better chance to escape in the back.

"Here, take my phone." I hand it to him. "It's got next to no battery left, so fingers crossed it doesn't crap out. Maybe this guy's got a charger."

Oscar thanks me and puts his hand on my shoulder with a solid *thunk* like we're saying goodbye before heading into battle.

Hallie and I climb into the bed of the truck. We nestle ourselves side by side between the mountains of bags, our arms and legs mashed up against each other. Whatever is inside the bags is lumpy and hard and pokes into my hip, and I feel compelled to apologize for her discomfort.

"Sorry."

"For what?"

"I'm sorry I got you into this. I mean—you were waiting for a bus, and now you're in the back of a pickup truck on a reconnaissance mission for a stolen car. This was not as advertised."

She smiles. "It's better."

9
HALLIE

SATURDAY, JUNE 5, 1:45 A.M.

I manage to wait barely thirty seconds from the time we leave the gas station to ask Jack, "So your brother—he's a recovering drug addict?"

"Yeah." I wonder if his brother looks like him—tall and slim with the same wavy, coffee-brown hair, square jaw, and stormy-gray eyes—or they're complete genetic opposites in every way, like Dylan and me.

"That must be rough. I'm so sorry."

"Thanks."

"Do you have other siblings?"

He shakes his head. "Just the one brother. He overdosed on OxyContin. He'd stolen my dad's prescription pad. If I hadn't found him when I did, he probably would have died."

"Wow." I hug my knees toward my chest. "Well, obviously you saved his life, which is good. He's still on the planet. I'm sure he's grateful to you for that."

"I don't know. Maybe. I haven't spoken to him since it happened."

"How long has it been?"

"Almost two years."

I absently rotate my bracelet around my wrist. "Wow. I can't imagine not talking to my brother for that long. Dylan's a pain in the ass sometimes—he's thirteen—but still. That's rough."

Jack nods. "My parents kicked him out. He'd pushed them too far and nearly messed up my dad's career because you have to report stolen pads to the police. It's not like Alex didn't know what might happen. He wasn't oblivious; in fact, just the opposite. He was smart enough to know it was exactly what it would take to get my parents' attention."

Dale swerves slightly, and the contents of the bag dig into my hip deeper. I shift slightly to lessen the pressure. This truck apparently has zero shock absorbers. No doubt we will both be black and blue by the time we get wherever we're going.

"That's awful," I say.

"My family puts the *fun* in *dysfunctional*."

A laugh escapes, and I quickly slap my hand over my mouth. "I'm sorry, I didn't mean to laugh. It's not funny."

"I think you can find the humor in anything after a certain point."

We involuntarily bump against each other in the back of the truck for a while until Jack finally says, "So since I've completely overshared—because apparently you bring that out in me—it's only fair that I get to ask you a totally personal question."

"That seems reasonable. Shoot."

"Why'd you leave school before the end of sophomore year? I mean, you didn't move away, right? Did you transfer?"

I look at him with disbelief. "You really don't know?"

He shakes his head. "Should I?"

Oh boy. I angle toward him to look him square in the eye. "If I answer your question, you have to promise you will not treat me any differently afterward or feel obliged to ask more questions because you're worried about being impolite, because that's usually what happens. And I'm so over that. Do you still want to know?"

"With a build up like that? Probably twice as much now as I did before. And I promise." He cracks a half smile.

I lean my head back against the cab window. "So, the short version is...I had cancer."

"Holy shit."

I steal a glance at him, half expecting him to scoot over two inches like I might give him a virus.

"It turns out pregnancy, the flu, and cancer have a lot of the same symptoms: nausea, vomiting, fatigue, abdominal discomfort. So, when I spiked a fever and collapsed in the hallway one night, my mom rushed me to the hospital. I was expecting it to be one of the first two, which would have been crappy enough, but they ran all these tests and it turned out to be number three. I have this super rare condition that only like a hundred and forty people have ever been diagnosed with called Carney's triad. It mostly affects teenage girls, and it's when three different types of tumors grow in three separate organs of the body, usually the stomach, lungs, or adrenal glands. Most people present with it in one organ if they're lucky, but over their lifetimes, a small percentage get all three."

His mouth is hanging open. "Jeez. Did you have all three?"

I shake my head. "The one I had was in my stomach. They call it a gastrointestinal stromal tumor, or a GST."

"Did you have to do chemo or radiation?"

"The kind of cancer I have doesn't respond well to either, so they do surgery. They removed part of my stomach along with the tumor, and I have to take this gross medicine with all these nasty side effects like muscle pain, headaches, and weird rashes to keep it from coming back. But it doesn't always work the way it should. With Carney's triad, you can have a tumor in one place and have it removed and then years later another will grow somewhere else."

His eyes flit to my stomach reflexively, as if searching for evidence of what I've been through, and then back to meet mine. "But you're cured, right? It's gone."

I shake my head. "There is no cure. There's always a possibility it'll come back. I have regular follow-up visits where they monitor what's happening with radiography so they can see if new tumors are growing."

"Why didn't you come back to school after that?"

"By the time I was able to, I'd missed half of sophomore year. I ended up doing homeschooling. It was much easier than having to go back to school and have everyone talking about me, or worse, *not* talking to me because they don't know what to say. People are weird about stuff like that. Even the people you'd never expect to

- - 110 - -

behave that way. So, I did classes online and had to check in with an advisor once a week, which was actually great because I got to work at my own pace, and I was able to take the GED and graduate months before I would have normally."

He bobs his head, expressionless. I can't tell what he's thinking. But then his brow furrows, and he says emphatically, "That's ridiculous. That people act that way, I mean—not what you chose to do. I'm sorry you had to go through that. I probably would have chosen not to go back either."

"Sometimes perspective comes in ugly wrapping paper." I arch my back slightly, eyeing him. "You're not going to look at me differently now, right? Because you promised."

"Nope."

I smile. "Okay, good."

"But you're fine now, right?" he presses.

Oscar hastily slides open the rear cab window, and we're snapped back into the moment.

"The battery died and as luck would have it, Dale is the last human on Earth with a flip phone. Seriously—you should consider donating that back to 1995," he says offhand to Dale then turns back to us and adds, "At the last check, it appears like they're just up ahead off the highway on this service road. They haven't moved since we started tracking them, which can't be good because it means they either ditched the phone or they're dissecting my car like a frog."

Jack and I got so caught up in each other's stories that I nearly forgot why we're here. And of course, none of us thought to check if they sold chargers at the gas station. Dale picks up speed as he exits the highway. My parents would freak out if they could see me right now. Yes, this is ill-advised and reckless, but it's also a total rush.

Oscar passes Jack's phone back to him and says, "Oh, and by the way, right before it died, you got a text from someone named Natasha."

"I did? What did she say?" he asks a little too eagerly.

"I didn't read it," Oscar tells him, which makes sense because he was slightly preoccupied with trying to track his stolen car. "We should probably come up with some sort of plan for if the guys are still there when we find the car."

"A plan would be good," I agree.

Jack shoves his phone in his rear pocket. "It's about the element of surprise, and in the worst-case scenario, being prepared to offer them something they want in order to get what you want."

"I have that Target gift card you gave me," Oscar says.

"Probably not gonna be enough. Do you have a watch or anything?"

"Do people even wear watches anymore?" I ask.

"I have a watch. It's a digital Casio waterproof to a hundred meters." Oscar proudly holds up his wrist to show us.

"The thing is: we're not all that intimidating, but we need to give off the impression that we are," Jack says, reeling him back in.

"All that. Yes. But how the hell are we gonna pull that off?" Oscar asks.

We drive down a dark, narrow road that runs parallel to the highway. The truck hits another pothole, and one of the green bags awkwardly topples onto my leg, dislodging the tie and falling open. What looks like a human head peeks out of the bag. Jack and I simultaneously cry out and recoil.

The truck hits yet another bump, and the head fully emerges, along with naked shoulders.

"Holy shit!" Jack yelps and instinctively puts his arm across me protectively, as if that might do anything.

You know that moment they say happens when you face the prospect of imminent death and your entire life flashes before you? Yeah, that doesn't actually happen.

Instead, I immediately start visualizing the grisly way in which I am potentially about to meet my end. A guy that looks like Santa is going to chop us all to bits and bury us in a shallow grave behind some scrub brush on the side of the 101. I haven't even done anything worth doing with my life yet.

And then the body slumps sideways, revealing the face. The eyes are painted on and the hair is fake.

It's a mannequin. Jack and I start laughing. I lean forward and peel the rest of the bag away to reveal that it is more specifically a mannequin head and torso. No legs.

"That's creepy," I say. "What do you think he does with them?"

"Maybe he's building an army for the zombie apocalypse," Jack offers.

He loosens the tie on another bag and pulls it down, revealing yet another mannequin. There must be at least ten bags back here, and they all seem to have the same dimensions. A smile spreads across his face, and he lets out a laugh.

"I have an idea," Jack says.

10
JACK

SATURDAY, JUNE 5, 1:58 A.M.

This reminds me of a scene from one of my favorite films ever.

"Did you ever see the movie *Home Alone*?" I ask Hallie.

"The one where the kid's parents go on vacation and forget him, and he has to defend his house from the two incompetent burglars? Of course. Why?"

"Do you remember the scene where he sets up all the mannequins to make it seem like there's a party going on so the burglars wouldn't think he was there all by himself?"

"Yeah." Her eyes dart to the bags, and then her face lights up as she realizes where I'm going with this.

I yell through the slider window to Dale, "Hey, what's the story with all the mannequins?"

"Did they escape? I worried they might break loose and create a panic." He chuckles. "My friend makes things out of them—mermaid sculptures for gardens, coffee table bases, all sorts of wild stuff. She's very creative. Got a deal on them for her from a warehouse that was going out of business."

"Would you mind if we liberated the rest of them? It's dark, so I'm thinking if we set them up around the truck, it'll look like there's more of us and we're not messing around."

Dale snorts. "I like how you think. Have at it. If you dig in the corner there, you'll probably find some old ball caps. Feel free to throw some of those on them to make them look more authentic."

Hallie and I set to work taking the mannequins out of the bags and setting them up along the perimeter of the truck bed. We discover Dale's stash of ball caps in the corner under a folded furniture pad. The first one I pick up is red with a white cross on it and says "Orgasm Donor" in thick, black letters. Classy. There's no time to be judgmental, so I stick it on a mannequin head and grab a few more. The sayings on them are equally creative. It's like he bought out the clearance section of a Spencer's Gifts. Judging by the contents of his truck bed, Dale clearly has a sense of humor.

I toss a few caps at Hallie, and she follows my lead. There are just enough of them to go around. I turn a couple around backward for good measure because in every gang movie I've ever seen, there's always those one or two guys who wear them flipped around, too cool for shade. As long as it's dark and no one has stellar nighttime distance vision, it's definitely passable. The only problem is, the mannequins are still naked. Nothing says "quake with fear" like potentially having your ass kicked by a bunch of nudists in suggestive baseball caps.

"How about if we put the garbage bags over their heads like ponchos?" Hallie suggests. "Maybe in the dark they'll look like commandos."

"As opposed to going commando," I joke.

By the time we've finished, we've successfully created the illusion that we are an army of badassery descending on these car thieves to take back what's rightfully ours. Hallie and I fist bump. Dale pulls down Lucille from the gun rack overhead and places it on the seat between himself and Oscar, ready to spring into action. Even I wouldn't want to screw with us.

Suddenly Oscar shouts excitedly from inside the cab, "There it is!"

We turn around and peer through the windshield. I spy the giant Buddha head peeking back at us from the driveway of a small, dilapidated house. There are at least eight other cars crammed onto the driveway and on what was once a lawn before the drought and neglect took over. Dale turns off the headlights as we slowly make our approach.

There doesn't seem to be anyone around. The car is parked in plain sight as if we pulled into the driveway and left it there ourselves. It's anticlimactic.

Dale stops the truck and cuts the engine. Somewhere, a dog barks and pierces the silence.

All four of us cautiously and quietly get out of the truck, looking around in all directions for any signs of life.

The car appears to be in perfect condition—no dings or scratches or signs of forced entry. Oscar walks up to it and peers in the driver's side window. He tries to open the door and finds it unlocked. He lets out a loud sigh of relief and ducks in then turns around and straightens up, holding up his phone like a victory prize.

"Phone's here. No keys," he reports.

We spread out and check the perimeter around the car—on top of the tires and underneath—to see if they were dropped, but no luck. Oscar pops the trunk, and we follow him anxiously as he opens it. Our bags are there, seemingly intact and untouched. Weird.

"At least all our stuff is here," Hallie says as she unzips her bag, checking it. Oscar shakes his head and starts pushing our things to the side and then lets out a sigh of relief.

"Thank god." He pulls out a black urn etched with paw prints—it easily could have been a cookie jar for dog treats—and pops open the lid, checking to make sure its contents are intact.

The dog starts barking again, but this time more urgently, and moments later the front door to the house cracks open. The porch light flicks on, drenching us in light. A guy stumbles out. He's in maybe his midfifties and wears a faded flannel shirt over an old white tee, a pair of gray sweatpants, and stained construction boots that look like they'd hurt in an ass kicking. In fact, it's hard to tell in the light, but the stains might even be patches of dried blood. Or ketchup. Hopefully ketchup. A loud, yippy Chihuahua spills onto the porch in front of him, baring its teeth at us.

"Settle down, Princess," the guy says to the dog in a warning tone then cups his hands over his eyes like a visor. "What the hell's going on out here?"

Oscar closes his eyes and whispers repeatedly to himself under his breath, "*This is just an audition. This is just an audition.*"

"We should be asking you the same thing," Hallie pipes up, squaring her hands on her hips.

"You stole my car," Oscar says boldly, immediately in the scene with total focus. He's convincing as hell.

And now the guy really does not look happy. "I didn't steal nothin'," he says. Princess starts barking furiously. "Get off my property."

My heart is pounding a mile a minute. I'm fueled by pure adrenaline. "Not until you give us back *our* property," I say in what I hope is an equally intimidating tone. The guy turns his gaze on me, laughing. He doesn't take us seriously. Not that I blame him. We're not exactly what you'd call threatening.

"Like I said, I don't have anything that belongs to you, so you best be on your way back to the middle school or wherever it is you came here from." He crosses his arms, puffing out his chest and standing his ground. "Tired of you punks knocking on my door all hours of the night."

Sticks and stones. I'm not naive. I know things could easily change on a dime here. But...he doesn't appear to have a weapon, and given the circumstances, he seems like the kind of guy who might have pulled one out by now if he had it. There's also only one of him and four of us. Twelve, if you count the mannequins. *God, I'm hoping he's counting the mannequins.* I roll the dice that my instinct is spot on.

"Oh yeah? Then how do you explain his car sitting in your driveway?" I ask as I notice Hallie out of the corner of my eye reach into Dale's truck and grab Lucille off the seat. She holds it up toward her ear like she's at bat. She looks very convincing, but *what the actual fuck is she doing?*

"Who told you to come here?" the man asks with a jerk of his head.

"We've been watching you for a while," Oscar says, channeling every detective confronting a suspect in every crime drama ever. This seems to make the guy nervous.

Hallie takes a step forward. "If you hand over the keys, we'll happily be on our way with no trouble. Otherwise, we're not making any promises. Don't make the rest of us have to come out of the truck."

She doesn't seem the slightest bit worried that he might call her bluff.

The guy's eyes flick behind her to the silhouettes of bodies in the pickup truck bed. He looks them over suspiciously. They are rigid and unmoving, which makes perfect sense because they're made of fiberglass and plastic. He boldly takes a step toward the truck, squinting for a better view, and for a moment I worry he's going to walk over there for a close inspection. Then Dale moves the mannequins ever so slightly as if they are getting restless and are champing at the bit to jump into action. He throws his voice from behind the truck bed, dropping it an octave. "Just say when, and I'll take him out."

I have an uncontrollable urge to start laughing. It's a weird reaction I have sometimes during moments of high stress. My therapist, Carole, says it's not that uncommon; it's the subconscious mind's way of negating fear and attempting to restore emotional balance. This would be the actual worst possible moment for that to happen.

So naturally, it does.

Hallie looks at me like I'm a weirdo, and Oscar widens his eyes in this what-the-fuck-are-you-doing-man-he's-going-to-snap-and-kill-us sort of way, which only makes me laugh harder. I bite at the inside of my cheek to stop it, but I can't.

"What the hell is wrong with *him?*" the man asks Oscar, wide-eyed.

Oscar, in the role he's been waiting for, improvs and says, "He's unhinged, man."

It sounds like a line from a poorly scripted episode of *Criminal Minds*, and it amplifies the sheer ridiculousness of the situation, thus causing yet another nervous burst of laughter to escape. This, in turn, causes Hallie to completely lose it, and then I'm laughing at her laughing, and we both can't stop laughing. Then Oscar joins in, and I imagine the three of us must look seriously baffling.

Hallie winks at me, and that's when it hits me, they think I'm acting, and this is part of a plan I've come up with on the fly, and they are following my lead. It's so brilliant, I wish I'd actually thought of it.

It seems to be working unplanned magic. The guy looks more than a little freaked out, unsure what to make of us or how to respond, and I sense his bravado is weakening.

I seize the moment and step forward, grab the bat from Hallie, and say in my most menacing tone, "We can keep this simple, or you can make this difficult."

His jaw tenses, and he holds up his hands in surrender. I guess me laughing while holding a bat in my hand makes him take me more seriously. "Hey, whoa—look, I don't want any trouble here." Even Princess lets out a whimper.

"Excellent. Then give us the keys and we're on our way. No further questions."

"Right." The guy's brow knits together. He throws a tentative glance toward the cars and asks, "Which one is it again?"

"You're kidding, right?" Oscar pipes up and points to it. "The one with the giant Buddha head that says GoodCarma on the side?"

The guy's gaze settles on the last vehicle parked toward the back with its visible-from-space-because-it's-so-huge Buddha decal as if he's noticing it for the first time. I give the bat a swing, and then the guy swallows hard and says, "Hold up here a second." He reaches down, tucks the yippy dog under his arm, and disappears inside the house, the front door creaking shut behind him.

The four of us are left standing in the driveway looking at each other dumbfounded. The guy is gone, and we still don't have the car. None of us are laughing anymore.

What the hell just happened?

11
HALLIE

SATURDAY, JUNE 5, 2:11 A.M.

Oscar looks like he's about to lose the last shred of his sanity as he boldly marches up to the front door and starts banging on it urgently. "Hey, man! Give me back my keys, or we're calling the police!" he threatens even though I'm pretty sure he'll do no such thing. He turns around and looks at us, throwing his hands up in the air. "Is this really happening? Are we on TV? Do you see cameras?"

He legit starts peering in bushes looking for a camera crew.

"Hold your horses!" a voice calls from inside the house.

Snippets of dialogue filter out from behind the other side of the door in agitated tones saying things like "goddamn Buddha head," "truckload of gangbangers," and "blow this whole thing wide open." Our ridiculous act must have worked, because this guy is obviously worried. The only time I have ever heard anyone actually use the phrase "blow this whole thing wide open" other than in a very bad, low-budget action movie is never.

The amount of adrenaline coursing through my body is off the charts. That was such a rush, like an out-of-body experience. My heart is pounding. I have never felt more awake. But now that the guy has disappeared and we still haven't gotten the car back, it ebbs, and I start to feel nervous. What if he comes back with a gun? Who would even know we were here?

Suddenly, the front door opens again, and the guy reemerges flanked by an old lady with short, curly, white hair pushing a roller walker. She's wearing a baby blue velour tracksuit with white stripes down the sides and flashy gold glasses with the Gucci logo on the temples, and she's holding Oscar's keys. The guy leans against the door and says, "This here's Momma. Seems there's been a mix-up and she took your car home from the service station instead of her own when she went to fill up."

"Yep, it was a mix-up," the woman says and looks at her son.

The guy puts his hand on his mother's shoulder. "Sometimes Momma can't sleep at night, and she likes to take a drive and gas up the cars. As you can see, we got a lotta cars, and sometimes she gets confused easy and forgets which one she took." He chuckles, the picture of innocence, and says, "Well, seems that was all a big misunderstanding. So now that you have your car back, I don't think we need to involve the cops."

The old woman holds out the key fob and mumbles an apology under her breath like she's a teenager who's been caught out after curfew.

Oscar steps forward and takes it from her hand as the guy

pats his mother's arm lovingly and says, "Honest mistake. Okay, Momma, you've caused enough excitement for one night. Now go on inside and get to bed." As she shuffles inside, he turns to us, winks and says, "Sorry about the inconvenience. Y'all have yourselves a good night." And before we can blink, he hurriedly shuts the door and turns off the porch light, drowning the yard in darkness.

Once he's gone, we all exchange a look of disbelief.

Oscar then holds his key fob up as if examining it to make sure it's real. "Holy crap."

"I guess you can cross 'Have car stolen by an octogenarian' off your bucket list," Jack tells him as Dale emerges from behind the truck. Jack hands Lucille to Dale. "And thanks for your help. We couldn't have done it without you. The ride, the mannequins, this scary-ass bat—that was beyond fiction."

"Glad to help. Here I was, expecting a long, uneventful drive. It was an entertaining diversion. Just shows ya you never know what your night's gonna be. You all charge up your phones and hold on to your keys from here on in," he says with a chuckle. "If you don't need anything else, I'll be on my way."

"I think we're ready to roll. Thank you. Everything Jack said." Oscar pumps Dale's hand furiously.

I don't think as long as I live, I will ever be able to erase the image of Dale's truck driving off into the night with a truck full of poncho-wearing mannequin torsos in backward baseball caps.

As we settle in the car, I clear my throat, and I can hear a slight, unmistakable wheeze. My breathing is a little more labored, but I attribute it to the night air and the adrenaline rush. Nonetheless, I put my hand to my chest and can't help but wince. It's only for a second, but Jack catches it.

"You all right?" he asks me.

I nod. Before, he might not have thought anything of it, but now, after what I've told him, he's bound to worry it may be something more serious. That makes two of us, but I made the choice to be here, so I need to push through it.

Oscar adjusts the rearview mirror and says, "Not that I'm complaining, but anybody else question the validity of the whole Momma-is-an-accidental-kleptomaniac story?"

He presses the engine start button, and the car makes a clicking sound. He presses it again, and there's more of the same.

"Why isn't the car starting?" I ask.

"I have no idea," he says and continues to press it as if this next time might be the charm.

I look at Jack. "So, what are we gonna do?"

"Why are you asking me?" he asks.

"You've come up with the plans so far tonight, so it's looking like you're the unofficial brains of this operation," I explain. I'm not wrong.

"I'm no mechanic, but since we just got gas, my first guess is it's a dead battery. You probably need a jump start."

Oscar narrows his eyes as he checks the dashboard screen. "Nope. Dead empty. I never got to fill up. I went to the restroom first. Good to know I can get this far even with the tank on empty. People may knock them, but Kias get some great mileage."

"So where are we going to find gasoline just sitting around?" I ask.

We all realize at the same time that if we are surrounded by cars, there must be gas. Wordlessly we fan out looking for the telltale red containers of fuel. I find one in the waiting-to-be-featured-on-an-episode-of-*Hoarders* side yard by the sagging carport, but it's empty. We keep searching, but then Oscar whispers loudly to us to bring him the fuel can ASAP. I grab it and follow the direction his voice came from to find him crouched down on the side of a gold Toyota Camry, proudly holding a long piece of what appears to be two different lengths of plastic aquarium tubing.

"Look what I found." He waves them back and forth with his hand, super excited about this random discovery. "Life imitates art."

"What do you mean life imitates art? And how is plastic tubing going to help us?" I ask.

"I once had to audition for a heist movie as this guy who is siphoning gas from the big mob boss's car and gets caught, but I still remember how to do it. I need a rag or something to create suction."

"Are you sure you know what you're doing? You've actually done this in real life? You got the part?" Jack asks him.

"No, I did not get the part, which is *ridiculous*. But I did watch a how-to video on YouTube a hundred times to make sure I had it down," he assures us. "Acting is all about authenticity."

I spy a piece of red fabric by the chain link property fence out of the corner of my eye. It's an abandoned T-shirt, sun-bleached and riddled with holes. It's probably been there for some time and has found its purpose.

"How about this?" I offer it to him.

"Perfect." He attempts to open the gas tank, but it's tight and he can't get it to budge. "It's stuck. I need a jar opener."

"Where are we going to find a jar opener here? This isn't exactly Target." I say, as if that weren't obvious. I start to get nervous again.

Jack's face lights up. "I think I have the solution."

He pulls out his wallet and extracts the Pokémon condom I saw him holding at the restaurant, tears off the wrapper with his teeth, then wraps the end of it around the gas cap and twists. It resists for a second and then turns with ease.

"Brilliant," Oscar says. He wraps the thin fabric around the base of the shorter tube and then shoves the other tube into the tank along with the first one, filling in the space around it with the T-shirt. "Let's give it a go."

He leans forward, blowing hard into the short tube. Nothing happens. He blows again. Nothing. He pushes at the fabric, making sure the seal is tight, and blows a third time and then like magic we hear the gasoline start to flow from the car into the canister.

"Well done," I compliment him.

Oscar grins. "And people say there's nothing of value on YouTube."

We are nearly finished pouring the gas into the tank when the front door cracks open and we hear Princess being released into the yard for a middle-of-the-night pee. All we need is that dog to start yapping again and that guy to catch us on his property siphoning gas without an army of half-naked mannequins and Dale's bat.

The guy yells, "Stay out you damn rodent. I swear as soon as Momma goes, your days are numbered."

He slams the door closed, and Princess lets out a whimper.

Oscar narrows his eyes. "I hate people who are mean to

animals. Nikki loves animals. Especially dogs. She'd rescue every last one if she could."

"We better get going before she picks up our scent," I whisper.

Too late. She's heading in our direction.

Oscar quickly caps the gas can and puts it to the side. Even if it's not full, it's enough to get us down the road enough to buy more. Oscar and I climb into the car and Jack's coming around the side to get in when we hear a low growling sound at his feet. It's Princess.

"Hi, Princess, nice doggy," he says gently, moving slowly toward the rear passenger door. He reaches his hand out and puts it on the handle. Princess stops growling and sits down, watching him curiously and then yawns. As he's edging himself backward to sit down, Princess walks over to the car and cocks her head sideways, looking up at him.

"I can't close the door with her standing there," he tells us.

Princess looks back toward the house then back at me, whimpers again, and starts wagging her tail.

"I think she wants to come with us," I say.

Princess lets out a single yip as if agreeing. I try to shush her. She gives a little whine, and I suddenly understand the full meaning of the term *puppy-dog eyes*.

"We can't steal his dog," Jack reasons.

"He stole our car," I refute.

"Technically Momma did," he says as Princess hops up on her hind legs, paws against the instep of the open doorframe.

"Look at her, she's practically begging. This jerk doesn't deserve her. He called her a rodent," I say, and then I get an amazing idea. "Oscar—you should give her to Nikki. Tell her you rescued her, which isn't *entirely* a lie. The charm of a live dog might be more romantic than a dead one, plus it would be symbolic. Think about it: Terrapin represents your old life together, but Princess could represent your new one."

"It's true—nothing says 'take a chance on our future' like gifting someone a stolen Chihuahua," Jack volunteers.

"Brilliant!" Oscar cranes his neck to look at Princess and grins at the scrappy junkyard dog. "Princess, today's your lucky day. Welcome aboard!"

He summons her to jump in with a curl of his hand, and Princess readily accepts. We should get the heck out of here before anything else can happen. Once in the car, the dog immediately sets to work sniffing everything. I offer my hand to her, and she contemplates it then begins furiously licking it. It's like an ad for why to use hand sanitizer. Trust established, Jack hastily closes his door as I pull Princess into the space on the seat between us. She rotates counterclockwise in a circle twice and then curls up into a ball like she belongs here, leaning her head against my thigh. In fact, I swear the dog is smiling.

Once we're in motion, I check my phone for any word about Owen, but I can't get reception. Even with that delay, it's still looking like I should be able to make it to San Francisco to catch my bus with no problem. I can't wait to see the look on his face when I walk in that door and we meet for the first time. Wait until I tell him about the mannequins and now the Chihuahua. I'm sure he'll appreciate the levity.

"I can't believe we just stole a dog," I say finally. "I've never stolen anything in my life."

"She's not stolen—she's rescued, like you said. We liberated her," Oscar says.

"You're right. We're offering her a better life," I say as I rub Princess behind her ears. That I can make peace with.

Jack stretches and says, "Well, I don't know about you two, but theft gives me a hell of an appetite."

As if on cue, an oasis with a neon gas station and fast food signs appears in the distance. My stomach gnaws with hunger in anticipation of the grease and carbonation.

Oscar picks up speed and it's not long before we find ourselves in the drive-through lane of a twenty-four-hour Taco Bell. Despite it being around three in the morning, there's a huge line. Apparently, all there is to do in the middle of the night around here is steal cars and dogs and eat fast food.

"The beauty of Taco Bell is you can get a ridiculous amount of eats and feast like a king for around twenty bucks," Jack says as he tears the wrapper off his first Soft Taco Supreme. "It's the kind of food you pay a little for up front and a lot for later, but right now it is the stuff of dreams." Princess props herself up on his leg and attempts to take a bite. He whisks the food away just in time.

"Aww, she's hungry," I say, pulling her off of him. "We need to get her something to eat." Jack reluctantly puts his taco back in the wrapper, and while Oscar tops off the car with gas, Jack and I quickly run into the mini-mart. I tuck Princess under my arm like a football. They don't seem to have any dog food, because why would they? We opt for a mini-mart hot dog, which looks fresher than the ones from the place where the car got stolen. Princess wags her tail when she sees Jack reaching for it. I add a bottle of water, Jack pays the attendant, and now everybody's happy.

Back at the car, I tear the hot dog into bits, and Princess eagerly wolfs them down. After I get her settled, I take a bite of my chicken soft taco, savoring every bite. I never get to eat this stuff anymore. At home, Mom tries to cook super healthy.

Jack lathers his soft taco in Fire Sauce and stuffs a quarter of it into his mouth. I shovel my nachos into my mouth like someone is about to take them away from me. I offer him one, but he declines, as he has his own order in the bag along with three more soft tacos and a MexiMelt. Oscar attempts to eat his burrito with one hand while navigating us back in the direction of the highway with the other.

"Do you ever wonder how many people you've walked by a million times at school might have turned out to be amazing friends if you'd only struck up a conversation?" he asks me.

I smile. "Only all the time, but not even just when I was at school. I like looking at total strangers and making up whole stories about them in my head."

"Like you did with me earlier. It's called profiling. I do it too."

"In fairness, you gave me lots of material to work with."

"Well, now you have even more. So, what's the story in your head about me now?" he asks. I grin. "C'mon, you can't tell me you don't have one by this point."

"Oh, absolutely."

"What is it? Let's hear it," he demands, and we both laugh.

"Well, obviously you're on the lam, afraid of being exposed as a total fraud after being caught not recycling a plastic water bottle despite being president of Earth Club. Unable to live with your crimes, you've decided to go underground and make things right by dedicating your life to creating eco-friendly, biodegradable, sustainable packaging. And then you will write a bestselling novel about the whole ordeal that will be turned into an Emmy-award-winning Netflix series starring everyone who is anyone in young Hollywood."

"Wow, you're good," he tells me and raises his eyebrows.

"It's a gift," I say as I cut a path with my chip through the remaining pool of semi-coagulated nacho cheese in my plastic cup.

I worry that he might turn it around and press me for more of my story, but he doesn't. We whiz past a sign saying San Francisco is still another two-hundred-something miles ahead. "Factoring in the strong probability of a bathroom stop or two, that puts us in San Francisco sometime shortly after sunrise," he announces as he unwraps and takes a bite of his second taco.

There is a very distinct *pfffft* as someone lets one rip, and then the car suddenly smells like ass. We all sit there awkwardly frozen silent for a minute, unsure what to say but all clearly smelling it when it happens again.

We simultaneously realize that this malodorous scent is coming from Princess.

"Naturally I steal a dog that's a farter," Oscar says, cracking up.

Jack and I burst into laughter. "It's probably the hot dog," I say as I plug my nose, fanning the air in front of me.

"No, it's *definitely* the hot dog," Jack concurs. Princess toots again and looks at me, tongue wagging happily. "From adorable to biohazard in sixty seconds."

All windows are rolled down simultaneously at warp speed.

I close my eyes, tilt my face toward the incoming rush of fresh air, and breathe in deeply, laughing to the point of tears. I don't even care about the heaviness in my chest, because it feels amazing to laugh like this. I can't even remember the last time I did.

12
JACK

SATURDAY, JUNE 5, 3:30 A.M.

We make an emergency pit stop for Princess to take a bathroom break on the side of the road, which is a good call. Her gastrointestinal issues hopefully remedied, we're on our way again.

I still need to charge my phone. And I'm dying to text Ajay. This night tops any of his brother's wild college stories, hands down.

I dig for my charger in my backpack and plug it in before connecting it to my phone. The home screen takes forever to come to life, and the earlier text notification from Natasha pops up on the screen. Amazingly, I'd forgotten all about it. It looks like there have been a couple more since, one as recently as twenty-six minutes ago.

I can't bring myself to look at her messages. I don't want to engage. Her push to be friends as if nothing happened feels like a manipulation to assuage her guilt. It's annoying actually. It will be what it is in its own time; it can't be forced.

More likely, we'll keep in touch for a while, but the gaps between talks will naturally grow further apart until at some point they stop. Natasha probably did us both a favor.

"Aren't you going to read it?" Hallie asks, angling toward me.

Like that poster in my therapist's waiting room says: you can't focus on the road ahead if all you're doing is looking in the rearview mirror. New day. New me. It's all about forward momentum.

"No." I should delete them without even reading.

She peers at my phone. "It's from that girl, right? I could read it for you if you want and tell you if you should read it."

I think about it for a second and then hand my phone to her. "Why not?" Hallie turns her attention to the phone screen, and I gaze out the window until I can't stand the silence and have to look at her for a reaction. "It doesn't even matter. It is what it is."

"I get it. Caring about someone is a risky proposition. Disappointment and heartbreak are inevitable." Her eyes stop scrolling, and she suddenly smirks.

Uh-oh. "What? Is it bad?"

She clicks off my phone and places it facedown on the seat between us, sighing dramatically. "She likes emojis."

"She does. Sometimes she will hold entire conversations in them. So are you going to tell me what she said?"

"If I tell you, my guess is you'll want to respond right away. I think you should leave it alone for a while. Let her sweat it a little, you know? Otherwise you'll look desperate."

It's sound advice. I think I've looked desperate enough for one day.

"Trust me, I know about desperate." Hallie tells Oscar and me about the guy that made her swear off love as if it were gluten. As soon as she starts to describe him and recount their undoing, I know she's talking about that guy I saw her with that night at 7–11.

"Ryan Mandry. He was a senior. We'd been together on and off since beginning of my freshman year, but I'd only ever met his family once. They had a ton of money—his dad owned all these car dealerships—and I think they had a certain idea of the sort of girl they would like their son to date. Let's just say I wasn't it."

"But you're the heir to the Pancake Shack. Not swanky enough for them?"

"Ha! Definitely not."

"I'm guessing this doesn't have a happy ending," I say.

She considers it and shrugs. "Depends on how you look at it. Sometimes it takes something awful happening to see someone's true character."

I huff a laugh. I can relate. "Yep."

She goes on, "Ryan was spineless and cared too much about pleasing his parents, and nothing proved that more or showed everyone's true colors like a good old-fashioned cancer diagnosis."

Oscar's eyebrows knit together. "Don't tell me he bailed. I will turn this car around and find him."

"Oh, he bailed all right—but not before his parents offered me five hundred dollars to break it off with him and leave him alone. He was leaving for college, and it wasn't as if they liked me, so they didn't want his focus to get caught up on me. They even tried to convince me that if I really cared about him, I would want what was best for Ryan."

"That's pretty messed up," I tell her. "So, what did you do?"

A lock of violet hair falls forward. She tucks it behind her ear and continues. "Naturally, I told them I wanted at least a thousand."

I can't help but laugh. "For real?"

"No, I told them to go screw themselves. But then I told Ryan what happened and expected him to be outraged. Instead, two days later he broke it off—said I was too much for him. My dad literally threatened to break both his legs if he saw Ryan anywhere near me again."

"So—you're too much, and apparently I'm not enough," I tell her. "We're yin and yang. We balance each other out."

She laughs. "Right? So happy endings are subjective. We didn't end up together, but that's a good thing."

Oscar slams his hand against the steering wheel in disbelief. "Jesus. What the hell is wrong with people? Who breaks up with someone right after they tell them they have cancer? I know I'm totally pushing all the driver/client boundaries here saying so, but that gets my blood boiling."

"I'm pretty sure we broke the driver/client boundaries a while back when we hitched a ride from a stranger, repo'd your car, and stole a dog," I assure him.

"Karma has her way in the end, don't you worry," Hallie says. "When word got around that we'd broken up and that I had cancer, people thought he was a total jerk for breaking up with me."

"Which, of course, he was," I inject. Princess whimpers a little in her sleep, and we all silently pray this will not lead to another episode of flatulence. I hover my finger above the electric window button as a precaution.

"Obviously. But get this: one night he calls me and begs me to meet him at 7–11. He has to talk to me. I don't even know why I went. I thought maybe he wanted to apologize. I still hate the part of me that hoped, despite everything, that he might even want to get back together. And then...wait for it..."

"How could it get any worse?" I ask.

"He was worried about what people were saying, so he wanted me to tell everyone that we mutually agreed to break up and that we were still friends, that everything was cool. He even asked if we could take a selfie together to show we were all good and post it on social media so the rumor mill would die down. Because if it's online, it must be true." She rolls her eyes.

I saw her knock his phone violently out of his hand that night. It's what drew my attention to her in the first place—the noise of it falling and cracking against the asphalt and how the guy didn't even flinch, like he knew he deserved it. Now everything about that night resonates differently with me.

"A *selfie*?" Oscar says, his mouth hanging open.

"A selfie," she affirms and then turns to look at me, casually adding, "You know what's weird? I swear I saw you there that night."

My stomach lurches. If I recognized her that night, it makes perfect sense she recognized me too. I should explain myself. "I—"

Princess cuts me off by loudly ripping another one, and the

noise startles her awake. She yawns, lets out a single bark, and then sits up, tail wagging, tongue hanging out the side of her mouth, panting and ready for adventure.

"Here we go again," I say as we depress the window buttons with lightning speed.

"She might be thirsty," Hallie says reaching down for the bottle of water and a small paper bowl the clerk gave us at the mini-mart.

Oscar cracks his window again. "Well, good god, whatever you do, don't give her anything else to eat."

Good point. All we need is Princess getting the runs in the back of the car.

Princess furiously laps at the water in the bowl, and Hallie gently strokes her bony back. I'm ashamed that she knows I saw her visibly upset and that I left like a total coward.

"If I'd known what was going on, I would have kicked his ass," I say, although I think we both know that ass kicking is not my strong suit.

"But somebody might have filmed it, and then it would have ended up on YouTube, gone viral, and you might not have gotten into Columbia," she says. She puts Princess's water bottle on the floor, pulls the one I'd bought her earlier out of her purse, and takes a sip.

"And thus, the course of history would have been changed. Because if I hadn't gotten into Columbia, I wouldn't be here right now having an existential crisis, and therefore the entire course of all three of our lives would have been completely altered," I counter. "And we might not have ever met up again."

I take another swig of my soda, but it's near the bottom, so it's mostly crushed ice and air. It goes down the wrong way, and I end up coughing. *Smooth.*

Hallie hands me her water bottle. "Here, no carbonation. It'll help."

I make the mistake of pausing and looking at the bottle instead of just accepting it from her. I don't even know why I did it. It's only a split second, but I can tell by the flicker of sadness in her eyes that she notices my hesitation. It was an involuntary subconscious reflex, a human response to putting oneself at risk. But it's ludicrous—there is no risk. I don't even need to be premed to know you can't catch cancer from sharing a bottle.

I reach for it and take a long sip. It's important to me that she knows I'm not scared of her.

"Thanks," I say as I dab excess water from my lip with the cuff of my sweatshirt. Her eyes soften as I hand it back. I sense that may have been a test of sorts, and I'd passed.

"Any time." She lifts the bottle to her mouth in the same spot where my lips had been moments before and takes another drink from it before putting it away to show me she's not scared of me either. It's like we've kissed but not really.

I don't even know why my brain goes there.

"You know what's weird? You're literally one of the only people who ever read anything I've written."

She scrunches her nose. "How come?"

I shrug. "I'm not great with criticism. I mean—who is, right? If someone tells you that your imagination sucks—where do you go from there? That's some debilitating stuff, like telling someone their baby is ugly."

She laughs and covers her mouth with the tips of her fingers. "I don't recall your writing sucking. Didn't you write that short story about the old man who hated dogs that dies and gets accidentally gets routed to dog heaven because it was the new angel's first day on the job?"

"You actually remember that?"

"Sure. It was hilarious."

I can't hold back my smile. I ask her, "Do you ever wish you could look into the future and know what's going to happen?"

She thinks about it for a moment. "That information would only be useful if I were also given the ability to change the outcome. Which you couldn't, of course, because if you're looking into the future, this is de facto what happens, right?"

"So, you wouldn't want to know if you were about to make some epic life-changing mistake?"

Oscar chimes in, "In my opinion, there are no mistakes. Sometimes something seems like the worst thing but is in fact the best thing. You just can't see it until down the road. So, it may seem like a mistake, but in fact, it wasn't." He raises his index finger at the last part for emphasis.

"Exactly. I think you have to go on faith that everything is exactly as it is supposed to be, or it's easy to get overwhelmed. We are the sum of our choices." Hallie curls a tuft of hair behind her ear.

"But what about the things we don't choose?" I ask.

"I think they happen for a reason, even if we don't know what it is. The choice is how we choose to react."

"Isn't that the truth?" Oscar asks. "It's like my ex Nikki—she's the sort of person that rips through your life like an F5 tornado and leaves behind as much damage. But who's to say I'd be any better off if she hadn't? Maybe Nikki pointed me in the direction I needed to be."

Hallie nods. "The sum of *her* choices influenced the sum of your choices."

"Precisely. Which is why I need to stop this wedding. It's my fault she ended up with Kevin, so I need to undo it." He says the name like it's poison. The conversation quickly morphs from waxing philosophical back to the present.

"What happened?" Hallie asks. She's unapologetically nosy, but I'm curious now too. Might as well all put our personal crap on the table tonight.

"I was too caught up in myself. I took her for granted. Kevin saw a window and swooped right in, and I practically handed her to him." He shakes his head. "If I don't make this right, I have to live my life knowing this person is still walking around on the planet with someone who isn't me, you know?"

"I hope it works out. So, what are you going to say?" Hallie presses him.

His eyes shift between the road and the rearview mirror. "I figure the right words will come to me in the moment. I don't want to overthink it."

"So true. Sometimes you just have to go with the flow. Like tonight, for example: right before we picked Jack up, I was going back and forth in my head about visiting my friend Owen. I was considering cashing in my ticket and going back home. I literally asked the universe for a sign." She turns to me. "Then you got in the car, and the fact that we'd seen each other earlier and then here you were again going to the exact same place as me—you felt like a sign. I was *supposed* to go. So here I am."

Wait—what? "You decided to go to Medford because of me?"

"What can I say? I'm a believer in signs."

"Oh, me too, girlfriend," Oscar says reaching his hand up for a high five.

Admittedly, it does feel as if there's a reason our stories entwined.

There's something freeing in talking to people you know you're probably never going to see again. There's no expectation or judgment. No sense of obligation to fix each other or solve each other's problems. You can be real with each other because there's no emotional investment in the outcome of things. Everyone accepts each other for who they are, and it's enough. It seems like all three of us needed that tonight.

At some point the sky transitions from midnight black to a deep violet. We descend upon the outermost fringes of a predawn Silicon Valley. The sides of the highway slowly populate with familiar chain restaurants, quadrangles of office parks, and, most importantly, the promise of an open Starbucks. I spy the beautiful, big, green-and-white, two-tailed mermaid logo like the siren she is and let out a whoop of joy.

This moment feels damn close to perfect. Not just because coffee is in my immediate future, but also because I have no idea what I'm doing and for once I don't care. All I know is, for the first time in a long while, I truly feel happy. I'd forgotten what it felt like.

But perfect can only last so long.

13
HALLIE

SATURDAY, JUNE 5, 6:04 A.M.

As we turn in to the Starbucks parking lot, I start coughing again, but this time it escalates, and I can't stop. I press my hand firmly against my chest and drain the last sip from my water bottle.

"You okay?" Jack asks.

"Yeah. This happens sometimes."

"It sounds pretty bad. You should get checked—you don't want it to turn into bronchitis or walking pneumonia," he suggests.

"Yeah, probably," I say and then look away from him as Oscar pulls the car into a space right in front. Not telling Jack the whole story is starting to feel like lying.

As we climb out of the car, he asks me, "Is it okay that you're traveling like this, then? I mean—back at the station, you said no one knows where you are, right? Aren't your parents going to be worried as hell?"

"Aren't *your* parents going to be worried as hell?" I deflect as I tuck Princess under my arm.

"Parent," he corrects me as he holds open the door to the Starbucks. "And right now, I'd rather ask for forgiveness than permission."

Oscar beelines for the restroom while Jack and I fall into line behind a handful of early risers. The smell of freshly brewed coffee, the whir of the grinder, and the *psssssh* of the steamer assault my senses. I realize I have been up for over twenty-four hours.

"Me too. And they don't know where I am because if they did, they wouldn't have let me go, and frankly, that should be my choice. Because I'm still living in their house and they are financially responsible for me, they feel entitled to some say even though I'm eighteen. And there isn't a lot of privacy. I didn't want them to freak out and worry over nothing. It was this way, or it wasn't going to happen."

"I can see how they might be overcautious since you were sick before. At least it's because they care."

"Believe me, I know. My cancer became the central point of their lives. They've given up so much already that the thought of putting them through more is awful...I hate it."

"Well, it's not guaranteed to come back. There's only a chance, right?"

He seems so genuinely concerned. As soon as I say the words out loud to someone else, it will become real. Hot tears well up at the corner of my eyes, and I try to blink them back. I do *not* want to start crying. I look away. He gently touches my wrist. "Hallie?"

I look down at my bracelet. "I had a follow-up visit a couple of days ago, and they saw something unusual on the scan, but they weren't sure what it was. It looks like it could be a pulmonary chondroma—a tumor on my lung—so my doctor wants me to come back on Monday for another scan to check, and we'll basically go from there. I haven't told my parents because, until I know definitively, why turn their lives upside down again?"

The barista cheerfully asks Jack for his order.

His face is ashen as he responds, "Uh...coffee, black, no room please. And whatever she wants."

Jack once again insists on paying. I start to dig for my wallet. "You don't need to keep buying everything for me. I can handle a cup of coffee."

"No, I got it. I want to. That was the deal." We migrate toward the end of the counter to wait for our drinks. "I don't even know what to say. I'm...wow. That sucks." He looks so sad.

"It wasn't clear, which is why they want to do another scan. And if it's something, at least we're catching it early." I'm trying to reassure myself as much as him, repeating the words the doctor said on the phone.

He shakes his head. "I'm so sorry. Here you are listening to me complain about my first world problems, and meanwhile you're sitting with this."

"Our problems are just different, is all. Everyone's got their crap they're dealing with. It's not a contest. Seriously—you promised a few hours ago that you wouldn't treat me any differently."

He nods and forces a smile. "I did. And I won't. I promise."

Oscar joins us, and I bring him up to speed. I feel better after opening up to them, particularly since they're both nonjudgmental and caring.

We get our drinks, and the conversation turns to Owen as we're walking back to the car.

"So does Owen have the same kind of cancer you do?" Jack asks as he climbs in.

"No, he has something called a *non-resectable osteosarcoma*—bone cancer but the kind where the tumor cannot be removed entirely by surgery. The five-year survival rate for that kind is significantly lower. He made it two and a half. He just turned nineteen. He won't ever see twenty." That's the part that keeps cycling in my brain. The part that worries me too.

Jack's phone buzzes on the seat where I'd left it facedown earlier. It keeps buzzing, and he looks at it then at me like it's a bomb he is awaiting my permission to diffuse.

"Do whatever you want," I tell him.

The buzzing is clearly making him anxious. He clicks his lock button without checking it and shoves it in his pocket. The vibration stops. A minute later a single buzz lets us know there's a voicemail.

The freeway lanes multiply, and the rolling hills and office parks give way to urban sprawl. Signs appear for alternate highways that branch like arteries to all different parts of the city.

Oscar pipes up, "Maps says we're a half hour from the bus station in San Francisco. It's not far from the waterfront, so it depends on traffic cutting through the city."

Princess wakes up and yawns, then turns herself in a circle and resettles, leaning against my thigh. I stroke her head. After I get out of the car in thirty-ish minutes, I won't know how things turn out for Jack or Oscar. Or Princess. It's like being on the last chapter of reading a mystery and someone has torn out the rest of the pages.

Jack must be having a similar thought because he says, "Are you guys on social media at all?"

"I'm on Instagram," Oscar says.

"Me too. I mean—it seems weird that after all these hours of shenanigans we just exit each other's lives forever, doesn't it?" Jack looks at me and smiles.

"For sure. TheOscarGoes2," Oscar tells him. "Follow me, and I'll follow you back."

"I see what you did there. Nice." Jack opens up Instagram to search for him then turns to me. "How about you? Are you on Instagram?"

I shake my head. "I'm not on social media."

"Seriously?"

"Seriously. I think it's so self-destructive. Everyone ends up comparing their lives to everyone else's highlight reel and feeling depressed. Its only redeeming quality is the plethora of silly cat videos."

He laughs. "How do you know I don't exclusively put up silly cat videos? Or pictures of adorable baby animals? Hamsters in tiny crocheted sweaters and hats?"

"Tempting," I say with a grin.

And then he says, "No, seriously. It'd be cool if we could keep in touch. Can we at least exchange email or something?"

I chew at my lip. "I don't think that's a good idea."

He digests that and nods, looking slightly wounded. "Okay. I guess I just figured that—"

"What, that because I told you my deep, dark secret and that story about how my ex-boyfriend broke my heart, you're under some obligation to keep in touch with me or you'll look like a jerk?"

I know it's unfair to unleash on him, but I can't help it. I can see he's struggling to figure out how to react.

"No, because I want to."

I want to too, but that's exactly the reason I won't. He's a great guy. It would be easy to get lost in waiting for him to text or call. And I'm afraid of that feeling of potentially soul-crushing disappointment if or when he doesn't. I'm afraid of hoping.

"I don't expect you to understand," I tell him, "but I think it's better this way. Let's just enjoy now without introducing expectations that it needs to be anything more than this."

Left with no choice but to accept my answer, Jack shrugs and smiles as he tucks his phone away again. "Fair enough."

Princess rests her head against my hand, nudging at it with her nose. I scratch behind her ear, which makes her left front paw rotate in small circles. I envy the simplicity of her life. Eat, drink, poop, and love. I don't know why it needs to get more complicated.

Fog hangs lower and blankets everything the deeper into the city and the closer to the waterfront we get. It engulfs the tops of buildings and bridges. San Francisco is famous for it. It's hard to imagine it's summer when it looks like the dead of winter outside. I wish I'd brought a jacket.

The light changes to red as we approach the bus station, and

I'm grateful for the extra couple of minutes. "So, after you drop me off are you heading to your brother's place?" I ask Jack.

"Yeah. If it's even the right address. I'll probably get breakfast somewhere first. I could use some time to formulate my thoughts."

"Are you nervous?"

He shrugs. "I don't know what to expect."

"I think the best way to avoid disappointment is not to expect anything." Easy to say. Hard to do. I need to listen to my own advice.

There's a lot of construction happening around the bus station. It's an eclectic mix of gentrified and brand-new buildings, long sidewalks, and parking garages. We turn the corner onto Folsom Street and the station comes into view. Princess, as if sensing my imminent departure and protesting it, puts her paw on my arm and looks up at me.

"Here we are already," I say, straightening up and pulling my purse strap over my shoulder. Jack's shown me one of the best nights of my life, but even more importantly, he's treated me like a normal person. For a moment, I second-guess my decision to not exchange numbers, but I catch myself. I turn to him and say, "It was nice catching up with you again."

"You too," he says.

Now we're at the part where I'm supposed to exit the car. Except I don't. I stare out the window at the terminal and then turn to Jack and find myself saying, "I have nearly five hours before my bus leaves. I'm just going to be sitting here. I could come with you if you want."

14
JACK

SATURDAY, JUNE 5, 6:49 A.M.

I temper my excitement about this latest development, so I don't come across as too eager. "That would be great!"

She smiles back. "Cool."

"So—I guess we're both getting out here," I tell Oscar.

"The band is breaking up," he jokes as we begin to gather our things and grab our bags from the trunk. Princess, excited by the sudden flurry of movement and change, lets out a series of farts that sound like gunfire from an AK-47. Parting ways just in the nick of time.

"Oh man." Oscar rolls down all the windows and hops out of the car along with us. "This is going to be a long ride to Berkeley."

"Well—good luck with breaking up the wedding and winning Nikki back. I hope Princess seals the deal, although I'd be careful about what you feed her between now and then," Hallie tells him as she comes toward us around the side of the car. "I feel like we should hug. I mean—we're kind of friends now—right?"

"Absolutely," Oscar says as they embrace. "I hope things work out for you—on all fronts."

"Thanks, you too," she says as she breaks away.

Oscar turns to me and extends his hand. "Thanks for the unexpected adventure, mate. I say trust your gut. And keep choosing your own ending."

It's a reassuring mini pep talk at the perfect time, exactly what I need to hear.

"I'll be first in line for my autographed copy!" he adds as he climbs back into the driver's seat and I realize that he's talking about my book and not my life.

He raises one hand out the window to wave goodbye then pulls away from the curb into the oncoming traffic. Exit stage left.

Hallie watches Oscar drive away and says, "Isn't it weird how people come into our lives—could be for a year or a day—and then they just disappear? Or you meet someone and it's as if you've always known them."

"Yeah."

We store her suitcase in a locker at the bus station and then check the departure screens. *Delayed.* The estimated time of departure is now 1 p.m., and I worry that she's going to flip out again like she did last time, but she seems to take it in stride.

"Unreal," she says. "Looks like you're stuck with me for a little longer."

"Challenge accepted," I say.

"So—breakfast then?"

Which is how we end up winding our way through the downtown streets in search of a place open this early that isn't another coffee chain. A few blocks away, we stumble upon an open taqueria with a giant red-and-white WE SERVE BREAKFAST sign out front. The building seems a little rundown, but this place has an A rating and a line, so hopefully it's decent.

I hold the door open for her. A set of bells tied to the door handle jingles to announce our arrival. We order two breakfast burritos and coffees at the counter and then settle in at a weathered-looking, red wooden table with a wobbly leg near the window.

"You know this is probably going to be the best breakfast burrito you've ever had in your life." She reaches for the bowl of creamers, pours one into her paper coffee cup, and then stirs it with her spoon. She nudges the creamer bowl toward me. "Want some?"

"No thanks, I take it unadulterated." I pop the lid on my cup and am pleased to discover the cup is filled to the brim.

"Right. Black, no room."

"Exactly."

"When I heard you order it this morning at Starbucks, all I heard you say was 'blacknoroom' like it was one word, and I was thinking maybe that's some fancy preparation. That is truly the difference between a caffeinated and an uncaffeinated mind."

I laugh and look around. "Wow—my dad would have loved this place. He was always a fan of a good hole-in-the-wall joint. He used to like to watch that Guy Fieri show on the Food Network—*Diners, Drive-ins, and Dives*? If ever there was an episode where it featured one within a two-hour radius, he would take me with him to check it out. He'd order exactly what Guy Fieri ordered every time so he could see if he agreed with the hype. It was pretty funny."

"That sounds fun."

"It was one of the things we used to do together. My mom was always busy with her practice and writing her books, and Alex never wanted to go. Gourmet breakfast was wasted on him. He ate a bowl of Captain Crunch for breakfast every single day. Sometimes he'd eat it for lunch or dinner too. In fact, I wouldn't be surprised if he's sitting somewhere eating a bowl right now." I laugh at the memory, but then my thoughts flip to my final image of Alex, forever seared in my brain.

She notices the change in my expression. "You okay?"

"Yeah. I was just thinking how the last time I saw my brother, he was unresponsive and sprawled out on the bathroom floor. I was scared he was going to die. And then when he didn't, I was relieved and also pissed off, which was confusing." I swallow the lump forming in my throat.

"And then you never spoke to him again after that?"

"Nope. After my parents sent him off to rehab for the third and final time, they told him not to come back, and he cut off all communication." I blow on my coffee and take a tentative sip.

"Do you think he did it on purpose? Overdose, I mean?"

I shrug. "I've had that thought. It wouldn't surprise me."

"Does he know you're the one that saved his life?"

"Not sure. For all I know, he might hold that against me."

"Well, it's about time you find out," she says. An old guy with a comb-over and a grease-stained apron emerges from the back and delivers us two red plastic baskets filled with the most amazing-looking breakfast burritos in the history of breakfast burritos. It's pure food porn. Then again, maybe I'm just really hungry. I'm running on the anti-food pyramid of birthday cupcakes and Taco Bell.

I tear into my burrito. "The last thing I ever said to him was pretty awful. We'd been having a celebration dinner for our mom because she'd been asked to be the guest speaker at some fancy women's retreat near Big Sur. Alex made some crack minimizing her work, saying the retreat would be a bunch of middle-aged women in the woods masturbating their way to enlightenment."

I realize I should explain who my mom is in case she doesn't know. Hallie's heard of her but doesn't seem to care, which is a welcome change.

"That must have been interesting on career day," she says with a smile.

"You have no idea. Anyhow, Alex was provoking my mom—trying to get a rise out of her like usual. She'd left the table crying, and my father sat there stewing, caught between them, until he got up and left too. Everything was so amplified. I yelled at Alex, 'Why do you always have to make everything turn to shit?'"

She looks nonplussed. "Maybe it's good you said that."

I take another massive bite. "How so?"

She has another sip of coffee and daintily cuts into her burrito with a plastic knife and fork, making me seem like a Neanderthal. "When people say things in the height of emotion, they're half-true. Part of it is meant to hurt the other person, and the other half is their own pain about the situation. That's where you need to start."

It sounds like something my therapist, Carole, would say.

"I was thinking more along the lines of *hello*," I tell her.

"No—I mean—maybe that's where you start a dialogue with yourself to get to what you *really* want to say to him. Not just the facts and the experiences, but how those things made you feel. It might be uncomfortable, but if you can't be honest, then what's the point of coming all this way to see him?"

"What if he doesn't want to talk to me? What if he shuts the door in my face?"

"What if he does? Just because you want him to react a certain way doesn't mean he will, and you should be prepared for that."

"How do you know all this stuff?"

She shrugs. "I watch a lot of *Dr. Phil.*"

My phone buzzes in my pocket again. I keep ignoring it. The more persistent the attempts get, the more annoyed I am by the intrusion. I reserve the right to not want anyone else getting in my head right now. It's one of the few things I have control over.

"Let me handle it," she says and holds her hand out, palm up for my phone.

"Wait—what are you going to do?"

"Will you please trust me?"

I hand her my phone, and she busies herself reading.

"Who was it?"

"A missed call and voicemail from Mother Ship, another text from Emoji Girl, and one from someone named Ajay telling you that Emoji Girl is having a meltdown trying to reach you and that he beat your high score on *Pac-Man.*"

"Did he say what his score was?" He's been trying to beat mine unsuccessfully for years.

"I'm glad to see you have your priorities straight," she kids.

"Did you know that *Pac-Man* was originally called *Puck Man* but when Midway started manufacturing the game in the US for Namco, they changed the name to *Pac-Man* because they were worried about vandalism and people changing the *P* into an *F*?"

"I did not." She types something on my phone and hands it back to me. "I sent each one a thumbs-up—the response that needs no response."

"A thumbs-up?" I raise my eyebrows and laugh.

"It's positive acknowledgement that lets someone know you're alive, and that's all you really owe anyone at this point."

She's not wrong.

She takes a bite of her food, and a dab of sour cream remains on her lower lip. I fight the urge to reach over and wipe it off. Instead I point to my lower lip in the universal mirroring pantomime for "you've got stuff on your face," and she removes it with her napkin.

"Do you ever think about that?" I ask her. "How much you owe anyone?"

"All the time."

"I mean—none of this is supposed to be happening. I'm not supposed to be here right now. You're not supposed to be here right now. But the thing is—why not? Shouldn't we be wherever we want to be, doing whatever we want to be doing? Within reason, of course."

I pour some Cholula on the edge of my burrito.

"Define reason." She pulls out a wad of napkins from the metal dispenser on the table.

"I can understand it in certain contexts. Like—if your parents are paying for college, don't fuck around and party for four years and get all Ds. You're in a relationship, so don't sleep with someone else. You decide to have kids, so show up for them. But does my brother *owe* me something for saving his life? Do I *owe* it to my parents to go to Columbia or become a doctor? Do I *owe* it to Natasha to be friends?"

"Exactly. It's like everything else we've talked about. At some point you need to let go of what you thought should happen and live in what *is* happening. Like with Emoji Girl."

I'm giddy at how much she would hate that nickname. "Natasha?"

"Whatever." Hallie smiles and takes another sip of coffee. "If she'd been open to giving the whole long-distance thing a shot— if your conversation with her had gone another way—I bet you wouldn't be standing here right now."

I rock my head side to side, evaluating that. "True. I most likely would have stayed at the party with her, maybe gone somewhere else after. Probably not San Francisco though."

"Exactly. But you *are* here. So maybe it's like Oscar said: she was a catalyst for moving you toward where you are supposed to be. I believe people come into our lives for a reason, but it doesn't mean they're supposed to stay there forever."

"Oooh, you're good. My therapist would love you," I compliment her.

She beams, encouraged. "*Maybe* this girl hasn't figured out yet that even if the odds are against things working out, it doesn't mean it isn't worth trying. She doesn't realize that everything is temporary. You—me—this burrito."

"*Especially* this burrito," I say and tear off another piece.

"The real question is: What do you owe *yourself?*" Hallie shifts in her seat and tucks one leg under herself, staring at me.

"Oh—is that an actual question you're asking me?"

"Like the whole college thing. It sounds like it's a big deal to your family for you to go to Columbia. Did you always want that too? Or did you feel obligated, like you owed it to your parents to go if you got in?" She adds another creamer to her coffee. I seriously don't understand how she can drink it like that. At least she's not adding sugar.

"The idea of doing anything else was not even up for discussion," I say. "I bought into the whole idea that certain schools are better than others and that if I didn't get into Columbia, it meant I'd failed somehow. But now I'm realizing that's bullshit. It doesn't matter where you go; there are great teachers and opportunities anywhere. It's what you put into it. And I don't necessarily believe that success equals happiness."

"Depends on the person's definition of success."

"Exactly." This girl freaking gets me. "But I think you're giving Natasha far too much credit for why I'm here. Like I couldn't handle the rejection and so I went off the deep end. It's not like that. But it certainly made it easier to leave."

I yawn, and it makes her yawn.

She points her fork at me. "If you hide away what you think and feel and are just who others want you to be, it's not the real you anyway."

I could never have this sort of conversation with Natasha in a million years.

After breakfast, we spill back out to the street. There are still a solid four and a half hours before she has to be back. "Where do you want to go?" I ask.

"Let's just walk," she says.

So we do. And when we step off the curb and jaywalk, dodging traffic like we're in a game of *Frogger*, she takes my hand.

15
JACK

SATURDAY, JUNE 5, 8:03 A.M.

A few blocks down by the waterfront, the vibe is totally different. It's more upscale and alive with a different sort of pulse. Money juxtaposed against raw poverty in full display. We join a stream of early riser tourists, joggers, and vendors receiving deliveries. The city is waking up. I'm wired despite the lack of sleep.

"I like the idea of having no particular destination. Then I'm never disappointed if I don't get there," she tells me.

I pull the hood up on my sweatshirt against the chill. Hallie smiles and takes a final sip of her coffee and throws the remainder in a nearby trash can as we pass it.

I steal a glance at her. Hallie makes me want to talk about stuff I never discuss with anyone. I feel safe to open up to her, like I know she's not going to use it against me or judge me. But the thing is, if I want her to know the real me, I need to tell her the whole truth about what happened the last time I saw Alex. The part that I've never told anyone.

"So...remember how I told you the last time I saw my brother, I found him on the floor OD'ing?"

"Yeah."

I cast my eyes down to my feet; I can't look at her as I say it. "The thing is—when I found him—I didn't call for help right away. I stood there in the doorway thinking how much less stressful everyone's lives would be if he weren't here—specifically mine—and I could make it happen. I felt drunk with power. It was only a few seconds, but it felt a lot longer."

After what seems like an eternity of silence, I finally dare to look at her. Her face is a blank slate. Not even the slightest reaction. "So, what stopped you?"

"He saw me. He looked right at me. He knew I was there."

"And if he hadn't?"

"I honestly don't know." I'm not proud of my answer, but it's the truth.

"You guys didn't get along?"

"No, we did—for the most part, anyway. He didn't get along with my parents, my mom specifically, and every time he'd act out, he amplified the tension at home. It put a lot of pressure on me. In the moment, something in me snapped."

She takes that in, and then shakes her head as if refuting it. "But you obviously chose not to let him die. You did the right thing. So why are you still beating yourself up about it?"

"Because I have to live with the knowledge that I'm the kind of person who'd consider letting my brother choke to death in a pool of his own vomit so my own life would be simpler." It comes out in one big burst sounding a little more defensive than I intend. I look directly at her. "Sorry. If I've freaked you out now and you want to go back to the bus station, I totally get it and zero offense taken."

"If I haven't been freaked out by this point, do you think confessing you're human will push me over the edge?"

I crack a smile, relieved. We keep walking and talking, putting distance between the bus terminal and us. That felt good to get out. I've been carrying this around a long time.

Hallie rubs her arms for warmth, shivering against the cold. I offer her my sweatshirt, which she eagerly accepts.

"Can I ask you a kind of personal question?" I ask her as I hold the left sleeve for her to feed her arm into it.

"Ask away."

"Are you scared of dying?"

"Scared? No. Angry maybe, for all the things I might not get to do or that might not happen and for how it affects my family. How about you?"

"I don't know. It's inevitable. No one gets out of here alive, right? It seems like lately all I'm doing is getting through the days, and when it's like that, I'd almost welcome it. Not so much that I want to die as much as I want to stop feeling so shitty, you know what I mean?"

"I do." I knew she would. "And sure—there's a whole extra layer to it because of the cancer, but the truth is the odds of my dying young or suddenly are probably not that much higher than yours. You could get hit by a bus crossing the street or struck by lightning. You never know when your number is up."

"True. So, what keeps you going?"

"It depends on the day. I suppose if all I did was focus on that I'm sick, I might never get out of bed. And I'm not gonna lie: I have those days too. A lot, actually. No matter what I do, what pill I take, what surgery I have, what foods I eat, it can keep coming back. Sometimes it all seems pointless and I wish it would just happen so it's over and everyone can get on with things. I'm incredibly good at feeling sorry for myself and raging at the universe."

"Yet another thing we have in common," I say.

She smiles and stops walking. "But then there are the days between—the ones where I feel okay, great even, and I remember how cool life is and am grateful to be here. To get to watch an amazing sunset, run barefoot on the grass with the sprinklers on, eat ice cream on a hot day, cook with my Mom, make a new piece of jewelry, experience something new for the very first time, laugh until it makes my stomach hurt, or walk around a strange city talking to a cute boy." She blushes, and we exchange a smile before she turns away and starts walking again. "That's the stuff that keeps me going."

The compliment warms me more than my missing sweatshirt ever could.

"I think that's what's missing for me—there are no days between."

She looks at me questioningly. "You never have a good day? Surely everyone has good days. Even the guy who is cleaning the shit out of the porta-potties at Coachella has good days."

"I mean—yeah, I guess, but I'm never completely happy." I shrug. "To be honest, I'm not sure I've ever been. There's always some part of me that's dissatisfied. But it's worse since my dad died."

I feel a crushing sensation in my chest as I picture my father. But not like his hospital staff photo with his perfectly combed salt-and-pepper hair and starched white coat. I picture him in his Pink Floyd T-shirt and basketball shorts grilling some burgers and dogs in the backyard for the Fourth of July or wearing his absurd blue and white wig to every Dodgers game, even the ones he watched at home on TV. I can't believe I'll never see him like that again.

"Everything feels broken," I continue, "and not the kind of broken that can be fixed. Like the kind of broken that stays broken."

"But sometimes broken things can be put back together differently. It may not be what it was before, but that doesn't mean it can't be something else potentially good."

"I don't know. I've spent the last year and a half existing in this foggy state, going through the motions, trying to get through the day. I'd been so depressed and anxious that I'd often go to sleep and not care if I woke up. Right after my dad died, I started having panic attacks, and I was diagnosed with generalized anxiety disorder, which is a fancy name for saying I constantly worry about things, even when there is little or no reason to worry about them. The world suddenly became an unstable place. I can't seem to find the same joy or meaning in anything, and I'm scared it's always going to feel this way. I'm just sort of lost." I take a deep breath and puff out my cheeks. "To be honest, right now, with you, is the best I've felt in a long time."

"Me too," she says and squeezes my hand.

"I feel like I can say anything to you. Maybe that's because we're not planning on being in communication after this, and while I'm sad about that, there's also something in it that's very freeing. So, thank you. I'll take it."

"I feel exactly the same way."

I try to shake it off and lighten the mood. "We've still got a few hours, and we're in this amazing city. We should do something cool, go somewhere."

"I'm up for anything," Hallie says with a smile.

And then suddenly I know exactly where we need to go.

The wave organ is not as close as it looks on Google Maps. I spring for a cab to save some time since otherwise it's a good thirty-minute walk. I'm going through money alarmingly rapidly.

Once we get to the entrance, we still have quite a hike because the wave organ itself sits on the end of a jetty that juts out into the bay. The long path is lined with some sort of weed with yellow flowers that smell like black licorice. The path appears to disappear into the water.

"Are you sure this is it? I would think we would at least see it," I reason.

"That must be Alcatraz." Hallie points toward an island in the middle of the bay. The prison sits atop it like the imposing fortress it is. "I hear the bay is infested with sharks. They say that's why even if the prisoners managed to escape, they would most likely not survive."

"Yeah, but they're mostly leopard sharks and brown smooth-hound sharks, which don't have much interest in attacking people.

Great whites tend to stay farther out in the Pacific Ocean." Hallie cracks a smile. "Sorry, was I being Human Google again?"

She points toward our left where the bottom half of the Golden Gate Bridge rises from the bay and disappears into the clouds. "I wonder why they call it the Golden Gate Bridge when it's actually orange."

I nod in agreement. I could tell her it's actually named for the Golden Gate Strait, the three-hundred-foot-deep stretch of water that runs under the bridge linking San Francisco Bay to the Pacific Ocean, but instead I say, "Amazing how many things don't make sense but we are forced to accept them anyway."

Even if we never find this thing, it's worth the walk for the view. As we draw closer to the end of the jetty, stairs appear as if out of nowhere leading us down a good six or eight feet. The land here isn't visible from above. In a radius around us, carved granite and marble slabs are interspersed with PVC pipes that pop up like periscopes at varying elevations. It looks like something out of a science fiction movie.

I smooth my hand over the cool granite and remember that Hallie had said it was built out of stones from a demolished cemetery. Markers of people that died, long forgotten. Repurposed. Someone has graffitied one of the slabs of marble nearby with something unreadable in red spray paint.

We are the only ones here. I don't hear anything that sounds like an organ, just the cries of seagulls and barks of far-off sea lions blending with waves slapping against the jetty.

Hallie climbs on top of one of the granite-and-stone benches and leans in to one of the periscopes. She grins, calling me over excitedly.

"Put your ear against it. It's like listening to a seashell." She moves aside for me to take her place and positions herself at another tube.

Mostly I just hear the sound of the water swirling along with the distant sound of a ship's horn and the cacophony of the birds. I keep my ear there and close my eyes and think about a time when I was with my family in Hawaii when I was little. My dad held a seashell to my ear and then to Alex's and told us to listen for the ocean. Instantly it conjures the weight of a brick on my heart, and I open my eyes again.

"It's not high tide," Hallie says. "We probably aren't going to hear much. That's disappointing."

Add it to the list. "It's a cool place though. I bet a lot of people don't even know it exists. They're busy wasting their time on all the touristy stuff."

We climb lower and see the intake pipes nestled amongst the mossy stones. We follow them back up again to a large, partially enclosed alcove with numerous tubes leading into it. It's called the *Stereo Room* because the sound rushes in from different sides all at once. We stand side by side listening to the muffled rumble of the water, hoping the universe gives us a break and rewards us after our having come all this way. It's very peaceful and hypnotic.

I turn to look at Hallie. Her eyes are closed, and her forehead is lined as if she was making a wish. And then as if sensing my eyes on her, she opens them and we just stand there looking at each other, not saying a word, listening to the muffled rumble of the water, and energy passes between us.

Natasha perceived vulnerability as a form of weakness—a

nasty side effect of her parents' ugly divorce. I suppose I knew from the get-go I would never get what I needed from her, but that didn't stop me from bashing my head against the wall trying and then beating myself up for getting exactly what I expected. I realize that's not what a relationship should be like. I never had a healthy one to compare it to. Not that *this* is a relationship, this mash-up of sorts with Hallie. It's just pure, honest connection. No pretenses. It's nothing I've ever experienced, and I like it. It makes me feel hopeful, though I'm not sure about what specifically.

A breeze kicks up. She takes my hand and puts my palm gently against the center of her chest and closes her eyes. She's not angling for me to feel her up; she wants me to feel her heart beating. It pulses rhythmically under the weight of my fingertips. This is the most personal, totally nonsexual moment I have ever shared with anyone.

The spell is broken as a breeze kicks up, pushing water into the pipes. There's a variegated baritone grumble as it regurgitates back into the bay. It doesn't last but a second or two, and the best way I can describe the sound is someone emptying a can of chicken soup while playing a didgeridoo. It's that unique. We listen for it to repeat, but it doesn't, which makes it all the more magical, like the universe made it happen just for us. We're two people in the wrong place at the right time.

I notice a man and a woman around my parents' age walking down the stairs, and the moment morphs into a shared space. Hallie is still holding my hand to her chest. I smile awkwardly and retract it. She smooths out the front of her shirt. The couple winds their way toward us, all friendly smiles.

"Good morning!" the couple says as they descend upon us. "You guys hear anything?"

Before I can answer, Hallie shakes her head and reaches for my hand, leading us out of the enclave. "No, it's low tide."

Perhaps she's hoping it will discourage them and they'll leave, or maybe she wants to keep what we heard our secret. We check out a few more tubes and then, with one more look at the view, we start to walk back up the jetty toward the city.

"I want to come back again one day at high tide," she tells me.

"How about high tide one year from right now?"

She laughs. "How would we know when high tide is a year from now? Unless you actually do, which wouldn't at all surprise me."

"Amazingly, I don't. I'd have to actually google and find an almanac. I'm serious, though—how cool would that be?"

"Very." She smiles thoughtfully and then adds, "But a year is a long time. A lot can happen."

"True." I wonder if she means actual events taking place or if she's worried she won't be here a year from now.

"How about six months, then? That would be December fifth."

"I'll have to check my calendar, but I might be able to squeeze it in."

"Excellent." I pull out my phone and Google high tide on December fifth this year in San Francisco. "Are you a late-night person or an afternoon person?"

"I'm a whenever person. Why?"

"You have a choice. High tide occurs at twelve fifty-six a.m. and again at eleven thirty a.m."

She puts a finger to her chin thoughtfully. "I say twelve

fifty-six. Potentially fewer people. And then we can walk around the city and get a late-night bite somewhere."

"Sounds perfect." I enter it into my phone calendar so that she can see. "That's a date."

Well, at least we have a plan to see each other now. That's something.

I pluck one of the yellow flowers lining the path and sniff it. The smell reminds me of biscotti.

"That's anise," she says. "The flower you're holding. The stems and leaves smell like licorice. It's an herb." She rubs one of the leaves between her fingers and then holds it to her nose.

"See? Now look who's Human Google."

"Finally brought down by botany. I knew you were too good to be true."

"You got me." I give the flower another sniff and then toss it into the water. A group of pelicans fly by and make a synchronistic nosedive straight down, scooping up breakfast in their orange bills.

"What time is it?" she asks.

I check my phone. "Nine fifty-six. Not a lot of time."

She wiggles her eyebrows. "Enough to get a small tattoo."

16
HALLIE

SATURDAY, JUNE 5, 9:56 A.M.

A Google search yields that the only tattoo parlor for miles that opens before noon is only a few streets from here, so we take it as a sign, confirmation that this is an excellent idea. I love the idea of putting stories that I choose on my skin, rather than the ones the scars leave behind. The fact that Jack is totally down to get inked too only makes it more meaningful.

"I always wanted to get a tattoo, but my parents told me I had to wait until I was eighteen," I tell him. "Specifically, I've always wanted a dragonfly tattoo—dragonflies are symbolic of change and transformation. They are born in water, and as they mature, they change colors and can fly in the air. They make a complete metamorphosis, ever-adapting to their changing environment and transcending their former selves, just like the soul. Something about them has always resonated with me and given me hope."

"It's weird; ever since my dad died, I see dragonflies all the time. It almost feels like your getting that particular image is like some sign he's actually here and that he knows what I'm doing and he's okay with it. Does that sound strange?"

"Not to me," I assure him. "In some Indigenous traditions, they are thought to be a link between here and the spirit world, so people often report seeing them or butterflies a lot after a loved one has passed on."

His expression brightens. "Maybe that's what I'll get too. For my dad."

Even if I never see him again, I kind of like knowing we'll both be out there in the world somewhere walking around with matching dragonfly tattoos. On the way Jack tells me, "I once heard this horrible story about this guy who went with his girlfriend and they were each going to get their names tattooed on each other's chests. The tattoo artist tried to talk them out of it, but they insisted, so the guy goes first, and the tattoo artist puts the girlfriend's name in huge letters across his chest. When he finishes and it's her turn, she turns to the guy and says, 'This'll teach you to sleep with my best friend. I want to make sure you'll never forget me for the rest of your life,' and walks out."

"Oh my god!" I crack up. As we get to the shop, I ask him, "So are we really doing this?"

He nods and smiles. "I think we are."

Inside, we are informed that there is an eighty-five dollar minimum. It's like the air has been sucked out of a balloon. I didn't expect it to be free, but I had no idea that tattoos cost that much. Jack immediately says that it's no problem and hands the shop owner a credit card for both.

"No way. Coffee and a burrito are one thing, but this is too much."

"Breakfast burritos and coffee are on you in December, how's that? Seriously, I want to. I like how every time we'll look at them, we'll think about this day. Proof this wasn't all just a dream. We were here."

He's so sincere that I can't argue. "Deal."

Jack grins as he settles into the chair. Annika—my tattoo artist—has bright, red hair, and every visible square inch of her except her face is covered in tattoos. I take this as assurance somehow that she knows her craft. I barely flinch as she skillfully inks my wrist. I look over at Jack, who is clenching his teeth as the needle repeatedly pricks his skin. Later, he holds up his right thumb, showing me the small, dime-sized dragonfly right below the knuckle.

"So *that* just happened. My therapist, Carole, would totally approve, which is good, because my mother won't. She'll hate it. Honestly, in a way that makes it all the more appealing."

We get a quick rundown of how to care for our new tattoos, and then we're back on the street hailing a cab back to the bus station.

"I love it," I tell him and flip over my wrist, looking at mine through the protective plastic wrap. It feels like I got stung by five wasps, and the skin is puffy and red in a halo around the design. "I'm so glad we did it—together, I mean. I might not have had the guts to do that on my own, and I've always wanted to."

I then explain to him why I chose it.

"Well, anyway, I can honestly say I would *definitely* not have done that without you. Getting a tattoo was not part of the plan."

"You mean your plan that is not having a plan?"

"Exactly. The very best kind."

We exchange smiles, but his eyes look sad, and once again I feel the weight of my imminent departure. I have to keep reminding myself that this friendship we've developed over the last twelve hours—it's temporary. Whatever this connection is—we're not going to get to keep it.

Once again, we're back at the bus terminal. When he walks me inside so I can grab my bag and say goodbye, we discover that my bus is now delayed another hour until two p.m.

"This is a joke, right?" I ask, feeling déjà vu as I sit down with a thud on the nearest bench. At this point I'll be getting to Medford after midnight, which will be problematic.

I haven't checked my phone since the time I tried but had no reception. I suppose unconsciously I didn't want anything to stand in my way once I'd made the decision to go. As I power it on, my screen is immediately littered with text notifications.

I scan them rapid-fire. They are all responses to a group text from one of my friends on the board chat, the first of which was sent about three hours ago. My stomach starts swimming as I read them.

"As someone once told me, just send them a thumbs-up—positive acknowledgement that lets someone know you're alive, and that's all you really owe anyone at this point," Jack suggests playfully.

Time stops.

I press my fingers to my lips, and a tear silently rolls down my cheek. *No, no, no, no.* The immediate shock quickly gives way to a deep sadness that courses through my body.

"Are you okay?" Jack asks as I shake my head. He sits down beside me on the bench, placing one hand gently on my shoulder and angling himself toward me. "Hallie, what's wrong?"

Another tear breaks free. My voice catches in my throat. "Owen's gone."

The tears start rolling one after the other, leaving burning trails down my cheeks. I knew this was going to happen, but now that it actually has, I'm gutted. My mind races to process that he no longer exists on the planet. I've never known anyone that's died before, and losing Owen suddenly makes the reality of my situation ten times more real. That could just as easily have been me. Cancer doesn't give a crap whether you're eight or eighteen or eighty. I suddenly feel alone, far from home, and unsure of what to do next. A sob escapes, and Jack puts his arms around me, drawing me to his chest. He whispers, "I'm sorry."

I cry into his T-shirt. He says it again.

My chin quivers. When I pull back, he has tears in his eyes. I know he understands the emptiness I'm experiencing.

"How did you find out?" he asks.

"I got a group text from someone else on the boards. Apparently, it happened late last night. He took a turn for the worse and had his whole family around him, and then he took the meds, and he went to sleep. It was very peaceful."

I dab at the corners of my eyes with the cuff of his sweatshirt. It smells like lavender laundry detergent.

"So, what are you going to do?" he asks. "Are you still going to Medford?"

"What would be the point? It's too late." I shake my head and look around the bus terminal. "It's not fair."

"I know." Grief is grief, and we understand each other's language. "For what it's worth, I honestly believe you can still tell him everything you wanted to say and he'll hear you. I get lots of signs from my dad that he's still around. Like those dragonflies. Or sometimes I'll find pennies right after I'm thinking about him. It's happened too many times for me to think it's purely a coincidence. I think they want us to know they're alright. And I believe they are. It's the ones left behind that have a hard time with it. Relationships in life don't really end, even if you never see the person again. Every person we've connected with lives on inside of us somewhere."

"I believe you," I say and sniffle. "Owen was one of the most positive people I've ever known. No matter how sick he got, he had the best attitude. We were going through this together. He was who I talked to about stuff. But him dying—it's surreal. Scary, you know?"

He lifts my hand and places it in one of his then covers it with his other hand. I wipe away my tears with my free hand and look at him. He's so genuine and sweet. It's exactly why I don't want to exchange numbers with him. I don't want to have to experience the pain of discovering he's anything less than perfect. I'd rather leave what this is or isn't to fate. It gives me something to hold on to.

Jack looks at me and asks quietly, "You wouldn't ever consider doing what Owen did, would you? Assisted suicide?" Before I can answer, he adds, "Sorry, you don't have to answer that if you don't want to. It's none of my business."

I sniffle. "No, it's okay. If I knew there was nothing more that could be done and I was in pain all the time? Maybe. I don't know—it seems selfish to put everyone through so much additional stress and prolong the situation when you know how the story's going to end. I'm grateful to have the option should I ever want it, anyway." I look around the terminal and sigh deeply. "I guess the universe is telling me it's time to go home."

"Right."

I don't move. My feet feel anchored to the floor. "The idea of being alone right now and sitting with my thoughts for hours after this devastating news is overwhelming."

"So, hang out and come with me to look for Alex."

Our eyes meet. "Really?"

"Yeah. I mean—if you want."

I would never have asked, but honestly, I'm so grateful for the offer. Being with Jack makes me feel safe right now. "I don't want to be in the way. I can take off when you find him. I could keep you company until then though, and then I'll get a ride back here."

"That'd be great."

I change my ticket to the 8:00 p.m. bus to Los Angeles while he pulls up a map on his phone to his brother's last known address.

17
JACK

SATURDAY, JUNE 5, 10:58 A.M.

My brother lives near Chinatown, sort of up a straight line and over a few blocks from here. It's about a nineteen-minute walk and close to the same by car with current traffic, so we opt to hoof it.

Hallie leaves her bag at the terminal again, but I bring my backpack with me because I have no idea what's about to unfold and where it might lead me.

We head down Folsom to Fremont, turn left on Battery and right on Bush until we reach Grant Street and the famous green-tiled Dragon Gate arch that leads to Chinatown, guarded on either side by giant stone lions. With every step, my nerves ramp up.

As we walk, I try to imagine for a minute that Hallie and I are here just being tourists too. Two friends exploring the city, shopping and eating and talking and laughing like life is completely normal.

It's amazing how different the neighborhood becomes as soon as we pass under the archway. The buildings are all three to four stories high with shops on the ground floor and apartments above. They are painted different colors, and many are run-down. All the signs are written in Chinese and English. Red lanterns dangle overhead strung from rooftop to rooftop. Souvenir shops overflow with Buddhas, trinkets, and I Heart San Francisco merch.

The air smells like incense and something else—garlic and ginger maybe?—from the gazillion Chinese restaurants competing up and down every neighboring street. Interspersed between the numerous fresh fish and produce markets are bakeries, tea shops, and foot massage parlors. It's as if we are on a bustling street in Hong Kong, not miles from redwoods and the Golden Gate Bridge. The building numbers start to climb as we head north in search of Alex's last known address.

"You okay?" Hallie asks.

"Yeah, why?"

"You have this look on your face..."

"I'm fine. Just a little nervous." I'm reassuring myself as much as I'm telling her. "How are you doing? About Owen?"

"I'm okay. Thanks for checking."

"Of course." I look at the number on the nearest building. We're getting super close. Just a little farther down. "Thanks for coming with me. It means a lot."

"Anytime." She smiles and gives my hand a light squeeze.

Unfortunately, it's the hand with the tattoo, so it's less comforting than it might have been otherwise, but the gesture grounds me.

And then we find it. It's an unassuming, faded-green three-story apartment building that has seen better days above a psychic reader storefront. It is flanked on either side by Top Ming's Beauty Salon on the right and Hop Sing Trading Company to the left. I scan the names at the buzzers, but everything is written in Chinese, because of course it is.

"How do I know which one is his? If it even *is* his?" I ask. I highly consider pressing them all. That seems to work in movies; someone is bound to be trusting enough to let me in.

I ask three different people passing by if they can translate the buzzers for me, and not one of them speaks English. Finally, a woman passes by who understands my request and rambles off a bunch of Chinese names, none of which sound like Freeman.

"If he lives here, there has to be *someone* who knows who he is or at least be able to tell us where we can find him," Hallie reasons.

The thought occurs to both of us at the same moment. We look up in unison at the dirty, purple wooden sign with gold lettering of the business on the ground floor of Alex's building. A large crystal ball and stars painted underneath the Chinese words with an English translation that reads LING PO, PSYCHIC, ALL ANSWERS REVEALED.

"*All* the answers? That's a tall order. She must be good," I say.

"It's worth a shot."

I imagine there are subspecialties in psychic arts like there are in medicine. Like: you can specialize in talking to the dead versus telling the future or palmistry or tarot or reading tea leaves.

I don't doubt there are real ones, but there are more charlatans who say ambiguous statements that have a high likelihood of being applicable to any situation or person. Stuff like: "I see an elderly gentleman—a fatherly figure—and he seems to be standing on the grass" and the next minute the person is connecting the dots and believing it's Grandpa from beyond the grave because he used to love golf.

The minute I see Ling Po, I know she's the real deal. She looks like Edna from *The Incredibles* with a short, jet-black bob and ginormous glasses that magnify her eyeballs to twice their size. All the better to see the future with. She's probably somewhere in her late fifties or early sixties. She's sitting at a table inside an otherwise empty room like she's been waiting for us to arrive, puffing on a cigarette that she jabs out as we enter.

The walls are painted red, and a thick, crimson-colored velvet curtain hangs floor to ceiling from a rod behind her like a backdrop. White Christmas lights rim the ceiling. There is a painting on one wall of a hand with an eye at the center of the palm, and on the other a giant yin yang symbol surrounded by dragons. It feels authentic except for Adele playing faintly in the background.

"Come in, come in," she says in accented English and fans us toward her with her hands. She lights a stick of incense and turns off the music. "I'll tell you everything you need to know."

"Hi. Actually, I was looking for someone and was wondering if you might know of him? I think he lives upstairs, so maybe you've seen him?"

She blinks her eyes. "Do you have a picture?"

I don't. Not a recent one. And as far as I can tell Alex isn't on social media. I honestly have no idea how much he might have changed physically in nearly two years. "He looks a lot like me, just taller and fuller. Blue eyes. And his hair is longer. Not long-long, but like shaggy long. But then again it might not be now. I haven't seen him in a while."

"Hard to find a person if you don't know what he looks like." She smiles and reveals a gold tooth.

"Right. I think maybe he lives here in this building—or at least he used to. This is the last address I have for him, so I thought you might have noticed him."

She narrows her eyes. "You a cop?"

I laugh. "No, I am definitely not a cop." Amateur detective, crime fighter, and dog kidnapper, yes, but cop—no.

"You want a reading or not? I'm busy. Lots of customers."

I look around. The place is dead empty, every pun intended. Unless she's seeing spirits. Maybe I'm underestimating her.

She lights another cigarette and exhales her drag in my direction. I fan it away and explain, "I'm just trying to locate my brother."

She remains tight-lipped, staring at me as if I haven't spoken. After a moment she eyes my pocket where my wallet is and then looks back at me. I get it. This conversation is over until I fund it.

"Never mind—we're sorry to have taken up your time," Hallie apologizes and tugs at my sleeve.

"Hold on a second," I tell her and then fish out my wallet and lay a twenty-dollar bill on the table in front of Ling Po. "You're a psychic, right? You should be able to tell me where he is."

"Reading thirty-five," she says firmly, and I extract another twenty.

"Do you have change?"

"No change," she says as she pockets it. Alrighty then. She comes to life like a pinball machine after a token has been inserted and motions to the two chairs in front of her. "Sit, sit."

I look at Hallie, and she raises her eyebrows and smiles as she takes a seat. I follow suit.

"Give me your dominant hand," she instructs and reaches for it. She studies my palm and then runs her fingers lightly over it, tracing the lines.

"I see you on a journey. You come from afar. You're looking for something."

So far, I'm not impressed, but then again, I've probably only gotten fifty cents worth of my reading. But then she says, "Your heart line is chained. Indicates emotional trauma. You've suffered great emotional loss, depression. Someone close to you, yes?"

It's the sort of thing she has fifty-fifty odds of getting right because who doesn't have some loss or depression at some point. "Yes."

She smiles. "This person takes care of you in this life. An adviser of some sort. A man of great importance and influence, not only to you but to many."

"My father. He died recently." A lump forms in my throat.

A knowing grin spreads across her face as she nods. "Yes, I sense male energy surrounding you. Helping you on your journey. Even in death you look to this person, want to feel his approval."

I get a chill down my spine. She could simply be reading the cues from my body language and responses to draw conclusions, but when she adds, "He gives it to you," it's as if I can suddenly sense him here in the room. It's exactly what I need to hear and what I never fully felt from him. Tears fall from my eyes, and I quickly wipe them away with my free hand and apologize.

Ling Po moves her finger to the line below it that curves down across my palm at an angle. "Your head line shows you are a highly creative individual. Crosses in the line show a crucial decision ahead that affects your fate. Fork in the road. You must choose."

Okay, that's a little uncanny. I unconsciously shift closer in my seat, trying to decipher how she can extract that meaning from a simple palmar flexion crease. "Is there any indication which road I should take?"

"Each road is the right one. Different outcome. Both have challenges to overcome. Everything in life is an opportunity to learn. Learning is not just in school. Trust your intuition."

So that's super helpful.

Her finger moves again across my palm and then rubs back and forth against another line. "I see you have had your heart broken many times. You hold on to people long after they have served their purpose, and this causes you pain. Purpose is not always what it seems. The universe works in mysterious ways. It is all part of necessary life lessons. Sometimes someone is there for a short time, sometimes a long time. No matter. All the same. All necessary." She points to two small lines on the side of my hand just beneath my pinkie finger. "Only when you let go, love will come. Happiness will come."

I think I saw that last part once in a fortune cookie. Or maybe it was in my mom's book.

When I think about it, everyone I've ever been close to has

broken my heart at some point. I suppose I've come to expect it. Perhaps what Hallie said earlier is true—not every person is meant to stay there forever.

She traces a faint line down the center of my right palm. "This is your fate line. See how it breaks? This means external forces heavily influence your life. You find escape in your imagination."

She puts my hand down and smiles and doesn't say another word. She's like a toy that's run out of batteries. That's when I realize she's done and still hasn't told me anything about where I might find Alex.

"Wow—that's pretty amazing that you can tell all that from my hand," I say and shift in my seat. "So...is there anything there more specifically about my brother? Because I was thinking when you offered the reading that maybe you had some information about him."

"Please—he's come a long way, and it's urgent he finds him," Hallie interjects impatiently.

Just as I'm thinking it's possible Ling Po is waiting for me to re-feed her meter before giving me the information I'm looking for, there is the sound of a door opening and the red curtains that rim the room part. A young Asian woman who looks to be in her early-to-midtwenties enters, holding a tray with a small, clay teapot and a single cup. She looks out of place, dressed in a cropped Pogues T-shirt and a pair of denim shorts, her jet-black hair swept up into a long ponytail.

She nods to us and averts her eyes as she puts the tray down to the side of Ling Po on the table. Ling Po speaks to her in Chinese, and the young woman glances at me and straightens then responds to her. They go back and forth for a minute, and then ultimately the young woman trains her eyes on me. She gestures gently with her head in the direction of the door from which she came.

"Follow me," she says in perfect English.

18
JACK

SATURDAY, JUNE 5, 12:22 P.M.

This holds no higher level of what-the-fuckery than anything else that has happened today, so of course I do. I thank Ling Po and follow the girl through a hidden door to a back stairwell. I feel slightly like Alice following the White Rabbit. That could also be because I'm going on my thirty-second straight hour of being awake, and everything has taken on an almost psychedelic quality. Her ponytail swishes back and forth like a metronome as she climbs the stairs.

"I'm sorry—who are you? And where are we going exactly?" I ask and turn around to check that Hallie is behind me. Safety in numbers. Hallie seems unfazed by the fact that we are following a total stranger up a back staircase without knowing exactly what we can expect to find at the top of it. We could disappear off the face of the earth right now and no one would know where the hell we are. It fits perfectly with the rest of our day.

"I am Mei, Ling Po's niece. She told me you're looking for your brother."

"You know Alex?" I ask her eagerly.

"I knew him. Yes."

"Knew? As in you don't anymore? Did something happen to him?" I didn't expect that. What if I'm too late because he's finished the job he started back then and I'll never have the chance to see him or give him Dad's letter? Mentally, I begin preparations for the worst possible news.

"Come inside and have some tea."

I'm not big on tea, but I'll drink it if it means Mei will tell me where my brother is. We reach the second floor, and she opens the stairwell door, which leads us out into a regular hallway, right in front of a scratched, wooden door with a brass 2 hanging precariously from it at an angle.

Unit 2. This is where Alex supposedly lived.

If he isn't here, then where is he?

She unlocks the door. It's a smallish one-bedroom apartment decorated like a college dorm room, with tapestries and rock band posters on the walls, milk crates repurposed as bookshelves, a bright-orange couch with a matching overstuffed chair and a giant TV across from them that takes up half the wall. A small gray cat meows as it sidles up to my leg before moving on to take up residence on top of a small, wooden kitchen table.

"Please—sit down." Mei motions to the couch as she goes into the tiny galley kitchen. She reemerges holding another teapot and some cups on a tray and places them on the small coffee table in front of us.

"Thank you," I say, accepting one. Hallie does the same. All this past tense has me confused. "So—this address is the last one I have for my brother. Did he used to live here?"

Mei nods as she pours us each a cup of tea. "He stayed here for a few months. We were friends. We met at Higher Ground."

"What's Higher Ground?" I ask. It could be a dispensary for all the name tells me. If it isn't, it would be a great name for one.

She straightens and looks at me cautiously. "I'm sorry—he's your brother and you don't know what Higher Ground is?"

"The thing is—Alex and I haven't spoken in a long time," I explain. "I've only recently found out where he is."

"Wow." She takes that in and nods. "Well, Higher Ground is a transitional housing facility. Alex and I both lived there after we got out of rehab. After that, he stayed here with me for a while. It was only supposed to be long enough to find a job and get on his feet, but it ended up being around seven months. Then it no longer became a feasible situation, and he left."

If he stayed here around seven months after treatment, it means he would have been living here when Dad died, which would also explain why this was the last address Dad had for him. It would also confirm my growing suspicion that Dad had stayed in touch with him, or at least kept tabs on him.

"So where is he now? Is he still in San Francisco?" Hallie asks.

"The last time we spoke he was, yes."

"When was that?" I ask.

"I bumped into him downtown about a few months ago."

"What—one month? Four months?" How am I supposed to find him?

"Do you know where he works?" Hallie asks. "We could go there."

Mei shakes her head. "I don't know. He's had a few different jobs. I think he was a busboy somewhere in Union Square, and then he worked at a dry cleaner in North Beach. Like I said, I haven't spoken to him in a while. In fact, if you find him, please tell him I say hi and hope he's doing okay. And please tell him I am too."

She casts her eyes downward, but not before they betray her sadness at their lack of contact.

"Is there a chance he might *not* be okay?" I ask.

Mei shrugs. "When you're a recovering addict, there's always a chance you might not be okay. It's a day-to-day kind of thing. As far as I know, he's clean and committed to his sobriety."

"Right." I try to imagine what sobriety must look like on Alex. Mostly when I saw him, he was sleeping, high, coming off a high, or looking for one. I know how much this last year and a half has profoundly changed me, so it's not a stretch to imagine it would have affected him significantly too.

"I wish I could be of more help. That's all I know."

"It's more than what I had, so thanks," I tell her.

"Anyhow—he left a few things here, and I've been holding on to them in case I got to see him again. I suppose it makes more sense that you should take them. You can give them to him when you see him."

"Well, seeing him hinges on figuring out where he is," I say.

"That still puts you at greater odds of seeing him than me."
Mei reaches down to the bottom shelf of her bookcase and extracts
a small, cardboard shipping box, the lid flaps straining to break free
under a single piece of Scotch tape. She puts it on the table and
gives it a slight nudge in my direction.

I reach tentatively for the box and open it. Inside is a deck of
erotic playing cards and a harmonica, which sit on top of a vintage
Japanese version Legend of Zelda: Ocarina of Time shirt from 1998
that is identical to the one my dad brought me once from Comic-
Con that coincidentally went missing. I knew it. Underneath that
is a folded piece of paper jagged at the edges where it was ripped
from a spiral notebook. Shoved in the crease of the fold is a robin's-
egg-blue paper bookmark for City Lights Bookstore with the name
"Malcolm" written on it in all capital letters.

I unfold the paper and cast my eyes on my brother's unmistakable chicken-scratch scrawl.

It's exhausting trying to be happy while
simultaneously believing you don't deserve to be.
News flash! No one is perfect. Distrust most of
all anyone who makes you think they have all the
answers and knows what they're doing. Everyone
is pretending on some level. Conforming to please.
You can't look to someone else to tell you how to
be happy. That shit comes from within. You are
entitled to be anyone you want to be. Just be
authentic.

It must have been a journal entry he'd torn out. Or a note he wrote for someone. I might as well have written the words myself for how much I feel them. Perhaps Alex and I are operating on more of the same frequency than I'd thought.

"By the way, I'm sorry about your father," Mei offers by way of condolences.

"So, Alex knows then?" This confirms what I'd suspected earlier when I discovered the letter, which only makes this more confusing. Obviously, my mother must have told him, but he wasn't at the funeral. And she kept perpetuating the story even after Dad's death that she didn't know how to reach him. Why would she keep lying to me, especially at a time when I might have benefitted from having him to talk to?

"Yes, of course. He was quite shaken by the news."

Was he? Why didn't he reach out to me or respond to my texts or emails?

Hallie asks what I don't have the balls to. "So how come he left?"

Mei's expression darkens slightly, and her shoulders hunch forward, like a balloon deflating. "At Higher Ground they advise that people who are in recovery should not live together because one can easily trigger the other if they backslide."

"Did he start using again?" I ask. My stomach bottoms out at the thought. It wouldn't take a rocket scientist to see why he might backslide if that happened around when Dad died.

"No. I did. And it nearly caused him to." She gives a tight-lipped smile, clearly ashamed. "Like I said, I'm clean now, but once that happened, he knew that it was no longer a safe space, and he had to go. I can't blame him."

I'd automatically assumed Alex would have been the one to screw things up. It sounds as if for once my brother was trying to do the right thing.

"I'm sorry," I say because this topic seems to make her sad. I pull out the bookmark and turn the printed side to face Mei. "Do you happen to know who Malcolm is?"

Mei shakes her head. "It might be someone he works with. Or maybe someone who works at City Lights?"

"Is this anywhere near here?" I'd heard of City Lights. It's one of the most famous bookstores in this country and known for publishing Allen Ginsberg's controversial poem "Howl" in the 1960s. It was the epicenter of the Beat Generation movement. All the big authors of the time—Kerouac, Burroughs, Ginsberg himself, and other greats—were frequent fixtures there. I love a good bookstore. So did my dad. Alex never struck me as much of a reader, but maybe he loves bookstores too. It wouldn't be the first time he surprised me today.

"Yes, it's not far. It's on Columbus Street, about a ten-minute walk from here."

Hallie looks at me and smiles. "I think I know where we're headed."

We walk up Grant a few more blocks and then cut through the aptly named Jack Kerouac Alley that empties out onto Columbus Street adjacent to the bookstore. The Transamerica Building looms to our right and there to the left, big windows overflowing with tomes, is City Lights Bookstore.

The wood floors creak under our feet as we enter. This place seems to go on forever, stairs leading up and down, alcoves off to the sides. I've never seen this many people inside a bookstore when it wasn't the holidays. It gives me hope for humanity. I could easily get lost in here for hours. There's so much to explore, but I can't get caught up in that right now. I'm on a quest to find Malcolm.

But as I turn a corner, I come face to face with an endcap display of my mother's book. There's her heavily Photoshopped face staring back at me with a perfect smile. It stops me in my tracks.

"What's wrong?" Hallie asks.

"That's my mother."

"Your *mother* is here?" she starts looking around.

I shake my head. "No—the person on the cover of that book. It's my mother."

Hallie reaches for a copy and reads the title aloud. "*Love Your Vagina, Love Yourself.* I think I saw her on Ellen."

"Not at all completely embarrassing." I wince as she starts to thumb through it. "Yep, nothing like being a teenage boy just trying to low-key it through high school and then your famous sex therapist mom writes a book critics call 'groundbreaking' with the word *vagina* in the title."

"Groundbreaking. That's impressive."

"It's weird—people love her, like she's some revolutionary thinker with all the answers. She can't even pick a restaurant for dinner. She's one of the most miserable people I know. Out in the world, she acts like she's some authority on happiness, but at home she'll lock herself in her bathroom with a gin and tonic and a pack of cigarettes, crack the window, and have a good cry."

"Who doesn't?" Hallie returns the book to its place on the shelf and follows me in search of an employee. "I take it you two aren't super close?"

"More like we coexist in the same space. Like if you saw us together in private, you wouldn't necessarily know she's my mother. In public, she's the doting parent who boasts proudly of my achievements, but the minute we're back home, we barely talk."

We continue to wind our way through the store. The shelves are crammed full and are close together, making the space cramped and hard to navigate. There are chairs everywhere, inviting people to sit and read, and the signs on the walls urge them to think. My inner nerd is like a kid in a candy store.

I glance at the name tag of each employee, but none match the one I need. I wind my way back toward the front room, hovering near the register so I can ask if a Malcolm works here. There's a huge queue of people waiting, and I immediately sense the stink eye from people assessing if I'm about to be that guy who thinks his time is more valuable than everyone else's.

I opt to make my way to the end of the line. An employee walks by and accidentally bumps me.

"I'm so sorry, my friend," he says and rests his hand on my shoulder. He's probably somewhere in his early thirties with shoulder-length deadlocks and a pierced nose and reminds me of a late '80s Lenny Kravitz. Just as he's about to walk away, I catch a glimpse of his name tag.

"Malcolm?" I ask.

He turns toward me with a smile. "I'm him; how can I help you?"

Bingo.

He looks like the kind of easygoing guy who is prepared for and unfazed by any request, no matter how obscure. I'm sure he's expecting me to ask him where I might find books about muckraking or essential Latin American feminist poetry. My phone vibrates in my pocket, but I ignore it.

"My name is Jack Freeman. This might sound weird but—I'm trying to locate my brother Alex. I found this City Lights bookmark amongst some stuff he left behind at his old apartment, and your name was written on it, so I'm hoping maybe you know my brother and can point me in the right direction to find him."

He smiles cautiously. "You're Alex Freeman's brother?"

"Yeah. Does he work here?"

"Well, well." His eyes light up, and he smiles as he studies me, which is a little unsettling. "Nah, he doesn't work here. He comes here sometimes though."

"So, you know him?" Excitement courses through me. "Does he live around here then?"

Malcolm puts a hand on my shoulder again. "I'm about to take my break. Wait for me in the Poetry Room. I need to give these books to a customer, and then we can talk. Gimme two minutes." He points in the direction of the Poetry Room as he walks away.

I look at Hallie, who shrugs and follows me up a creaky, wooden staircase to the Poetry Room to wait for Malcolm. True to its name, it's a small nook crowded with chairs and windows and floor-to-ceiling bookcases filled with nothing but poetry. There's a lone patron in here, and in the time that we're waiting, she leaves.

I direct my attention to the shelves. There are separate sections for anthologies, Beat poets, modern poetry, the list goes on; I had no idea so many kinds of poetry existed. In high school we touch on the big names, the famous ones, but there are thousands of volumes here by voices I've never heard of, each with something to say, waiting to be discovered and heard.

I'm wondering how long it would take to read every one when Malcolm arrives, apologetic for having to keep us waiting. He extends his hand, and I shake it, then he turns a chair around backward, sitting directly in front of me. "I'm so glad you came. I thought we should talk more privately. I'm Malcolm Sinclair."

I gesture toward Hallie. "This is my friend Hallie."

Malcom smiles. "It's great to meet you both. I'm Alex's sponsor."

"Sponsor?" I parrot back.

He looks at me with confusion. "I'm sorry, I thought you knew."

What he's saying clicks. "Oh—*sponsor*—like as in you're who my brother has to check in with to help him stay on track."

"It's all voluntary. He doesn't *have* to do anything, but statistically those in recovery who seek out a sponsor in the first six months post-rehab have a better chance of staying sober. I'm someone he can count on to listen to him and support him no matter what. We share common bonds of addiction and recovery. I love your brother." He puts his palm over his heart.

"That's really cool," I tell him.

He leans in slightly. "Right now, understandably, Alex is worried about interacting with anyone or putting himself in situations that might trigger him to use again. He has worked hard at his sobriety. I am honored to be part of his team. It's taken a lot of dedication to following the twelve principles of NA."

"Good for him." I nod and then sit back in my chair.

"It will mean a lot to him that you've come. He speaks of you often."

"He does?" This, of course, is startling news to me, because I haven't heard from him in a year and a half, and the last time we saw each other, he looked right at me as I considered letting him die.

Malcolm nods reassuringly. "You seem surprised by that."

"I guess I am. But in a good way."

"You showing up is obviously a huge life event for Alex, one which I think would be good for him. This is going to have a great emotional impact for you both."

I nod. "So, you can put me in touch with him? He must have changed his phone number, and he's not on social media."

"I think it would be best if I reach out to him directly first. Connecting with people from the past can be a huge trigger, especially family members." The way he emphasizes *especially* makes me wonder exactly what he knows about my parents and me.

Malcolm chats with us well beyond the end of his break. He's very easy to talk to, so I can see why my brother would trust him. At this point Malcolm knows Alex better than I do. He takes my number and says he'll text me once he reaches Alex. It's unsettling having a gatekeeper—a total stranger—standing between my own brother and me.

So, with nowhere to go yet, the only thing to do is wait. I've been like a Ping-Pong ball bouncing all over the city, and the sleep deprivation is starting to kick in. Everything has taken on the surreal tinge of an out-of-body experience.

"How are you doing?" I check in with Hallie. "These last few hours have been all about me."

"No, it's a welcome distraction, trust me. And I'm fine. A little hungry maybe."

"Well, we've got time to kill, and we're close to the best Chinatown in America. I say we find something to eat."

"Sounds good."

We head back toward Chinatown. As we wander past a busy hole-in-the-wall restaurant called Yum Yum Dim Sum, the smell of soup dumplings wafts out. I'm suddenly famished as well. With a name like that, we can't help but stop, regroup, and test that claim.

The place is packed and although the atmosphere is best-described as sanitary-lite, we grab the only seats left at the counter. As we order, my phone starts vibrating incessantly in my pocket yet again. This time, I grab for it and answer without even checking the caller ID, thinking it's probably Malcolm and he's decided to call instead of text. It isn't.

"Hello?"

"*Finally!* Jesus, Jack, I've been trying to reach you for hours. Didn't you get my voicemail?" Natasha sounds more annoyed than worried. Like she has a right to be either. I'm guessing she was the source of the buzz in my pocket earlier.

I jam my finger in my ear because I can barely hear her over the din of the restaurant. It would never occur to her in a million years that perhaps I don't want to talk to her, that my not answering was intentional.

"I emojied," I tell her. Hallie raises her eyebrows and mouths, *Emoji girl?* I nod, and she covers her mouth with her hand, suppressing a laugh. Natasha's not nearly as entertained.

"Yeah, and what the hell was that about? I write this forty-page apology *over text*, and then I'm *freaking* out because I went by your house this morning, but your car wasn't there and you weren't home, so I went back to Carly's house, and it was still there. So then I started *freaking out again* because I didn't know where you went, and you seemed really upset, so I felt bad, and then *hours* go by and you send me a *freaking emoji*," she says and then takes a breath.

Hallie motions toward a little boy maybe five years old who is shoving an entire dumpling in his mouth. It makes me laugh.

"What—you think what I said was *funny*?" She's pissed. "This whole night I've been worried you might've done something drastic. I know you can be reactive sometimes."

My smile instantly disappears. "Whoa, slow down a sec. *Drastic? Reactive?* You broke up with me on the grounds of being statistically doomed according to an article in *Teen Vogue Online* and then told me you're going to UCLA, which you've actually known for months. I think that definitely entitles me to some kind of reaction. I'm sorry if that feels a little drastic to you."

Hallie nods and gives me a thumbs-up.

"See? This is what I mean. You make things a bigger deal than they need to be."

"Jesus, Natasha, how could you stand to be with me as long as you did? It must have been hell for you. You're such a martyr."

"That's not what I'm saying."

"I'm pretty sure you just said that."

She sighs deeply. "I know you've been super depressed lately, and I'm worried about your ability to handle it on top of everything else, and I don't want to be the reason—"

"Wow. That's it right there, isn't it? You're relieved that I'm okay, but more because you don't want that guilt hanging over your head that if I wasn't, you might somehow be responsible."

"I didn't say that, Jack. You're twisting my words. You always do that."

"Let me ease your mind. I'm fine. I'm more than fine, actually." Ironically, this is the finest I've felt in a long time.

A fire engine roars past with sirens blaring. "Where are you? You can't be in New York already."

"Why does it matter?"

"Jack—what was I supposed to think?" Her voice cracks and sounds shaky as if she's crying.

"That I'm so torn up over our breakup that I'd possibly kill myself? That's giving yourself a lot of credit, don't you think? Everything isn't always about you."

"You don't have to be mean."

"That's funny, you telling me how I should behave."

She sniffles. "I deserve that, I guess. I'm just scared, Jack. We could pretend like we weren't moving in two different directions for only so long. I didn't know what to say. I only knew it had to be said."

"No, you're actually right," I say as the chef puts a bamboo steamer filled with piping hot dumplings in front of us, and I shove one in my mouth without delay.

I can picture the confused expression on her face. "You agree with me?"

I speak with my mouth full. "Yeah, like you said, what's the point of dragging it out? Sounds like more drama than an episode of *The Bachelor*." I move my mouth away from the microphone and say to Hallie, "Holy crap, these are bomb-ass dumplings."

"Right?" Hallie says as she swishes hers in a pool of soy sauce.

"Are you *with* somebody?" she asks. There's a sudden softening to her voice.

"Yeah," I tell her. "I am."

"You spent the night with someone to get back at me," she says matter-of-factly, the momentary softness replaced by a chill worthy of a polar ice cap.

"Technically, I guess I did, but it definitely had nothing to do with you and everything to do with me. I didn't realize I owed you a check in or *anything* really, for that matter."

"Wow." She sighs dramatically. "You're angry."

"Of course I'm angry. I'm allowed to be." I realize my voice is elevated when a few people glance in my direction. I lower my voice and bow my head. "I'll get over it, but a lot of crap just happened, Natasha. You had time to think about all this, so you can't expect things to go back to the way they were in one day. Or maybe we never get there. Because that's the thing, Natasha— you made your own choices, but you don't get to choose the consequences."

Hallie fist bumps me and grins as she mouths "Burn."

Natasha doesn't respond.

"Hello?"

Silence. *Did she seriously just hang up on me?*

I pull the phone away from my ear in disbelief, only to discover that all my googling and mapping has drained my battery yet again, and my phone is now out of juice. As in dead, most likely mid-rant, and I have no idea how much of that she actually heard. Well, at least she can't call back. But the satisfaction is short-lived as I realize it also means I won't be able to get Malcolm's text.

19
HALLIE

SATURDAY, JUNE 5, 2:38 P.M.

After lunch we hurriedly set up camp in the first Starbucks we find so Jack can plug in and charge his phone long enough to buy him a few more hours. He settles into a soft, brown leather chair in the corner and anxiously checks his phone as it flickers back to life.

There's nothing. He looks crestfallen. "It's been over an hour already. Maybe Alex doesn't want to see me."

"Stop it. You don't know that. There are a million reasons why he might not have texted yet," I assure him. "I'm going to order some drinks so they don't yell at us for sitting here."

It occurs to me as I stand in line that I never asked him his drink order because I already knew it. Something about that makes me smile, but it also feels potentially dangerous.

The line is long and moves slowly, and it practically lulls me to sleep. I glance over at Jack. He's stretched out in the chair with his eyes closed, his phone resting on his lap. I wouldn't say this to him, but maybe he's right; it could be that his brother *doesn't* want to reconnect. I'm sure he'd have his reasons, but my chest physically aches for him at the thought.

By the time I get our drinks and head back to where Jack is sitting, my chest still aches for real. I set the drinks down on the table and clear my throat, which sets off another chain of coughing like earlier this morning. Every time I cough, my throat spasms, and it feels like someone is stabbing a knife in my chest. Jack's eyes fly open, and he's immediately on his feet, looking absolutely terrified, like I'm going to drop dead on the spot. I press my fist to my heart.

"Are you okay? Do you need me to get you water? I can get you water." I nod. He turns toward the counter and frantically yells, "Can I please get some water?!"

A girl rushes out from behind the counter with a plastic cup filled with water and hands it to me. I grab it from her and take a huge sip and then another, trying to ease the irritation in my throat. Jack, clearly not knowing what else to do, pats my back gently. By the time I calm down, there are tears in my eyes, my face is no doubt beet-red, and everyone in the place is staring at me.

"You okay?" he asks again softly. I nod.

"Yes, sorry." I wave to everyone so they can go back to whatever it was they were doing before I hacked up a lung. "I'm okay. Sorry."

My chest hurts, although not as badly as before. I'm pushing myself too hard, and my body is starting to react. I realize I'm long overdue for taking my pill. I reach in my purse, digging for the bottle. I run my fingers over the surface of every object inside but don't feel the round plastic cylinder.

"You don't have to apologize to anyone. Do you need more water?"

"No, I'm okay for now, thanks," I tell him as I sit down to search more thoroughly. Where the hell is that pill bottle? I was sure I threw it in here. I remember seeing it sitting on the edge of my desk, but then Dylan came home, and I'd gone out to see him before I'd had a chance to take it and finish packing. I must have left it there.

I start to get scared. I know what I'm feeling is all tied to my health, so it's not going to get better. More likely it will get worse. Owen's dying is a wake-up call that this isn't going to go away. I have no choice but to deal with this. I'm surprised by the realization that for the first time in a long time, I want to be here.

I don't want to alarm Jack. I know he's got a lot on the line right now, and the last thing he should be thinking about is me. As much as I love being here, the signs are all pointing toward home.

A rumbly vibration emanates from Jack's seat. His phone seems to have lodged itself in the crevice between the arm and seat cushion of the chair. He fishes it out and flips it over.

He looks at me. "It's a text from Malcolm."

"What did he say?"

He reads it, and his face lights up. "My brother is down to meet me tonight at seven thirty, after work."

"That's fantastic! I'm so happy for you."

"Thanks. Looks like an address somewhere in Berkeley. That's across the bay, and with rush hour and everything, I guess it makes sense to head in that direction soon and wait it out somewhere in that vicinity instead. But your bus is at eight. That would put you much farther away. You'd get there and be close to having to turn right around again." He frowns.

"True." I'm suddenly freezing and completely depleted. I involuntarily shiver.

"Are you cold?" he asks.

"Mmmm. I'll be fine once we get outside. It's like an icebox in here." I'm still wearing his sweatshirt jacket, and I zip it all the way up and tuck my hands under my arms.

"It really isn't."

The sheer exhaustion in his eyes matches my own. Seven thirty is still a good four hours away. The idea of being on the go for that long in my current state is a little daunting.

My words jumble with his as we both start talking at the same time. He laughs.

"I'm sorry. Go ahead," he says, and I shake my head.

"No, you."

"I was going to say that you shouldn't feel like you have to stay. You're obviously not feeling well. You should probably take it easy and rest. Honestly, it would be completely selfish and irresponsible of me to recommend differently."

I nod, relieved. "And I was about to say that this is a huge moment for you. I wouldn't want to compromise the focus in any way because you're worrying about how I'm doing or worrying about me getting back or whatever. Either way—we say goodbye now or in a few hours, right?"

"Right. It makes sense. We're just being logical about this."

"Absolutely." It seems to be what he wants. Unless he's saying this because he thinks it's what I want. I smile reassuringly. "I can get a cab back to the bus station and find a bench and read and hang out until my bus leaves. Maybe I'll get lucky and they will have Raisinets in the vending machine."

He sits down in his chair and leans toward me, resting his arms on his knees. He bites his lip. "Are you sure you're gonna be okay? I feel like a jerk for not offering to travel back with you to LA."

"Don't be ridiculous. I'll be fine. That was never the plan," I tell him.

"There was no plan. I can at least drop you off at the bus station and go on from there."

"That would be great."

"So, okay, good—that's what we'll do then."

"Yeah."

I hadn't even noticed music had been playing in the background until the song changes and suddenly "Dancing Queen" comes on. Jack and I lock eyes and smile, both remembering the sing-along hours ago.

"I guess this is kind of our song," he says. I know he's kidding, but it always will be the soundtrack that plays under the memory of this time together in my mind.

It's hard to know what to say after that. Despite briefly sharing the same path, at the end of the day we are indeed on separate journeys. Until now, I thought mine was about seeing Owen, but I'm realizing it was actually about stepping back and seeing myself. Talking with Jack has helped me understand that behind this mountain will always be another mountain, because that's just how life is. The key is not letting them stand in my way.

The temperature is starting to drop outside. Jack stops at a souvenir shop next door and buys me a black I Heart SF sweatshirt to wear so he can take his sweatshirt back. They only have bigger sizes, so it swims on me, but at least it's warm and cozy. As he puts his sweatshirt back on, I know that when I think of him, I'm going to picture him exactly like this, with the afternoon sun hitting his face and the city as his backdrop.

On the cab ride back to the bus station, I angle myself toward him in the seat and say, "There's something I want to tell you before I go."

"Okay." He looks nervous. He's probably wondering what I could tell him at this point that could possibly top cancer.

"I've felt more alive in these less-than-twenty-four hours than I have in a long time. For the first time in a long time, I'm excited to think about the possibility of the future and what it could bring, and I have you to thank for that. I think our paths were meant to cross."

He beams. "I feel exactly the same way. Maybe this sounds bizarre, but when I'm with you, it's as if I'm coexisting in some alternate reality, and in this one I actually feel good. Like the version of me I want to be. And if not for meeting up with you last night, I honestly don't know what I might have done if I'd gone home, all up in my head on the eve of yet another unwanted major life shift. Meeting you forced me to unknowingly take charge of my destiny."

I feel myself blush. It's probably the most amazing thing anyone has ever said to me. It's good that I'm leaving, because I am falling for him, and that can't happen right now. It's the absolute worst timing for both of us. It's not fair.

He looks deep into my eyes. "Thank you for the most perfect day between I could ever imagine."

I nod. "That was a good time."

He blushes and asks with a nervous smile, "So you sure you want to leave it like that? No contact, no communication, just show up six months from now and see if the other one does too?"

"The universe brought us together once—if it intends us to meet again, we will. No expectations. It'll be a surprise. Like a present our future selves get to unwrap."

Something to hold on to, something to hope for.

We arrive at the bus station for the third time today. The driver waits while Jack gets out of the car to say goodbye.

"So, this time this really *is* it," I say and then wrap my arms around his neck and pull him in for a hug. "It's weird to say goodbye."

"It is." We stand there like that, me resting my head on his shoulder. "I guess I'll see you in six months."

As I pull away, I kiss him softly on the cheek. His skin is cold against the warmth of my lips. If he turned his head ever so slightly, our mouths would touch, and so I pull away quickly to make sure he doesn't, even though a part of me wants him to. It would only make this harder than it is already.

"Bye, Jack." I take a snapshot of him in my mind and grin as I raise the handle on my Hello Kitty suitcase and walk toward the terminal. I refuse to look back.

20

JACK

SATURDAY, JUNE 5, 4:11 P.M.

Now I get what Natasha meant earlier when she said she cares about me enough to let me go. Even though it's the furthest thing from what I want, I want to give Hallie that.

How is it possible to spend less than twenty-four hours with her and feel like she knows me better than anyone who's been in my life the whole time?

I force myself not to look back as the car pulls away and heads toward the Bay Bridge and Berkeley. Unlike Oscar, this driver seems to prefer music at a low volume to conversation, which is fine with me. It gives me time to wrap my head around what's about to happen.

I check my phone and see that my mother has called twice. My phone buzzes with a text. It's from Ajay: **Seriously dude, you ok?**

I can't help but smile as I type: **Never been better.** Before I hit send, I add: **Hey, do you remember a girl named Hallie Baskin?**

He shoots right back: **Mayyyybe? Was she hot?**

I laugh. *She's definitely cute.*

🖤 **Name is familiar. Wait—didn't she get cancer and drop out or something?**

She's so much more than how he's summed her up, and I know she'd hate that he remembered her by her illness. I text back: **Too much to get into but took slight detour/road tripped with her to SF/on my way to meet Alex.**

He responds: **WTAF? Holy shiiiiiit!**

I watch the three bubbles appear that tell me he is writing more, but it takes forever, so I'm expecting a paragraph. I write back: **Exactly right** as his words pop up on the screen. **That's awesome! Glad ur not dead. I would feel guilty about beating your high score earlier. #backtogloating** to which I reply **#biteme** followed by **Details later** and click off my phone. It's too much to get into now.

I'm sure he's already texting Natasha the update. Not because he's a jerk; just the opposite. Because he's a genuinely good guy, and he wouldn't want her to worry. I don't want her to either, but I also don't want to text her, so I'm grateful. He's gonna flip when I tell him the whole story.

Writing *bite me* and thinking about Natasha reminds me of the bottle opener she gifted me sitting in my backpack. I take it out and look at it, then gently stick it into the seat back in front of me for the next rider to discover.

As I'm zipping up my bag, a glint of metal on the seat catches my eye. It's Hallie's bracelet—the one with the Latin inscription.

It must have fallen off, and we're too far away to turn around and give it back to her. She'll be so upset when she discovers it's missing. I carefully attach it on to my wrist for safekeeping. Having something of hers against my skin makes me even more aware of her absence.

She too is now part of the past, and I have to keep moving forward. Toward *what* is the question. But it's okay to not have that all figured out in a day. Or even a month. It seems like the sort of thing that you keep figuring out all your life, so taking a little extra time on the front end doesn't seem so irresponsible after all.

I hole up at a coffee shop a block away from the address Malcolm gave me. They happen to have an old-school, tabletop *Tetris*, and I easily set the high score in the couple of hours I'm there killing time. By the time I head over to see Alex, the sky is hued orange and violet and pink, and the evening fog has begun to roll in from the west.

I'm excited to see my brother, but I've also spent the last year blaming him in part for having a hand in Dad no longer being here. If not for what he'd done—getting into trouble all the time, lying and stealing, ultimately overdosing and nearly costing Dad his career—everything might have been different. Dad might not have been so stressed out. He might have paid more attention to his health, noticed warning signs.

I carry my own guilt about his passing too. On the final morning of his life, Dad and I had a heated exchange on his way out the door to go jogging about my wanting to apply to a few colleges as a creative writing major. It was not well received, and I'd sent his blood pressure through the roof. They call the kind of heart attack he had a *widowmaker* because the survival odds are so slim.

It's taken me until now to start to realize that neither of us is to blame for Dad's passing. Sometimes bad stuff just happens.

I'm snapped back into the present as a dragonfly skitters past me, brushing against my cheek before settling on a nearby bush. On every level, it feels like my dad trying to get my attention, letting me know he knows I'm here and wants me to stop dwelling on the past or worrying about the future and be fully present in this moment.

I stop in front of a two-story brick building adjacent to a neighborhood park. It's weird to know that my brother is somewhere inside.

There are some kids my age shooting hoops on a basketball court outside. Through the front window of the building, I can make out a pool table with several more teens around it. Looks like some sort of community center.

I am moments away from actually standing in front of Alex. Where do we begin? Suddenly all the things I want to say jumble up like a strand of Christmas lights in my brain. My stomach twists with anticipation, and my palms start to sweat.

I'm a little early, but I put my hand on the steel push bar on the door and enter the space. Barely anyone acknowledges my arrival except the twentysomething girl with Princess Leia hair doing her nails at the reception desk. She grins and dunks the brush in the jar of neon hot-pink polish.

"Hey, what's up?" she asks.

"I'm looking for Alex Freeman," I tell her.

She grabs the phone receiver carefully so as not to smudge her nails, cradling it between her chin and shoulder.

"Hey, is Alex back there?" There's a pause. "Oh, okay cool," she says. I can hear a muffled response as she hangs up. "He'll be right out. He's finishing up."

"What is this place?" I ask her.

"It's the Teen Outreach Center."

"What do you guys do here?" I ask. Nothing wrong with gathering a little intel.

"We provide programs for at-risk youth, from tutoring to community service projects, life-skill building, career training, and free counseling. Many of these kids are homeless or come from difficult backgrounds. For a lot of these kids, it's a lifeline."

I'm trying to figure out how my brother fits in here. Alex seems a little old for this place. The kids seem to range from about thirteen to seventeen. A peal of laughter emanates from behind the closed doors of a classroom or meeting space. I can make out a handful of teens seated in a circle through the door window. A moment later they all rise and the door opens, spilling their cacophony of voices into the common area. I scan their faces as they emerge, but none of them are Alex. The door closes behind them with a click as they scatter in different directions.

And then it opens again, and there he is. My breath catches in my throat. Jesus—I'd forgotten how much he looks like Dad.

There is no mistaking whether we're related. Our builds are similar—tall and lean—and we both have Dad's grayish-blue eyes. He looks different since I saw him last. His medium-brown hair is shorter now and brushed back off his face, not at all how he used to wear it. He looks older. My parents always used to be after him to cut it and clean up his appearance. Seeing him like this would make Dad happy.

We are both sporting slight scruff on our chins, which in my case is not by choice but circumstance, although I don't entirely hate it. Alex is wearing a gray, half-zip, mock turtleneck sweater and jeans, which are way more preppy than he ever dressed. He looks like he's making an effort.

Alex looks up and catches sight of me openly staring at him, and his face lights up with a smile. *Dad's smile.*

"Holy shit," he says as he crosses the room to me and pulls me into an awkward hug. "Wow, you grew up, little brother. Or should I say not-so-little brother. When did you get so tall?"

"Hey," I say as casually as if I'd seen him last Thursday, though actually it's been somewhere in the ballpark of ninety-six Thursdays.

He smells different too. I didn't hug him a lot then, but he was like Pig Pen from Peanuts, who always has a dust cloud around him. Except Alex's was more like cigarettes, Axe deodorant, and pot.

"Wow, it's really good to see you," he says. "It's been a long time."

"Almost two years. And yeah...the magic of puberty."

Alex laughs. "It's crazy. Let me get my stuff together, and then we can get out of here and go somewhere to catch up. Hang tight here for a sec. You thirsty? Can I get you anything to drink first? Water? Tea? Coffee?"

"I'm good, actually. I've had about forty-six cups of coffee today."

"Aaaah, pot head." He says with a grin as he looks me up and down.

I laugh. "What?"

"Pot head, as in you drink a pot of coffee a day. I can relate. Fellow card-carrying member." He starts walking away. "Be right back."

"Sure." I dig my hands in my pocket and look around aimlessly. The girl behind the counter smacks her gum.

"You guys look a lot alike," she says and blows a bubble. "I like Alex. He's a good guy."

I wouldn't know exactly. The last time I saw Alex, he wasn't at all what I would describe as a *good guy*. In fact, he was kind of a nightmare, but still I say, "Yeah."

He returns and says goodbye to the girl behind the desk, and I follow him out the front door into the early twilight. I'm positive the piece-of-shit green beater in the second row is going to be his before he even maneuvers toward it in the parking lot. The polar opposite of my BMW. He never cared about stuff like that.

"Do you mind if we stop and grab some food?" he asks. "I'm starving. I didn't get a chance to eat between work and here. Then we can have a chance to catch up."

"Sure. No problem. Isn't this where you work?" I hitch my thumb back toward the brick building.

Alex shakes his head. "I volunteer here. I like to talk to the kids. It's been a mutually good thing. But my regular job is at UC Berkeley. I also freelance fixing electronics and stuff on the side."

That comes as a surprise. "Wow. You're teaching? Don't you need a degree for that?"

"Actually, I'm a janitor. Or, as they say, a maintenance artist."
He smiles and shrugs. "But hey—it's respectable work and pays
the bills, plus I get to sit in on classes sometimes. Free knowledge.
It's pretty cool. And the electronics stuff is for fun. I always liked
taking things apart and understanding how they work."

It's true. His room was always loaded with half-dissected
computers, broken clocks, random electronics. For a while there,
my mom was convinced he was building a bomb.

Sure enough, we get to the green piece of shit and he unlocks
the doors. "I know a great pizza place a few blocks from here."

"Yeah, sounds good," I reply as I climb inside.

I am surprised by how orderly the car is. I would have expected
piles of clothing or balled up fast food wrappers, old drinks that
could double as science experiments in the cup holders. His room
at home was a biohazard. Carole once told me that how a person
keeps their personal space is an outward reflection of how they are
feeling inside. It would seem my brother has found enlightenment.

We drive down a block and make a left at the intersection.
His blinker makes a *dut dut dut* sound and I reflexively keep time
with the beat on my leg. *This is awkward this is awkward this is
awkward.* He's acting like nothing's wrong, and it's kind of weird-
ing me out.

"You must be about to graduate high school, right?" he asks.

"Graduated. Yesterday, actually."

"Congratulations. Sprung from the prison. So—you're off to
college in the fall, I presume."

"Yep. Funnily enough, I was supposed to leave today. I have
a summer internship lined up in New York at a biotech startup."

"I see you took a slight detour."

"Apparently."

"Got a girlfriend?" He looks amused by the idea, but I'm sure it's because he's still registering me as the kid I was when he left.

"Had. We just broke up. Also yesterday."

"Aaaah. Bummer. Sounds like an eventful twenty-four hours."

"You have no idea. Actually, I'm okay with it. We saved each other the part where what we had left became unsalvageable."

"That's the worst. So, what college?"

"Columbia."

He cracks a half smile. "Why am I not surprised?" Rather than praise for the achievement, his comment feels a little weighted with judgment about following the favored parental protocol. "I think Dad and Mom would have freaked if one of us hadn't ended up there, and we all knew that wasn't gonna be me. Thanks for taking one for the team."

He's joking around, but I wonder if Alex resents that my life seemingly has all the stability and opportunity his lacks. It seems like he chose it though. He was never willing to buy into our parents' advice.

I tell him how I've been anxious about leaving for college and have found myself increasingly ambivalent about going.

"I can appreciate medicine, and I find it interesting, but I don't know that I want to make a career of it. I like the idea of helping people though, making a difference in their lives. But it seems like there's lots of ways to do that, not necessarily just by following Dad's path at Columbia."

Alex tenses slightly at the mention of Dad. He listens intently, and when I've finished, he simply says, "Yeah," and nods like he can feel me, every word. "If you think there's nothing of value in having that experience, then it sounds like you're right to let it go. But I personally think there's value to be had in every experience. What's the worst that could happen?"

"What if I accidentally killed someone?"

Alex's brows knit together. "At Columbia?"

"No—I mean if I were a doctor."

"What if you saved someone's life?"

When did Alex get so pragmatic? "So, you're saying you think I should go?" He doesn't exactly have the best track record for making great decisions, but nonetheless it gives me pause.

"I didn't say that. I'm totally neutral here."

"I don't know—something about the magnitude of the commitment I'm about to make suddenly hit me, and it feels so... binding." I look out the window. There's a streak of bird shit in the shape of a J. Oddly appropriate, if not metaphoric. "Plus, after they couldn't save Dad, I lost faith in the system. It's a lot of time and energy to invest in something that I'm not sure I honestly want."

Two lines form across his forehead. "What's Suzanne got to say about that? I mean—she was cool with you coming to see me?"

Mom always hated that Alex insisted on calling her by her first name. "She doesn't know."

"Seriously?" He lets out a little chuckle.

"Yep."

Alex raises an eyebrow like he's surprised by my answer and nods with approval. "So, how'd you know where to find me?"

"I didn't until I found this letter Dad wrote you sitting in a drawer. Honestly, I didn't know if you were alive or dead. They told me you went to rehab and that you weren't coming back. That this was best for everyone, and I wasn't to contact you." My pulse accelerates. "But nobody ever asked me my opinion or if I was okay with that plan. I ignored them and texted and emailed you, but you never wrote me back. Like you didn't even care. And then they told me they had no idea where you were. You just disappeared. I mean—what the hell is up with that?"

He looks surprised. "Dad wrote me a letter?"

He brushes right over my feelings to focus on that. I don't want to make a big thing of it because I don't want to put him on the defense before we even get started. Better to ease into it.

"I have it with me, actually. He never sent it." I unzip my backpack, rooting through it until I find the envelope. I curl the edges and set it into the front cup holder. I can see my dad's scribbly handwriting. He used to joke that illegible penmanship was a prerequisite for becoming a doctor. "I apologize—I didn't know I'd be seeing you and I opened it."

I steal a glance at the letter, sad to let it go. I have Dad's personal mementos, but nothing with his actual words and thoughts meant specifically for me, like a conversation that could be replayed at will.

"It's okay. Thanks." He rests his fingers gently on the top of the envelope for a moment and a flicker of a smile crosses his face. "I'll read it later."

"So yeah—I went to the address on the envelope, but your friend Mei told me you didn't live there anymore."

"You saw Mei?" I can see her name produces the same effect

as snapping a rubber band at him. Momentarily startling and uncomfortable.

"Yeah. She gave me a box with some stuff you left behind, and that's when I found the City Lights bookmark with Malcolm's name on it."

Thinking about things left behind makes me remember the other stuff Mei gave me for Alex, and I reach into my backpack again to pull the rest of it out and stack each item one by one in the empty cup holder. "I also have your erotic playing cards, harmonica, and Legend of Zelda: Ocarina of Time shirt, which—I'm pretty sure—is actually mine."

He's quiet for a beat, drumming his fingers on the steering wheel, and then asks, "So what did Mei have to say?"

"Not much. Just that she hadn't seen you in a long time and she hopes you're doing well and wanted to let you know she is too."

"That's good." He puffs out his cheeks and then says it again as if to assure himself. Up ahead I see a neon sign for Vinnie's Pizza in the shape of Italy. It's got twinkling white bulbs around the border. He pulls up to the curb in front and parks. "I hope you're hungry."

"I'm always hungry."

And with that we exit the car and enter the territory of everything we're not talking about.

21
JACK

SATURDAY, JUNE 5, 7:59 P.M.

The smell of fresh garlic assaults my nose. There's sawdust on the floors, and the walls are lined with framed pictures of Italian movie stars. Without even trying a slice, I know this place is going to be amazing. Dad would have appreciated it. He was a pizza aficionado. Some of my favorite memories are of when he'd have a night where he wasn't on call and he'd take us out for a pie. It was one of the rare times we'd have dinner as a family, and for one hour everything felt perfect.

Out in public we seemed like a happy family. Everyone got along great. And then we'd go home and all scatter to our respective corners like roaches when someone flicks the light on.

I order two slices of extra cheese, pepperoni, and mushroom—Dad's favorite. Alex gets two slices of deluxe veggie, which takes me by surprise.

"Veggie pizza? I don't think I've ever seen you eat a vegetable in my life unless you count fries. Is this some side effect of adulting? Like you hit your twenties and suddenly develop a newfound appreciation for brussels sprouts and acorn squash?"

He laughs. "I'm trying to get healthier."

"You know it's still pizza though, right?"

"Don't bust the illusion." He winks. We sit at a table in the corner next to a signed picture of Sylvester Stallone from *Rocky*. Alex grins and taps his fingers on the table. "So—this is kind of weird, huh?"

"A little."

"I guess we have a lot of ground to cover."

"Yeah."

His expression grows serious. "But first I guess I should start by saying I'm sorry."

"Alex—"

He cuts me off and holds up his hand. "I brought a lot of shit on myself, but you didn't need to get dragged into it. That wasn't cool, and I hope you can forgive me. I also want to thank you because if you hadn't found me, I probably wouldn't even be here to apologize."

So, he *does* remember. But how much does he know? I can't have any sort of honest relationship with him going forward if I don't tell him the truth. "You shouldn't thank me. My intention in the moment wasn't as pure as you give me credit for."

"How so?"

I've never said it out loud to anyone but Hallie and that seemed to go okay. "I waited to call for help. On purpose. I'm not proud of it."

I wince and brace myself for his response. He nods and cracks a half smile. Not even a look of surprise. "I don't blame you. I was an asshole. I would have done the same thing. But the thing is: you didn't. So—what changed your mind?"

"Honestly? I got scared." I take a long drink of water, and Alex jiggles his leg restlessly, his eyes darting around the room. He reminds me of a bird, like at the slightest startle, he could just take off. I wonder if he's wishing he could.

"That I would die or that you'd get caught?" he asks with a disarming smile as an older guy with silver hair and a sauce-stained Kiss the Cook apron walks over with our slices and puts them in front of us on the red-and-white-checkered tablecloth. They glisten with oily perfection.

"Hey! Alex! How you doin'?" the guy says giving my brother a pat on the shoulder.

Alex lights up with a smile. "Hey, Sal! How's the machine working?"

"Great! No problems since you fixed it. It's been getting a lot of play."

Alex turns to me and says, "Remember how I told you I fix things? I've been working on helping Sal restore an old pinball machine for the last few months. It's around the corner by the bathroom if you want to check it out after dinner."

Sal motions toward me with his hand. "Who's this?"

"This is my brother Jack. Jack—this is Sal, maker of the best pizza in the East Bay."

"Who needs advertising when I got this one," Sal jokes. He pumps my fist and tells us to enjoy our meal before heading back to the kitchen.

Alex sprinkles red pepper on his pizza then stuffs it into his mouth ravenously. With his mouth full of food, he asks, "So, where were we? Oh, right—you thought about leaving me for dead but got scared."

"Right. Well, that and I probably wouldn't have been able to live with myself. But I learned I'm capable of actually thinking like that, which is even scarier."

He washes his food down with a sip of soda and says, "I think most people are capable of thinking like that. Didn't you ever have to read *Lord of the Flies*? The reason doesn't even matter; you didn't do it. But if you had, I would understand why. I'm sorry I put you in the position of having to make that choice. I was way out of control. But I'm not that person now."

"That's good." I want to believe him. "I'm not that person now either."

He smiles. "It's really good to see you."

I can't hold it in. I have to ask. I twist the Parmesan shaker around in circles on the table. "Why didn't you come to the funeral?"

He stops chewing for a second then wipes at his mouth with a napkin and swallows. "I didn't belong there."

"Of course you did. You belonged there as much as anyone. You're his son."

"It didn't feel right. It's not like he was there in that box. Besides, everybody grieves differently."

"Fair enough. Still, I wish you had been there."

I would have given anything to have had my brother to talk to during that time, no matter what happened between us in the past.

"The truth is, sending me away and not allowing me to come home was the right thing to do. In case you never noticed, I was a walking threat to everything Paul and Suzanne Freeman believed in, especially you. I wasn't a kid anymore. They made clear they'd pay for treatment but then I was on my own. I needed to figure my life out. It turns out going away was exactly what I needed. It gave me a chance to be alone and tune in to myself. Sometimes you need that space, and if you aren't willing to create it, then sometimes life creates it for you."

"Were you in touch with them at all?"

"I sent them an email telling them where I was staying, but we never spoke, no. That's how Dad would have known Mei's address. And then Suzanne contacted me when he died."

"Oh." Why did my mother withhold that information from me when I asked about him? She saw how much I was hurting and how I needed us to be a family again.

"How are you doing with all that?" Alex asks. "I mean—I'm sure this must be hard for you. You were close."

I definitely had a better relationship with Dad than Alex did, but I don't know if I would call us close in the way I think he means. It seemed as if Dad tried to connect with Alex, but he was rebuffed every time. Alex was always testing him to see how far he could push him before he gave up. By default, I was the good son, and I liked the attention, but to call us close would imply a level of unconditional love and understanding that I hoped for but never found.

"Depends on the day or the hour. It kind of fucked me up. Nothing makes sense the same anymore, you know? It wasn't supposed to be like this."

"How do you think it was supposed to be?"

I shake my head. "I don't know. Nothing turned out the way I'd imagined. It's made me rethink a lot about my life."

"Sounds like a positive side effect of a negative situation."

"I guess that remains to be seen," I tell him.

I'm actually grateful when he switches topics. "So, what are you into these days? Tell me about you."

"I'm pretty boring, actually. Mostly I listen to music, or hang out with friends and binge-watch TV, or play video games, or write." I give him the elevator pitch for my book. He seems impressed.

"I didn't know you wanted to be a writer."

"It's definitely something I'm pursuing." Saying that out loud feels like an affirmation, the first step toward making it so.

"Sure." He nods. "So what games are you into? *Overwatch? League of Legends? Counter-Strike?*"

"That stuff is fun, but honestly I'm a little more old-school: Mario, Zelda, *Pac-Man*, pinball."

"Nice!" His face lights up. "That's what I'm hoping to do eventually—make video games. I'm taking some classes to learn programming and design. Seems like that would be a cool gig." He grabs another slice of pizza and tears into it. "Hey—since you like pinball, we should play Sal's machine after. It's an old Simpsons. You familiar with that one?"

"Of course. It won 'Best Pinball Game of 1990' by the Amusement and Music Operators Association and brought pinball back from the dead. It's pretty fun."

"What was that game you were obsessed with at that arcade in the Valley we went to with Dad once? You had some unbelievable score but then the machine broke. I forget what it was."

"TRON: Legacy."

"Right. That was a fun time."

I remember the day he's referencing too, although slightly differently. Dad and I were supposed to go together, but at the last second Alex glommed along. Dad had to step outside for an emergency conference call and left us on our own for nearly an hour feeding quarters into a TRON: Legacy machine. I'd engaged multiball play and was threatening to overtake the high score when Alex decided to be a dick and slammed the side of the machine as a joke, which triggered the tilt mechanism, ending the game. I actually cried. I never realized how much I hold on to shit but there it is.

"So, let's see this machine."

He grabs the remainder of his slice, takes a final sip of his soda, and walks me to the back of the restaurant and into a dimly lit room with a sign above it that says GAMING PALACE. And by *palace* they mean a lone Simpsons pin table, a *Street Fighter IV* with a line of missing pixels across the center of the screen, and one of those machines where you put in fifty cents and get a bouncy ball. There's inexplicably a disco ball hanging from the ceiling, and it casts glittering lights on the walls.

"Just needed for me to solder a few loose wires, add a few flipper rubber bands, fuses and lights, and it was good as new. Now, I should warn you that I have spent a great deal of time with this machine. Therefore, you should prepare to lose."

"Not a chance," I challenge him with a smile.

He laughs, and with that, the ice cracks. I feel like I get back a small piece of something I lost. Something I wasn't sure I'd ever experience again. I can't let myself get attached to it. This is still too potentially combustible.

Over the next fifteen minutes, I completely let him kick my ass. As I drain my last ball, a smile spreads across his face, victorious. "What time do you have to head back?"

"I have no plans," I tell him. "I'm on no schedule."

It's true. I don't even know where I'm sleeping tonight, let alone what I'm doing tomorrow. It actually hurts my brain to think about it, so I try to focus on right now.

He grins. "I have someplace I want to show you I think you'll dig."

He won't tell me where we're going. Only that he's helped the owner out a few times and I'm going to love it.

We relax into being with each other a little more. On the drive, we talk about all sorts of random shit like what we're watching on Netflix to some song by some band he's really into right now, and then ultimately wind our way back to Mei.

"They say you shouldn't get into any relationships within your first year of recovery, so we knew it was dangerous to live together, but I didn't have a lot of other options. One night I came home from work and found her wasted and partying with some guy in the apartment, and that was it. It wasn't safe for me to be there anymore. I think that was probably the first time I've ever put myself first in the right way in my entire life." Alex averts his eyes and nods his head toward a brick building with a turquoise awning up ahead. "Here we are."

He slides into a parking space just past it. My jaw drops momentarily as I take in the front mural of pinball art and the large glass window that showcases some of the advertised more than ninety machines inside available for play. I seriously wonder if I've died and gone to heaven.

"What *is* this place?" I ask.

"The Pacific Pinball Museum. Four rooms with over a hundred machines from the 1940s on, an all '80s jukebox, twenty bucks for all-day unlimited play." I can see rows of machines lit up in play through one of the front windows.

As we enter the magical oasis, all thoughts of anything else fall away. I don't even know where to start. I wander through it room by room, taking it all in. The walls are decorated with vintage murals, and every square inch of wall space is taken up with machines. They have a Seawitch from 1980, and of course an Addams Family because that's the bestselling flipper game ever made. There's a Modern Pinball Room, separate ones dedicated to machines from the 1980s and '90s, and a fully working version of Visible Pin, the first transparent pinball game ever made. I run my hand over the front of the table. Ajay would seriously crap his pants with envy right now.

Alex points out the placards above each machine telling its history. There are so many here I've never seen in person. I can't help but laugh and come to a stop in front of an Elton John Captain Fantastic pinball machine from the 1970s.

"Have you ever played this one?" I ask him.

"I can't say I have," he says. "It does have Elton John on the bumper caps though, which is pretty awesome."

"It briefly made Bally the number one pinball manufacturer for a game that was basically about a celebrity, which is hard to believe, right? They sold like seventeen thousand of these. Bally produced about eighty machines before they realized the extent of how borderline pornographic the artwork was. They recalled what they could, destroyed the backglass, and remade it using stars to cover up some of what was going on." I point toward two people near the bottom of the screen by Elton John's boot. "Like that lady has her hand down that guy's pants, but you can't see it because it's covered over by a star."

Alex leans in closer to examine the artwork. "Well, I'll be damned. You sure know a lot about pinball."

"I like how it's never the same game twice. It's art, it's light, it's sound—it stimulates all the senses. There's nothing like it. I always thought it would be cool to open up a restaurant with the walls all lined with pinball machines, maybe a few classic uprights."

"So—you want to franchise a Dave & Buster's?"

I laugh. "No. Classier than that. A retro arcade slash restaurant and bar. A place to bring people together to escape reality, unwind and have some fun."

He nods approvingly. "I've seen stuff like that around. That would be cool. So, what's stopping you?"

"From what?"

"From doing that."

"Ummm...besides several hundred thousand dollars and the

fact that it's tricky to get a liquor license when I'm not even legally allowed to drink?"

"That's what investors are for. You don't need a fancy Ivy League degree for that; you need knowledge of the product. Maybe a good business partner. And passion."

I allow myself to imagine it for a moment. It's as viable an option as anything else at this point. "There would be a lot to learn about before it could become a reality. I'd have to spend the next few years researching pinball machines, writing business plans, doing market research, talking with experts, securing financing. I would imagine the first few years, any profit would be turned right back into buying more games, so I'd have to be prepared to do whatever on the side until it takes off."

"The fact that you even know what you'd need to do tells me you've actually thought about this." I totally have. He isn't wrong. He selects two-player mode and pulls back the plunger, setting the ball in play. "You asked me before if I think you should go to New York, and I didn't want to give you an answer, but I guess I am anyway. That look in your eyes when you're talking about pinball or writing that book or opening that arcade bar, that rush you experience when you play a game—you should feel that, but it should be about the work that you do, the people you hang out with, the food that you eat, the music that you listen to. If this doesn't seem like it has the potential to be that, I say don't go."

I laugh. "Seriously, who are you and what have you done with Alex?"

"Sorry—one of the side effects of rehab and step programs is it makes you think about all your shit and deal with it. My point being: you're under no obligation to be the person you were before—a month ago, twenty-four hours ago, fifteen minutes ago. You have the right to change course. No apologies needed. The only expectations you have to live up to are your own. Anyhow, that's my two cents." His ball banks off a bumper and goes straight down the drain.

My father always told me he loved medicine because he felt like he was helping people. We connected over that aspect of it rather than the mechanics of the job itself. And that's the part that's still important to me. Letting go of the original plan we built together doesn't have to mean letting go of that objective or falling short of it.

We play until closing, and they kick us out, the last ones to leave. By the time we get back to the car, it's after ten and the moon is out, a waxing crescent peeking out between a smattering of clouds. Our evening is winding down, and I have no idea if or when I'll see him again after this.

"Can I give you a ride back to the city?" Alex asks as we head back toward his car. "It's getting late, and at the risk of sounding like a total grandpa, I probably should get to bed. I have to be up pretty early for work. Where are you staying?"

Good question. "Actually, I haven't figured that part out yet."

"I just rent a room in someone's house. I don't have a couch or anything to offer, so I can't invite you to crash with me. There's a motel not far from me though, and it seems decent enough. I could drop you off there."

I'm slightly disappointed that I can't stay with him, but at this point I'm so exhausted that I only care about being horizontal soon.

"Cool. Maybe we could meet up in the morning for coffee or something before you go to work."

"Yeah, sure," he says.

Overall, I think tonight went really well. On the drive to the motel, I take in an awesome view across the bay of the Golden Gate Bridge and the city lights. "Wow." I've seen my share of city lights in Los Angeles but nothing quite like this.

"Yeah, that's what I say every time I see it," he tells me. "Kind of takes your breath away, doesn't it? Makes you realize we're just specks. I mean, amongst those lights are millions of people, and every one of them has crap they're dealing with. It puts things in perspective."

"Yeah, it does."

"So, when do you have to decide about going to New York?"

"By tomorrow at the latest. At least for the internship."

"But you don't start Columbia until the fall, right? You can always find another internship. You have some time to decide about the rest. Let it marinate. But just know—you don't ever have to be someone you're not for someone else's benefit."

We find ourselves behind a city bus, and my mind drifts to thinking about Hallie. She's probably somewhere a few hours outside the city on her way back to Los Angeles. I visualize her, fists curled inside the oversize sleeves of her I Heart SF sweatshirt, earbuds jammed in, staring out the window at the same moon.

We reach the motel—a dumpy, two-story, gray stucco structure on the corner of a busy intersection with a neon-pink VACANCY sign hanging in the office window. The kind of place where you probably want to sleep fully clothed on top of the sheets and the odds are fifty-fifty that the bed vibrates. Thankfully, it's only for one night, and I'm not picky. Right now, the prospect of sleeping far outweighs curb appeal.

He points to a diner across the street. "How about I meet you there tomorrow morning around seven? Is that too early? I have to be somewhere at eight."

"No, seven is good," I tell him as I collect my things.

"Before you go, there's something I gotta ask you," he says. The look on his face is serious.

"Yeah, sure, anything."

He puts the car in park and turns toward me. "What are you looking for from me exactly?"

"What do you mean?"

"I mean did you come here looking for forgiveness to absolve yourself from guilt so you can go on with your life? Or are you just looking for someone else to make the decision for you about what you should do so if it doesn't work out you can blame it on me? Because I've ruined enough lives through my errors in judgment, and I'm not up for adding to that list."

"I—"

He doesn't give me a chance to answer. "If you're only here to feel better about yourself, then consider yourself forgiven, but I also ask that you just go, no hard feelings. I'm not saying that to be a dick; I'm simply trying to protect myself. You're at a crossroads and looking to me for answers, and that seems like a huge responsibility."

Now that we're about to say good night, we finally get to the meat of it. I only wish it had happened earlier, so we had more time, but maybe it was by design. After all, he's kept his distance for a reason, and obviously I'm part of it. By the same token, every time he screwed up, it pushed the bar higher for me to compensate, to prove that we're nothing alike. At least not in the obvious ways. But he's always been unapologetically who he is, and I'm the one pretending to be someone I'm not to make other people happy. It makes me think about the piece of paper I found with his stuff and his words about being authentic.

"I came here because I'm trying to figure out my life, and I think in order for me to move forward, I have to start by going backward. Look at all the pieces one at a time and be honest with myself, which requires me to be honest with everyone else too. I've missed you, and this last year I've really needed you. I think about what happened with you every single day, and I wish I could go back and erase that moment. Maybe everything that came after it wouldn't have happened."

"But it *did* happen, and believe me, I think about it all the time too. Things can never go back to being what they were, so we all have to make our own peace with that. I'm out here trying to live my life, doing the best I can, but it's day by day, and if we're being honest, your showing up here, looking to me for answers—it brings up a lot for me, and it's a little overwhelming." He averts his eyes and stares somewhere straight ahead out his front window. I can see that despite whatever work he's done, he's no more at peace than I am. Grief has no timetable.

"I get it. I'm not under the illusion that because we've reconnected, everything is back to normal, because I know it never can be. And I'm not looking for you to give me answers. I just want you to know that if and when you're ready, I would really like it if we could be in each other's lives."

He considers what I've said. "I don't know if I can be the person you need me to be right now."

"I don't need you to be anyone but yourself."

He smiles and bobs his head as he kicks the car into gear. "Sleep tight, little brother."

"See you in the morning."

"Yeah. See ya." I watch his taillights as he drives off, and although it didn't go perfectly, at least it was a start. The door has been cracked open.

I wash my face and gently clean the tender skin where I got my tattoo. I lie on top of the covers fully dressed and let my head sink into the surprisingly comfortable pillow. It occurs to me as I'm falling asleep that Alex and I are the last remaining atoms and molecules of Dad left on Earth.

22
HALLIE

SATURDAY, JUNE 5, 11:11 P.M.
My eyes are fixed on the small sliver of moon in the starry sky as the bus heads down the highway toward Los Angeles at a steady sixty-five miles per hour. I'm physically exhausted, and by all accounts, I should be sleeping, but now that I'm alone, the silence is deafening, and my mind is on hyperdrive.

The bus is freezing cold, and the guy next to me fell asleep and is precariously close to leaning on my shoulder. I tuck my hands into the sleeves of the sweatshirt Jack bought me and lean my head against the window. I breathe against the glass. It fogs, and I draw an upside-down happy face in the condensation. I feel a pang of missing Jack, which is weird because we've only just met. I mean, sort of; not really. Being with him was the perfect distraction.

Without him here and being in constant motion, the reality that Owen is gone is finally sinking in. It's surreal.

Owen is dead. Owen died. Owen no longer exists.

My eyes well with tears. I dab them with the cuff of my sweatshirt. It's impossible to imagine he's not on the planet and that I'll never speak to him again. Of all the kids I've met on the message board these past two years, he and I connected in a different way than the others. He was probably my closest friend. He helped me find the light in the darkness. I'll miss his optimism and his twisted sense of humor. Having someone who understood me on so many levels was everything.

People say they understand, but they don't. They don't know what it's like to be a teenager and not be able to do all the stuff your friends do because you feel weak or nauseous, to be watching numbers and checking levels and getting invasive tests and taking pills that make you feel worse than the illness itself. To be terrified to let yourself care about anyone and leave yourself vulnerable. Once they find out I have cancer, let alone see the scars on my stomach and soon potentially on my chest, it inevitably gets uncomfortable.

My hand reflexively reaches for my bracelet to rub the words on the metal band, my reminder to be strong and believe in myself, but I only find the skin of my wrist. The bracelet must have worked its way up my sleeve. I dig higher, but it's not there. It must have fallen off somewhere. A momentary feeling of panic sets in, but then the thought occurs to me that maybe it's time. It's not enough to merely say *alis volat propriis* without living it.

It's time to take the training wheels off the bike. Something has to shift. Happily ever after isn't the sort of thing that's just going to happen to me; I have to go out there and *make* it happen.

I have cancer, but it's up to me if I let it to control my life or define me. It always has been. Attitude is key. I can't count on Owen or my parents or Jack or anyone else to make me feel okay about everything; I have to find that inside myself. While I'm here, I want to focus on enjoying as many days between as I can get instead of dwelling on what bookends them.

The guy next to me starts snoring loudly and wakes himself up. He adjusts in his seat, and I'm grateful for the extra two inches of space it creates.

I close my eyes and try to get comfortable. I'm still a long way from home. I'm hoping my parents will already be gone when I get back. Sunday mornings are super busy at the Pancake Shack. I'll have all day to think about what I want to say.

The motion of the bus lulls me to sleep, and the next time I open my eyes, the bus is pulling into the station in Los Angeles. I reorient myself, stretch, and collect my things, following the other passengers into the terminal. Everything is exactly as it had been the night before when I'd been there with Jack, except the faces have changed. I look over at the spot where we'd been sitting when he invited me to go with him. The seat is now occupied by a woman knitting a really ugly scarf. Raisinets Guy has moved on, and Tuxedo Guy must have found a ride. The older lady and her granddaughter are no longer stretched out on the bench where we'd been at first. It seems like I've been gone forever, but it's only been a little over twenty-four hours, and in that time so much has changed.

I've changed.

The rideshare drops me in front of my house sometime just before six. I don't see my dad's car in the driveway, so that's a good sign. I put my key in the lock and quietly close the door behind me so I don't wake Dylan; he wouldn't be able to keep his mouth shut.

As I tiptoe down the hall to my room, the door to my parents' bedroom opens, and my mother comes out, still in her pajamas. We are both startled. She clutches her hand to her chest.

"Hallie! You scared me to death. What are you doing home so early? Is everything okay?" A concerned look crosses her face. She reaches for my arm.

My whole body is pins and needles from the adrenaline of having been caught without time to prepare. I say the first thing I can think of. "Yeah, Lainie wasn't feeling well, so she drove me home." I feel awful for looking her in the eye and lying to her, especially while wearing an I Heart SF sweatshirt.

"So early? Gosh—you look exhausted. Did you guys stay up all night?" She doesn't even question any of it. That's how much she trusts that I would never keep something from her.

"Yeah. She has some sort of stomach virus, I think, so I was up trying to—um, help her." I try to change the subject. "How come *you're* here? Don't you have to be at work?"

"Dad is holding down the fort. I wasn't feeling well last night either, so I thought I'd play it safe. I wouldn't want to get the customers sick. He brought Dyl with him to bus tables, so he should be alright. Gosh, I hope you don't get whatever Lainie is coming down with. Or whatever I've got. Clearly stuff is going around. Make sure you pop some Vitamin C today."

"Yeah."

I freeze. I can't think of what to say next. She's worried I'll catch Lainie's imaginary virus. She has no idea it is so beyond that, and I feel myself cracking wide open. I break eye contact, and that's all she needs for her mom radar to kick in.

"Hallie? What's going on?"

It builds inside of me until it can no longer be contained, and then I completely lose it right there in the hallway. Mom's arms are around me in two seconds, and I'm certain if she weren't holding me so tightly, I'd fall straight to the floor. She strokes my hair and makes little shushing noises like she used to when I was little, and I fold into her.

Wordlessly, she makes us a cup of tea, and we climb into her bed side by side. I tell her everything: the phone call on Friday, Owen's post, taking the money from her tin, and my spontaneous trip with Jack to San Francisco. I find myself minimizing the Jack part, keeping the focus on going to see Owen unsuccessfully and coming home, as if Jack were a relatively unimportant part of the story. Mostly, I'm trying to convince myself, because if I get started talking about him, it will only make me miss him. I may never see him again anyway, so what's the point?

When I'm finished, tears are streaming down both our faces. I tell her I'm scared. Mom leans her head against mine, takes my hand, and squeezes it in her own.

"You've already given up so much and are working so hard. I'm so sorry," I sob into her neck.

"There is nothing to be sorry for. There is nothing we've given up that would ever be worth more than you being healthy, and that's never going to change. We'll figure it out." She curls my hair behind my ear and kisses me gently on my forehead.

We talk for a while more about the call from the doctor's office and my appointment Monday, and then finally she circles back to my trip to San Francisco. I was foolish to think I'd get off that easily.

"What were you thinking? Do you realize how dangerous that could have been, driving off with two strangers hundreds of miles from home without telling anyone where you'd gone? Who is this boy? And to visit yet another that you don't even know without having any emotional support in place to deal with what you might find when you get there?" And then she notices my tattoo, and her mouth falls open.

"I know. You have every right to be upset with me," I tell her.

"Honestly, I'm more upset that you lied to us or that you felt like you had to." She looks so hurt. It makes me feel even more awful than I already do.

"I felt like if you knew everything, you would stand in my way. Find a reason to talk me out of it based on fear. These last few years, I've been living my life under a microscope. Nothing feels like it belongs only to me or like I have final say. But I'm not a little kid anymore."

"I know that. But I'm always going to worry that you and your brother are warm enough when it's cold outside, that you've gotten enough to eat, that you have a roof over your head, that you're happy and healthy, because I'm your mom. You can't expect me to turn that off like a light switch just because you're suddenly eighteen."

"I know." And I do. I understand. She'll probably still be telling me to take a sweater when I go out when I'm forty.

"I mean—am I upset? Yes. Do I think this was smart? No. But whatever pushed you there, and in this way, you had your reasons, and we have to accept that. But I don't want you to ever think you can't be honest with us, even if we don't like it." She squeezes my hand again.

It's great that she's being so surprisingly cool about this, because it's exactly what I need, but at the same time, it's almost worse. "I really am sorry."

"For which part?"

"What do you mean?" I look at her curiously. She's got this unsettling smile. What was all that literally two seconds ago about accepting that I had reasons? "I said I was sorry a bunch of times. I meant it. I'm sorry for lying and for thinking that by keeping the truth from you and Dad, I was protecting you somehow."

"That's not what I mean. Are you sorry you went? Was it at least worth it?"

My mouth hangs open—I'm unsure how to answer. Mom goes on, "Because the girl I know spends every day holed up in her room with the blinds drawn like it's a cave. This same girl used to talk excitedly about wanting to travel the world collecting stones and making beautiful jewelry, would pirouette in the kitchen and could move a room to tears with her poetry and her art and in the next breath have them laughing. And suddenly she never wanted to leave her room. It's like she got sick and placed herself in a self-imposed prison afterward she refused to be drawn out from."

"It's seriously creeping me out that you're speaking about me in the third person. I'm right here."

She laughs. "My point is—I hope it was worth it, because believe it or not, I'm glad that you found something powerful enough to make you leave that room. I'm glad you gave yourself permission to engage with the world. I've wanted that for you for a long time. I hope you found something out there that makes you want to keep coming out of that room, because nothing is going to change if you just stay in there feeling sorry for yourself. This too shall pass. You have a whole life ahead of you to see and do and be whoever and whatever you want. I want you to believe that. Not just because I'm telling you—because you truly understand that."

I don't say anything. She cups my chin gently in her hand and turns my face to look at hers. "I know you're scared, especially because your friend died, but that doesn't mean that you're going to. This is just something you have to deal with in your life, but you have, and you will. You are strong. And most of all, you are not in this alone."

"Dad's gonna be upset that I took off like that," I say, anticipating he won't take it as well as she has. When my father gets scared, he gets angry. He acts the exact opposite of what he's feeling. I am already dreading the conversation we'll have when he gets home, but I've earned it.

"I'm sure he will be, but it's only because he loves you. If you speak to him from your heart the way you've spoken with me, he'll understand where you're coming from." She runs her fingers gently up and down my arm from my elbow to my shoulder and back again. She notices the tattoo on my wrist again and lifts my arm, taking a closer look. "So you got a tattoo."

I nod. I don't regret it. For a moment I think she's going to get upset about it, but then she smiles and says, "It's pretty."

"Thanks."

"Did it hurt?"

"A little."

She leans her head against mine. "Everything will be okay."

I want to believe her. I close my eyes. I'm still listening, but I can't keep them open a second longer. I'm completely spent. The pillow is so soft, and the blanket is so perfectly warm, and Mom stroking my arm like that makes me melt into the bed the same way it's done since I was little. After a few minutes, she gently shifts position, extricating her arm from mine. The mattress creaks and gives as she stands.

I feel like I should answer her question, that I owe her that much.

I call out to her groggily, "Mom?"

She turns around. "Mmmm?"

"It was totally worth it."

She smiles. "I'm glad."

23
JACK

SUNDAY, JUNE 6, 6 A.M.

Amazingly, I'm up right at six on the dot. I take one glance at the shower, and despite how gross I feel, there is no way I am stepping foot in that petri dish, so I make do with a wet washcloth and a bar of soap, and I lather on the deodorant.

The sky is gray, it's drizzling from the low-lying fog, and my sweatshirt is no match for the dampness. I bolt across the street to the diner and am waiting in a booth and nursing a cup of coffee by 6:47. I get a refill at 7:02. Alex still hasn't shown, but it's literally been two minutes. By 7:15 I'm growing concerned, and by 7:19 I'm also a little pissed. I pull out my phone and realize Alex doesn't have my number, nor I his, and I don't know where he lives or anything about him other than the address at the teen center. But he knows exactly where I am. He could easily find a way to reach me if he wanted to.

At 7:28 the waitress wants to know if I want to keep waiting or if I'd like to order something other than coffee. I get sourdough toast and a double side of bacon because bacon makes everything better.

At 7:46 the waitress comes to the table with a coffeepot in hand and asks, "Are you Jack?"

"Yeah?"

She hands me a green paper folded in half with my name written on it. "Some guy asked me to give this to you."

I take it from her and open it as she refills my coffee. On it is my brother's familiar scrawl.

> Trust the journey, little brother. Wherever it takes you, be authentic and you'll be all right. Best I can do for now.

Be authentic. He wrote that on the paper mixed in with his stuff at Mei's. He must have heard it somewhere and adopted it into his lingo. He always did stuff like that. If I'm Human Google, he was Walking Urban Dictionary. He'd discard words as easily as people when they no longer served him.

I look out the window toward the street, but there's no one there, only cars driving by.

"When did you get this?" I asked.

"Some guy handed it to the cook through the back door a few minutes ago and described you. You're the only one here that fit the description." She smiles and stops filling my cup. "Can I get you anything else?"

I'm not entirely surprised he didn't show. Still, I had hoped.

"No, I'm good. Maybe just the check please?" I look at his words again. *Trust the journey. Best I can do for now.* I can't help but smile. *For now* offers the hope there's a later, and I guess that has to be enough. At least I had the opportunity to tell him how I feel.

I finish my coffee and am sliding out of the booth to go pay the check when the bells on the front doors jingle, followed by a dog's yip. The noise catches my attention. I throw a casual glance in that direction and do a double take before breaking out into a smile.

"*Oscar?*"

He's the last person I expect to see, but I'd be lying if I said I wasn't happy for a familiar face. Princess starts wagging her tail furiously, although that might have less to do with her recognizing me than coveting my leftover slice of bacon. I spend the next hour continuing to caffeinate while watching Oscar eat steak and eggs as he tells the saga of how things unfolded with Operation: Wedding Breakup. Apparently, his ex lives somewhere down the street, and he's just come from a final drive by her apartment and decided to grab a bite before hitting the road.

"So, things didn't go the way you hoped?" I ask. Looks like I'm not the only one.

"Not exactly. I showed up at her place and parked right across the street. I had Princess in my lap, Terrapin in the trunk—I was feeling confident. I was ready to tell her she was making the biggest mistake of her life and I was here to save her from it and how great things could be if she'd only give me another chance. Before I even got out of my car, I saw her come down the front steps of her building with Kevin, and she looked so freaking happy. She never looked like that when we were together. Maybe early on, in the beginning, but not for a long time. I couldn't bring myself to move; I sat there and watched them walk down the street, and I thought to myself, *You're a supreme douche if you do this, Oscar.* Not because I might actually cause her to change her mind, but because if I truly love her, I should want her to be happy, even if I'm not the one that makes her feel that way."

I shake my head. "Man, I'm sorry. That's rough."

"Yeah, well, you know..." He sips his coffee. "Now they're married, so that's done."

"Did you go to the wedding? I don't think I could stomach watching that."

"No. I'm not a total masochist. I sat in the church parking lot and tortured myself by waiting until they came out. Then I went back to my friend's apartment and got stinking drunk and marathoned *BoJack Horseman* on his couch until I passed out, and now here I am. Have you ever watched that show? Brilliant but depressing as hell, and probably not the best choice at the moment. Can you pass the ketchup?"

I hand it to him. "For whatever it's worth, I think you did the right thing. It frees you up to meet the right person."

"But what if *she* was the right person?" he asks.

"This is the part where you just have to have faith in the universe." I find myself repeating Hallie's words to Oscar. "If you're meant to find each other again, you will."

"I guess time will tell, won't it?" He squeezes a blob of ketchup on his plate, and the bottle makes a loud farting sound that makes the waitress look in our direction. Princess lets out a single bark.

"So, what are you going to do with Princess now that she's not the cornerstone of your happily-ever-after master plan?"

The dog, who sits between us eating bites of Oscar's steak, perks up at the sound of her name. He scratches her between the ears, and her eyes form contented slits. "We've grown pretty fond of each other, actually. I think I'm going to keep her. At least I'd know she's being treated properly. Plus, guys with dogs are chick magnets."

"Note to self."

"So how about you? What brings you to this obscure dining establishment early on a Sunday morning?"

"I was supposed to meet my brother, but he didn't show up. So now I guess I've got to figure out how to get back to LA."

He nods and swirls a bite of egg in ketchup. "I'm about to drive back. Why don't you just come with me? No charge."

Which is how I end up back in Oscar's car, in the front seat this time, with Princess curled up on my lap, driving back to Los Angeles while contemplating life, love, and the mysteries of the universe.

As we reach the outskirts of LA, the sky glows an eerie orange from the lights and flames reflecting off the smoke particles in the air. Hard to imagine now, but after the first rainfall, these same charred hills will turn as green as Ireland. Life finds its way. If nature can figure out how to start from scratch after being devastated and scarred, so can I.

I remember at the last minute that my car is still at Carly

Ginsburg's house. As we approach her McMansion, I see it parked all by itself on the street. There's an abandoned red cup sitting on the trunk and another on the roof. Toilet paper dangles from a tree at the base of the driveway next to the exact spot where I stood with Natasha, unaware of the turn my night would take. It seems like eons ago.

When I get home, I don't even turn on the lights. I head straight upstairs to my room, where I collapse on my bed. In the darkness, I can make out the silhouettes of the two suitcases standing sentry by the door, and a rush of emotion overcomes me.

What am I doing?

This is real. This is the rest of my life, and it starts now. It's not too late to fill those bags and catch another flight, and yet the idea makes my heart pound faster in my chest, and suddenly it's as if I can't get enough air in my lungs.

I'm like a can of soda that's been shaken up and someone just pulled the tab. Everything bottled up inside me explodes. The tears come fast and furious, and I curl into a ball, fetal, my body lurching with guttural sobs and howls.

I miss my dad so fucking much. I wish he were here to tell me what the fuck I should do, to assure me that everything would work itself out and be okay. I have never needed him more, and he's not here. *Nobody's* here. I am alone, literally and figuratively.

I have never known how lonely I could feel until I felt the vast emptiness of the space my father once occupied. Our connection since he died is almost closer than the one we shared when he was alive. I know he was far from perfect, but all that bubbles to the surface are the good things that makes me physically ache: The gravelly sound of his voice. A random moment where I felt his love. How safe he made me feel in the world. The satisfied noise he'd make after his first sip of coffee in the morning. His repertoire of two jokes that he told all the time and how it used to drive me crazy. I'd give anything to hear him tell them right now. The pain of his loss is so profound, it lives deep in my bones and permeates every pore, infiltrates every thought, and sucks up all the oxygen in the room.

And my brother. To find him only to lose him all over again.

And my mother, somewhere halfway across the country, and who couldn't be bothered to show up for me the way I needed even one fucking time.

And Hallie, who'd only just met me but shared this amazing connection, and yet she had no problem walking away, not even wanting to keep in touch.

What is it about me that makes me so easy to leave? Because everyone I care about seems to eventually—if not physically, then emotionally.

I cough, and it makes me gag. The grief flattens me. I want it to stop. I want to feel like me again, but I don't even know who that is anymore.

I just want, more than anything, to close my eyes and wake up to find everything the way it used to be.

I dream that I wake up to the sun shining and the distinct smell of coffee brewing. It's an olfactory hallucination, of course, because I'm the only one here. I rub my eyes, stand up, and as I crack open my bedroom door, the smell only grows stronger.

I swear I can hear someone banging around in the kitchen. I tiptoe down the hall and hear voices. Male and female. *What the*—

I walk into the kitchen, and there's my mom, pouring a cup of coffee, adding a splash of hazelnut sugar-free coffee creamer and then filling a second mug black, no room, and putting it on the table. I see a hand reach for it, and I'd recognize my father's hand anywhere. Thin, precise fingers, the silver-and-gold band of his watch against his tanned wrists. But that's impossible.

My mother turns to look at me as I enter and says, "Oh, good, you're up. We were just going to check for a pulse," she says, like that kind of joke could be funny in our house.

"Dad?" I want to go to him and hug him, but I can't move.

"You okay, bud? You look like you've seen a ghost." He cracks a smile and takes a sip of his coffee.

And then Alex walks in, his hair askew in the way I remember from back when he gave zero fucks. He goes to the refrigerator, opens it, and takes a swig of OJ straight from the bottle.

"Alex! Cut that out! That's disgusting!" my mother chastises, which only encourages him to take another sip just to taunt her.

"Sorry, Suzanne," he mumbles and puts it back then steals a slice of bacon from the plate on the counter and winks at me.

"Stop calling your mother *Suzanne*. You know she doesn't like it," my father says.

Alex slides into the chair opposite him. "Sorry," he says and then adds quietly under his breath, "Suzanne." My father rolls his eyes as Alex snickers, and then all three of them are staring at me because I'm still standing there wide-eyed.

I try to move again, but my legs feel as if they have twenty-ton weights attached.

"I was just telling Mom that it was a beautiful day for a hike. Any interest in joining?" Dad asks. He was always trying to get me to hike with him, and I wish I'd said yes more often. Before I can answer, Mom responds.

"He can't until he finishes all his work." My mother lays the plate of bacon on the table and one of eggs and another of toast and then motions with her chin toward the table. "Sit down, Jack."

"Oh, right," Dad says and puts a spoonful of eggs on his plate.

"What work?" I ask.

She looks at me in disbelief. "What *work*? You have to finish taking all the tests for your college classes up front because they want to see how much they need to teach."

"That makes no sense," I tell her.

Alex shakes his head. "Why do you always have to look for things to make sense? Haven't you been paying attention?"

What the actual hell is going on?

"Is this real?" I ask. "Are we all sitting here in the kitchen having breakfast right now?"

My parents exchange a concerned look. My mother walks over to me and puts her hand to my forehead like I'm five years old and she's checking my temperature. "Jack? Can you hear me?"

Dad tells her, "Let him rest, Suzanne. He'll be all right. He has to figure out how to fly with his own wings." It's the translation of the Latin phrase on Hallie's bracelet.

Before Mom relents, she gets right in my face—checking my pupils to see if I'm high, I'm guessing—and when she backs up, I turn to look at Dad and Alex, but they're gone.

Someone is tapping my cheek, gently at first and then harder.

"Jack?"

It takes me a minute to orient myself to what is happening. I'm back in my room. The sun is shining in the window, and I'm still here on my bed in the clothes I've been wearing for the past two days. My eyes fly open, and I nearly jump out of my skin.

It's my mom. I let out a little yelp, and it startles her. She retracts her hand and clutches it dramatically to her chest.

"Oh, thank goodness. I kept saying your name, and you didn't respond. You've been sleeping since I got here, and it's nearly three."

"What are you doing here?" I scrunch my eyes against the light and sit up abruptly.

"I should be asking you the same thing," she says with a little more edge to her tone. She's entitled. She's tried to reach me about a million times, and I've ignored it, which was kind of an asshole move. Still, I'm disoriented and ill-prepared for this confrontation to take place. When I don't answer, she adds, "Alex called me. Apparently, you showed up out of nowhere having some sort of life crisis, and amazingly he did the right thing and let me know. He was concerned about you."

For a second I feel as if Alex betrayed me, but then I realize in his own way, he was probably looking out for me. He knew when he didn't show up, I'd probably go home and that it was the right thing to do. I could only run from my problems for so long—something he knows all too well.

"I'm glad somebody is."

I didn't mean to utter the words out loud, but it cuts to the heart of everything I'm about to say. She immediately looks hurt and confused as she stands up and faces me, arms crossed across her chest. "You think I'm not concerned? I called my editor on a Sunday night *at home* and let her know I needed to end the tour because there's a family emergency. If that doesn't qualify as concerned, I'm not sure what meets your criteria."

"You didn't have to come," I tell her.

"Of course I had to come. You're my son. So take a shower, because frankly, you smell like you crawled out of a sewer, and then come have a cup of coffee and help me understand what is going on."

I appreciate the buffer of being given time to wake up and refresh my brain before launching into everything with her. I take a long, hot shower and then throw on a fresh pair of jeans and a clean tee shirt and pad barefoot on the cool wooden floors, following the scent of my mother's Chanel Number 5 until I find her in the kitchen. There's a half-empty bag of Milano cookies on the table. I plop into the seat Dad usually occupied. "Okay, here I am. Let the lecture begin."

"Is that supposed to be sarcasm?" she asks.

"No, actually it *is* sarcasm." I shove a cookie in my mouth. It's slightly stale, but I eat it anyway. Her eyes lock on my thumb as she places a mug of coffee in front of each of us and sits down adjacent to me at the table.

"What's on your finger?"

"I got a tattoo."

"A *tattoo*?" She raises her eyebrows. In all fairness, I did tell her the other morning that I was going to get one. I just didn't know I wasn't joking. "This is quite serious, Jack."

"Not as serious as lying to me for the past two years about Alex, telling me you didn't know where he is."

"It's not that black-and-white, Jack." She sighs deeply and shakes her head. "At the time, it was what your father and I thought was best for everyone involved. It was for your own good."

"You have no idea what I needed. You never asked. Not then, not now, not ever."

"Part of being a parent is sometimes having to make impossibly difficult choices that on the surface seem like they're not caring but are actually just the opposite."

"Were you ever going to tell me the truth?"

"Yes, of course, but if you want me to be honest, I worried about him coming back into your life when you seemed so emotionally fragile. Despite that, I invited him to come to the funeral, except I didn't tell you so that you wouldn't be upset if he didn't show. When he didn't, he only proved to me that he still hadn't moved beyond only thinking of himself. So, hearing you're looking to him for life advice like he in any way has your best interests at heart has me, understandably, a little concerned."

"At least he was willing to try to help."

She tries to redirect the conversation as she doctors her coffee, pouring in her hazelnut creamer. "Look, Jack—I need you to explain what is going on. I can't fix anything if you won't talk to me, and hopefully it *can* be fixed. I'm sure changing tickets or calling your new boss is no problem. We'll tell them something came up and you'll be able to start later in the week. And worst comes to worst, we'll buy another ticket."

"But that's the whole point, Mom. I don't want *you* to fix anything. My whole life, everyone else has been thinking for me. Not once has anyone asked me what I want, so for the longest time, I've believed it didn't matter. But it does. I'm tired of feeling like being anything less than the person you want me to be is not good enough for you."

Her eyebrows form an agitated V, and she huffs. "Don't put that on me, like everything you've done is because I held a gun to your head." She averts her eyes to the plant in the center of the table and begins picking off the yellowed leaves. There's no short- age of things that have suffered from a lack of attention around here. "This is what you've always wanted to do."

"No, this what *you've* always wanted me to do, and I went along with it because it seemed to make you guys happy. But if I can't trust my own voice, why should I trust anyone else's?"

I've never stood up to my mother in my life, and my doing so takes her by surprise. I've got her full attention.

"Are you saying you aren't interested in being a doctor? Or you aren't interested in going to Columbia?"

Here we are. It's all come down to this moment. I need to make a decision, and the more I talk, the more my choice becomes clear. I shake my head. "All of it."

"I see. And what sparked this sudden change of heart?"

"It's not sudden. Since before Dad died, I'm realizing.

Honestly, it's always felt like if I didn't do this, you might not be proud of me—both of you." I take another cookie off the plate and crack it in half before putting it in my mouth. "For the past year, all I wanted to do was curl up in a ball. The future is suddenly imminent, and it doesn't look like I'd expected. It's like I've lost my sense of place and purpose and my ability to see anything good up ahead, and it scares me a hell of a lot more than letting go of this."

I feel a wave of sadness building offshore. I don't want to fall apart in front of her. She'll write it off as anxiety and start analyzing me, and I'll lose ground. It's more than that.

Predictably, she says, "Maybe we should talk to Carole about going back on an antidepressant."

"That's not the solution for me. I know they're amazing for some people, and they helped for a while, but I don't personally like how they make me feel. I want to have agency over my life and learn to deal with whatever happens without having to rely on meds to feel okay," I tell her. "I've been giving this a lot of thought, and I've realized I'm just not ready. Like life has kept moving forward but I'm standing still, and I need some time to catch up. I don't know if that's a few months or a year; but I don't want to rush into something that doesn't feel right. It seems unrealistic for me to have my whole life figured out at eighteen. And frankly, I shouldn't have to. Maybe I can talk to Columbia about deferring so if I decide it's what I want, that option is still there—I don't know."

Her jaw tenses. "That would be wise."

"Most of all, I want to be happy, to wake up every day and

feel good about who I am and how I'm walking in the world. And how I'm choosing to do that should be secondary for you because it's not *about* you."

She sighs deeply. She can't refute that, and she knows it. It's why my father also once said I'd make a good lawyer. "I think you might be making a very big mistake that you will possibly regret someday."

"Maybe. Maybe not. If you think about it, everything we do is potentially a big mistake we might regret deeply one day. We're always one decision away from changing our whole lives."

I know you can't hold on to anything forever. Not a person, not a situation, not a plan. Perhaps my problem is I keep trying.

We talk late into the evening. Really talk, like we haven't in years, if ever. I'm glad to find I haven't given her enough credit. She has her own feelings about everything I'm saying, but surprisingly, she's not discounting mine.

Before we call it a night, I ask her, "Do you ever wonder what your life would have been like if you'd made different choices? Would you be happier? Or would it have just been a different series of disappointments and heartbreaks?"

As she turns off the lights and we head down the hall to go to bed, she answers, "I think disappointment and heartbreak are unavoidable. But giving up the painful, messy moments that come from those choices would mean giving up the positive ones that came from them too."

I nod. "So—are you flying back to New York tomorrow? I mean—I know you still have three weeks left on your tour."

She shakes her head. "No. I want stick around here for a while in case you need me—which I know you don't, sounds like you've got this under control. But you know what I mean."

"I've always needed you, Mom," I tell her. She folds her arms around me, and we stand there like that for a long time.

24
JACK

WEDNESDAY, JUNE 23, 1:22 P.M.

I spend the first two weeks of summer mostly hanging out with Ajay, playing video games, applying for a handful of minimum wage jobs, and watching a lot of shows on Netflix.

Still, two weeks out from shooting off an apologetic email to my supervisor at the internship I won't be taking and another to Columbia University's admissions department to inquire about deferring, I'm not as relieved as I might have expected. I'm guessing it will take a while to sink in.

Today, I'm taking a break from organizing my bookshelf alphabetically to go the mall with Ajay. He needs to get some new clothes for his upcoming trip to Europe where he's spending the summer with his cousins in Paris, and I'm *that* bored that I've offered to tag along. Ajay thumbs through stacks of identical-looking tan shorts at five different chain stores until he finally settles on some and buys three identical pairs. We linger in GameStop for a while chatting up the guy behind the counter about Nintendo's *Breath of the Wild* sequel and then head to the Starbucks kiosk for rejuvenation.

"So, have you talked to Natasha?" he asks as we loop around the turnstile and enter the queue.

"Nope. Should I have?"

"No, it's just—you guys went out for a long time, and then it ended kind of weird. I don't know where that leaves me exactly. I mean—I'm friends with both of you."

"Has she asked about *me*?" I ask.

"I haven't actually talked to her since the day after Carly's party, when she was having a meltdown."

"Nobody's expecting you to choose sides. We broke up with each other, not you. We can be mature. We're all adults here."

"That's a terrifying thought," he jokes.

"Seriously, it's fine. I'm fine. Things could not be finer. I am the King of Fineland." We order, and Ajay doesn't even make a move for his wallet. He's distracted by something, and there's someone waiting behind us, so I pay. "No problem, I'll get it."

"Cool—so—if your paths crossed suddenly and without warning, you'd be totally chill?" he asks, his gaze remaining fixed somewhere over my shoulder.

I let out a single laugh. "Yeah, totally."

"Excellent, because she's standing at the counter right there waiting for her drink."

For a single beat, I wonder if Ajay is trying to prank me, but it's not his style to twist the knife. He's more about trying to embarrass me in public. And then I hear the barista yell out, "Triple venti, half-sweet, nonfat, caramel macchiato, extra hot!"

I'd recognize that high-maintenance drink order anywhere.

I scan the faces arcing out around the pickup area at the end of the bar and spot her copper curls, piled on her head in an intentionally sloppy bun. Our eyes lock as she reaches for her beverage. She's caught off guard, and the sight of me so clearly unsettles her that she knocks into not one but two people behind her as she steps back from the counter. Her face is as white as if she's seeing a ghost. In a way, she is.

We exchange awkward smiles, and I raise my hand in hello. For a millisecond, I feel a twinge of something I used to when I looked at her, but then I realize it's more of a conditioned response, like Pavlov's dogs. The truth is, I haven't thought much about her these last few weeks.

"Iced coffee for Cade!" the barista calls out, and my attention is now drawn to the guy standing to her left that I hadn't noticed at first. It takes me a minute to recognize him as he approaches the counter because he's wearing sunglasses and a wool beanie even though it's hot as Hades out. As he comes to stand alongside her, I realize it's Cade fucking Krentzman. The same Cade Krentzman from grad night.

"Hey, what are you guys doing here?" Natasha asks. Her smile looks pasted on.

"Well, it's the mall. Doing some shopping," I deadpan.

Cade takes a sip of his drink and nearly spits it out. He approaches the barista and says rudely, "Excuse me, I ordered this sweetened." The barista quickly apologizes and offers to remake it.

I can't help but look at Natasha and smile. She knows how I feel about people who sweeten black coffee and people who speak rudely to service workers. It's so many kinds of wrong. Her face is frozen, staring at me.

Cade looks at me over the top of his sunglasses, trying to place me. "Do I know you? You look familiar."

"We went to Madison together for the last four years."

I still clearly don't register. "Oh, okay. Right."

If Cade realizes Natasha and I used to date, it's lost on him. Or he's so cocky, he simply doesn't care.

"How come you're not in New York?" she asks me, visibly flustered.

"Change of plans. Change of heart. You know how that goes," I tell her.

Her cheeks flush. "So, you're *not* going to New York?"

"Not at this point. I'm taking a gap year, working, traveling, figuring stuff out."

"What about Columbia?"

"What about it?"

"You're not going?" She's looking at me in disbelief, her words dripping with judgment.

"I don't know. Probably not."

"*Why?*"

"The fact that you're even asking that question shows how little we know each other," I tell her and render her speechless. I'm not trying to be a jerk; I'm simply stating a fact.

"We should get going. The movie's gonna start," Cade tells her.

"What are you guys going to see?" Ajay asks.

"*Psycho in The Cellar*," Cade offers as the barista hands him his new drink. "It's supposed to be killer. Every pun intended."

He cracks up at his own joke, another pet peeve of mine. Natasha is turning absolutely scarlet. It's kind of fantastic. "Interesting. I thought you hated horror movies, thus further proving my point," I tell her. "Well, it was great to see you guys. Have a good summer!"

"You too." Cade presses Natasha's hand to his arm to steer her away, but she stays rooted in place.

"Maybe we could meet for coffee sometime and talk," she offers as an olive branch of sorts.

"Sure." It's the kind of vague thing you say to end a conversation even though we both know it probably won't happen. I'm ready to move on. Clearly, she is too, even if it is with Cade Krentzman.

On our way back to the car, I notice the mannequins in every store window display, and it makes me think of my night with Hallie. I tell Ajay the story on the drive home. I take the long way, which routes us by the Pancake Shack, which I do every day, hoping to steal a glance of her through the window as I pass, some sign she's okay. I'm still wearing her bracelet every day so I don't lose it.

"If you're so hung up on this girl, I don't understand why you don't go talk to her."

"I can't. I told you—she doesn't want contact until we meet up in six months."

He shakes his head. "And you're okay with that? I, personally, don't get the whole six months deal. This is real life, Jack, not the climax scene of a Hallmark movie. She wouldn't make some elaborate future meetup plan with you if she weren't interested, which lends itself to the strong possibility she's been regretting that decision ever since."

We reach the stoplight across the intersection from The Pancake Shack. The car is deafeningly quiet, both of us staring at it, and then Ajay says, "Seriously, my friend, I think you just need to go in."

"I think you just want hash browns," I tell him.

"I wouldn't complain."

"If I'm doing this, you're coming with me."

"Only if you buy me hash browns."

"I mean—it's reasonable to expect I'd be concerned that she's okay after what she told me, right?"

"This is what I'm saying. You're just checking in, and then when she sees you again, she'll be reminded of your irresistible charm and change her mind. In fact, she's probably waiting for you to storm the restaurant looking for her, so you can tell her to lay down her pancake batter ladle, set aside her apron and sweep her off her feet right now."

"Yes, I'm sure that's exactly how it will go. Who's Hallmark Channeling now?"

The light changes. The car behind me honks because I idle a second too long.

"You just gotta get it over with. It'll be like ripping off a Band-Aid," Ajay assures me.

We sit in my car in the parking lot for a full ten minutes before I work up the courage to go in. There's a HELP WANTED sign taped to the front door, which is ironic because the place is quiet as a graveyard.

My eyes immediately dart to the far back booth where I saw Hallie sitting before, but she's not there. No one is. The place is empty.

"This is a bad idea. Let's go," I tell Ajay as I jam my hands in my pockets and am about to turn around and leave, but he's having none of it.

"Band-Aid," he says like it's some code word between us.

He smiles at someone over my shoulder. I turn to face an older version of Hallie, except this woman's hair is brown and tied back in a ponytail. They even have the same smile. I'm guessing it's her mom.

"Table for two?" she asks pleasantly.

"Hi, um—yes, please," I tell her and awkwardly follow her to a booth where she slides menus in front of us. Up close she looks tired, like she's been through a lot, and from what Hallie's told me, she has. My eyes scan every inch of the restaurant looking for signs of Hallie, but as far as I can see, there's only her mom and a line cook in the kitchen.

"You know what you want, or you need a minute?" she asks.

"Uh—I'll have some buttermilk pancakes please. And a cup of coffee—black, no room."

"Triple order of hash browns, please," Ajay says as he closes his menu and wiggles his thick, black eyebrows at me.

"You got it," she says and walks off to put in my order. An elderly couple comes in, and Mrs. Baskin acknowledges them by name and seats them at a booth a few down from us. Must be regulars.

"I'm pretty sure that's her mom," I tell Ajay.

"Do you see Hallie?" he asks.

"No."

Mrs. Baskin returns with two mugs of coffee and puts them in front of us. "Food should be up in a minute."

"Why didn't you ask her if she's here?" Ajay says.

"I'm working up to it," I say.

At least, I'm trying to. Who knows what she's told her parents about me, if anything? Something about being here feels wrong, like I'm trespassing. Hallie had been very clear and certain about not wanting to see each other right now. I'm being selfish to walk in here unannounced and uninvited and steamroll over that in the hopes she's changed her mind. And if she does, she's smart and just as capable of tracking me down.

Most likely, she knew what might be ahead and she didn't want me to see her like that, which is completely her right. It's about as personal as it gets and not necessarily the kind of thing you'd be comfortable sharing with someone you've only first started getting to know. I can respect that.

In the aftermath of my dad's death, all I wanted was space. I didn't want to put on a happy face or be on display. For a long time, the first thing anyone asked about was how I was doing, and then after some time had gone by, people stopped asking, and that was hard too. As if they expected that by a certain point, I'd be over it. Healing—emotionally and physically—happens at its own pace, not necessarily the one everyone else is moving at. It's not the sort of thing that can be rushed. There's something in allowing yourself to be exactly where you need to be, whether other people understand it or not, that is essential to the process.

But I do understand it, and that's why I realize I need to leave.

"This is a mistake. We should go," I tell Ajay as I pull out my wallet to throw money on the table for the bill before it even arrives.

"Hold on—we just ordered! What about my hash browns?" Ajay looks like a two-year-old whose balloon popped.

"Seriously?"

"Dude, you need to relax. Just be cool."

Mrs. Baskin brings coffee to the elderly couple, and I can't help but overhear their conversation. The older woman asks Mrs. Baskin, "How is your daughter doing, dear?"

My ears perk up. They're obviously asking her about Hallie. Mrs. Baskin sighs and rests the coffeepot on the table.

"You're so sweet to ask. The surgery went well, but then she developed an infection in the incision site, so they've had to treat that with antibiotics and wait for it to clear up before she can come home. They're saying hopefully by the end of next week. And when she does, she has a long road ahead of her. She'll get tired easily and won't be able to handle much activity for several months. The biggest challenge will be keeping her from pushing herself harder than she should prematurely."

"No, you mustn't rush that sort of thing. Everything in its own time," the older man says.

"Exactly. My Hallie is the most strong-willed girl I've ever met, so if she gets an idea in her head, you can bet she's not going to let go of it. I'll have to tie her down."

They all laugh. Ajay looks me square in the eye. He's eavesdropping as well and raises his eyebrows. I imagine Hallie lying in a hospital bed with tubes coming out of her chest and a nasal cannula. I can visualize the fluorescent lights, the white square ceiling tiles, and the incessant beep and hum of machines. I feel a pull in the center of my chest. I don't want to lose it in the middle of the restaurant.

The older woman says, "I'm sorry for the complications but glad to hear she is on the mend. Please tell her we say hello, and we'll be praying for you all."

"Thank you. I sure will," Mrs. Baskin says as someone in the kitchen yells, "Order up!" On her way to the kitchen, two moms in workout gear come in with their giggly preschoolers in tow, a boy and a girl who are chanting, "Pancakes! Pancakes!" Mrs. Baskin tells them to sit anywhere they'd like as she goes get our food.

"There you go," Ajay whispers. "Feel better now?"

I look at him incredulously. "How could finding out she's in the hospital with post-surgical complications make me feel better?"

"Because at least you know what's going on. Mission accomplished."

Mrs. Baskin returns with our breakfast. The plate has barely touched the table before Ajay dives into his tower of hash browns, no waiting. As I reach for my napkin to put it on my lap, she catches sight of Hallie's bracelet on my wrist.

"Oh—I like your bracelet!" She lights up with a warm smile as she places my pancakes in front of me. "It reminds me of a piece of jewelry my daughter made that looks similar."

I casually rest my arm on my leg, taking it out of view, and say, "Thanks. That's really cool."

"I'm always telling her that she has a beautiful eye for design.

She sees a stone, but to her it's not just a stone. She can wrap metal wire around it in an intricate design and then suddenly turn it into a work of art. She's something." She wedges our check between the salt and pepper shakers. "No rush. Take your time."

No rush. Take your time.

There it is again, like the universe subtly asking me to pay attention. That's it entirely. There's no need to force things or rush them along at an unnatural pace. Not finishing breakfast, seeing Hallie, starting college before I feel ready, figuring out my life, getting over losing Dad or rebuilding things with Alex—none of it. *No rush, take your time.*

I pay the check, and before I leave, I gently unhook Hallie's bracelet and lay it on the table for her mother to find.

On the ride home, Ajay says, "You know what I think? I think you should come with me to Europe."

"Europe?"

"Yeah! It's going to be killer. My cousin Sanjeev's apartment is right in Paris. He's our age, totally chill. We'll use his apartment as a base and take the train all over because the countries are so close. One day we can be taking selfies on Abbey Road and the next, eating a baguette in Paris or checking out the Van Gogh Museum in Amsterdam. Oh—and you'll be so down for this—we can go check out the Computerspielemuseum in Berlin! It's a whole museum of playable video games. It'll be totally lit."

It reminds me of the Pacific Pinball Museum. That does sound pretty amazing. It's not like I've found a job yet or made any other plans. "I don't know..."

"Dude, what could you possibly be doing that would be more

about going with the flow than that? Seriously, my cousin won't mind. His dad, my uncle Dev, is a chef, and he's never home. We'll take you to his restaurant in Paris. It's awesome. C'mon, it'll be an adventure."

Maybe Ajay's right. Getting lost for a month might be exactly what I need to jump-start my thinking about what's next. I have enough in my savings to pay for my ticket, and a free crash pad makes it beyond feasible. Mom's busy all summer focusing on promotion and working on her new book anyway, and this way she wouldn't need to worry about me. There's honestly nothing keeping me here.

I reach in my jeans pocket for my phone to check the calendar even though I know it's empty. As I do, a small crumbled piece of paper dislodges from inside and tumbles on to my lap.

At first, I think it's a piece of a straw wrapper, but it's too wide. I unfold it and realize it's my fortune from Oscar's car. It's been through the wash, and the once-black words are now worn away and a pale, bleached-out lavender, but I can still make them out.

A ship in harbor is safe, but that's not why ships are built.

"I'm in."

25
HALLIE

THURSDAY, DECEMBER 23, 3:13 P.M.

There is no hell quite like a grocery store at Christmastime, especially in the produce section. People are clawing each other over the last russet potatoes, bags of pretrimmed green beans, and veggie platters to the strains of Wham's "Last Christmas." I've offered to pick up the groceries because I finally got around to getting my license last month. I'm still getting used to it, and it hasn't taken long for me to figure out why my mom cusses so much when she drives.

I dig through the bin of cantaloupes, searching for two ripe ones. My family has decided to throw out tradition this year and start a new one. We're making an eclectic buffet of everyone's favorite dishes, one of mine being Mom's melon gazpacho. It's off-season, and most of them are not quite ripe enough. I find a contender and push gently at the stem end of a second one, hoping it yields slightly. *Success!*

I hear a voice to the left of me. "Nice melons."

I freeze. My stomach flip-flops with anxious anticipation at seeing the source of that voice.

Even in this relatively short time, he looks different. His hair is short and tucked into a navy-blue Columbia University baseball cap, his chin now covered by an artfully trimmed beard that makes him look older, and he seems to have grown even taller. It makes me aware of how much time has passed. The minute he smiles, and his eyes crinkle up at the edges like that, I'd recognize him anywhere. My heart feels like it's beating out of my chest.

"Hey," is all I can manage. There's so much to say, and I have no idea where to begin.

By the look on his face, he doesn't either. "I almost didn't recognize you for a sec without your violet hair."

"I let it grow out. Back to my brunette roots," I laugh, suddenly self-conscious, wondering if he thinks it looks better this way.

"It looks good," he replies with an appreciative smile.

"Thanks. I like the beard. Very distinguished," I say as his hand reflexively touches his chin.

"Right? Totally what I was going for. I'm still getting used to it. I've had it a few months now. So..."

"So..."

We share an awkward laugh. "It's funny running into you here."

I smile. "It's a grocery store."

"Yeah, but it's not *my* grocery store. In fact, this is the third grocery store I've been to because apparently there's been a run on pancetta, and there's literally no point in eating brussels sprouts without pancetta, which my mother insists on making because she's on this domestic kick, so I volunteered as tribute to brave the crowds, and here I am." He holds up his package of pancetta like a prize. His face softens. "And here *you* are, fondling melons. It's nice to see you."

"It's nice to see you too." If only he knew how many times in the last six months I've thought about him and regretted not keeping in touch. Eventually I'd managed to convince myself he thought I was a jerk for doing that after everything we'd been through, which I was, and that he'd probably changed his mind about wanting to see each other again anyway. I figured that was why he left my bracelet on the table at The Pancake Palace.

Self-sabotage as a form of control. I am the grandmaster. Or at least I was. I'm trying not to be anymore.

I realize I'm standing there awkwardly clutching two canta-loupes to my chest, and I lay them down in the top section of my grocery cart. I nod my chin in the direction of his hat. "So, did you end up going?"

He reaches up and touches the bill of his hat as if he's first noticed he's wearing it and grins. "Ha! Nope. This was my dad's. I just like to wear it."

"Wow." I bob my head, impressed.

"You sound surprised. Did you think I would?"

"I don't know. It was a lot to walk away from."

"It was a lot to take on." He shrugs. "I think I made the right choice."

"I'm glad." The conversation is so stiff and surface-level

- - 279 - -

compared to the easy-flowing banter we had the last time we saw each other, even though there's no shortage of things to talk about. It's almost like starting over from scratch.

He follows me as I move toward the cucumbers, placing one in my basket. "So—what are you doing? Are you here in LA, working, or…?"

He rakes his fingers through his hair and says, "Yeah, I've been working as an office temp, answering phones, filing papers, running errands, that sort of thing. Saving up money. Plus, I'm also writing, applying to colleges. I'm actually thinking I might want to go to Berkeley."

"Oh, that's awesome." I maneuver my cart to the fresh herbs section in search of fresh mint and cilantro.

"Yeah, I really liked it up there. I got in once, so I hope that's a good sign I can get in again, even if it would be for a different major. Berkeley has an amazing writing program, plus they also have this cool thing they do where you start in the summer, but then you spend fall semester in London and come back for spring semester. It's also near my brother, and it would be nice to be closer to him."

"Totally. How'd that go? Was it good?"

He nods. "Yeah, it was. I mean, it's the kind of thing that takes time. But I think we'll get there. At least we're talking now. So how about you? What are you up to?"

I tell him, "I've just started working part time at a jewelry store, learning about the business and helping in the shop with simple repairs and stuff like that. It's been very interesting and fun. Ultimately, I'm thinking I want to get certified as a gemologist, but that's a way off. I have to save up. I'm looking into getting a degree at community college. Plus, it turns out there's all this free scholarship money if you're a cancer survivor. Silver linings, right?"

"Wow! That's fantastic. Yeah, there's all sorts of stuff out there. You just have to search for it."

A woman turns her cart down the aisle, forcing him to inch closer to me to let her by. I breathe in the familiar lavender smell of his laundry detergent. It reminds me of the time I borrowed his sweatshirt, and the scent had lingered on my clothes. More than once on the bus ride home to LA I'd put my sleeve to my nose and let the smell fill my senses, just as it does now.

He grins and shifts his weight between his feet. "So...I have a confession to make. I came by the restaurant once. I left because I realized I had no right when you'd asked me specifically not to, but I wanted to know if you were okay. To be honest, that was a lot to sit with, not knowing how you were. I, uh—overheard your mom telling this couple that you'd had surgery."

My stomach flip-flops again with guilt about how I'd handled everything. "Yeah. I know. She told me."

His brow creases with confusion. "Your *mom* told you?"

I nod. "When I came home from San Francisco, I explained to her how I knew you and how you'd been at the restaurant that morning I'd left because it was your birthday. After you left her my bracelet, she realized it was you. Thank you for that, by the way." I pull back the cuff of my fuzzy, gray sweater and show him it back on my wrist. I throw two limes in the cart on my way to the avocados and red onions for Dylan's request: Dad's famous guacamole dip.

"Wow. Right. So—you're okay now? I mean—you look great."

"My cancer is in remission with the battle scars to prove it," I tell him with a smile and a thumbs-up.

His face lights up. "That's awesome. I'm glad to hear it. I mean—I didn't know—I didn't know what to think." And then two lines set in on his forehead. "Especially after you didn't show."

Which he could only know if he did. I stop in my tracks. My stomach roils. I turn to face him. "Jack—"

He smiles, holding up a hand, assuring me, "No, it's okay. I almost didn't either. I probably wouldn't have if I hadn't already been up there at the time, checking out Berkeley. I mean—it was a nice idea in theory, but it was unlikely. A total long shot, right? That stuff only happens in movies. Lots of logistics, stuff happens, plans change, but we weren't in touch, so it's not like the other would know."

"I know. And about that—" I begin to say, but he cuts me off.

"To be honest, I wasn't sure if I'd gotten the time wrong, so I showed up at both high tides just in case."

I picture him standing there just after midnight on that peninsula in the freezing cold waiting for me. And then later he came back a second time. My stomach churns. I'd convinced myself he wouldn't show up for all the reasons he said and more. I wish I could rewind and do it differently. I deserve to feel every bit as awful as I must have made him feel. There are a million things I could say, excuses I could make, but for now all that comes is, "I'm sorry."

"No, seriously, it's all good because here's the thing: I *knew* you wouldn't come. And that's not a judgment. I'm not upset or holding on to it in any way. I get it because I tend to be cherophobic too."

"Cherophobic?"

He smiles. "Let me Human Google that for you. Cherophobia is the irrational fear of joy. Being convinced that happiness is impermanent and always expecting things to fall apart and go wrong instead of believing they might actually go right. But I figured what the hell, and I took a chance. Because what if I didn't show up and you did?"

He huffs a single laugh, but the look in his eyes is pure hurt. An older woman shopping nearby for tomatoes turns and glares at me disapprovingly. He isn't wrong. I'd done exactly what I was sure he'd do to me. "I'm sorry. You deserved better than that."

"So did you," he says.

"I wanted to be there. I honestly did."

"Like I said, I get it. It's all good. Besides, you once said if we were meant to find each other again, we would, right? Well—here we are. Aisle twelve. Produce."

Glaring Tomato Lady is clearly eavesdropping, taking way too long to make her selection. Jack picks up on it too. He winks at me, reaches out and grabs a beefsteak tomato, then hands it to her. "This looks like an excellent one, don't you think? Plump and juicy with smooth skin?"

She looks at him with surprise, accepting it from him and scurries away. I can't help but smile. It makes me remember how much he made me laugh. I find myself asking, "What are you doing right now?"

"Procuring pancetta," he says, holding up the box again.

"I mean after that."

He shakes his head. "Not much."

"Do you want to go somewhere?"

"With you?"

"Yes, with me."

"Absolutely. Where?"

"Does it matter?"

"Not in the slightest."

Jack follows me home and waits in the driveway while I go inside to drop off the groceries and tell my parents I'll be back in a few hours.

My heart is beating a mile a minute as I climb into the black, leather front seat of his car. Definitely a step up from Mom's Toyota Sienna. The familiarity of being with him in this sort of enclosed space comes rushing back.

He grins at me.

"What?" I ask.

"Where should we go?"

By this point, the sky is growing dark and all the Christmas lights and decorations kick on. "I don't care. Maybe we could just get a hot chocolate, drive around, and look at the lights or something," I suggest.

"I'm down with that," he says as he shifts the car into reverse. "It's funny, you made me think of this memory from when I was a little kid. My parents brought a thermos of hot chocolate, packed my brother and me in the car, and drove out to this one street in the San Fernando Valley to look at all the lights. People would come from all over. It was actually famous."

"Candy Cane Lane!" I tell him excitedly. "My parents took Dylan and me there a few times too."

"I can't believe you know it. That's so funny."

"It's actually a big thing. It's on Yelp. That's totally where we should go!"

"Let's do it."

We zigzag our way up Laurel Canyon to Mulholland where we can see all the twinkling lights of the city on our left and the San Fernando Valley on our right. As we cut down through the hills, past homes dangling on cliffsides, I ask, "So how about you? Tell me everything. Don't leave out a word."

He smiles. "Well, after I decided not to go to New York, I ended up spontaneously going to Europe for the summer with my best friend Ajay, and meeting his cousin Sanjeev and his uncle Dev. Their apartment is a cramped, unspectacular shoebox in a neighborhood littered with graffiti a few blocks from the Louvre, but it's freaking Paris. Ajay and I spent a month having a blast traveling all over. And then I got to thinking how incredible it would be to stay on for another month or two and just plant myself at one of a hundred amazing-looking sidewalk cafes I'd seen and drink copious amounts of espresso and write."

"That's literally, like, a fantasy," I tell him.

"Exactly. But there I was, and suddenly this was my life. Ajay's cousin Sanjeev invited me to stay with him. It didn't seem right to hang around without contributing anything, especially with Ajay gone, so I helped his uncle Dev out at his restaurant at night in exchange for room and board. Sanjeev taught me about spices and cooking and how to make a seafood paella that would knock your socks off."

"Wow. Did you just keep pinching yourself?"

"Right? For one solid month, I'd spend half the day writing and the other half getting lost in museums and exploring Paris. I highly recommend it. It doesn't have to be Paris; just getting outside your normal day-to-day reality gives clarity and perspective. It lets you hear yourself think."

"Sounds amazing. So, did you finish your book? I want to read it!"

"Almost. I'm about two-thirds done with the first draft, but I've realized that whatever I do, it needs to be creative, and that I want writing to be a key part of it. It also made me decide that no matter where I end up next, I don't want it to be Los Angeles. I've lived here my whole life. I want to experience different places."

I ask him more about his book as we wind through the Starbucks drive-through and get two venti hot chocolates. According to the GPS, Candy Cane Lane is minutes away. "So, do you know how you want it to end? Do the guy and girl find each other?"

"That's the beauty of a choose-your-own-ending novel. There isn't just one. Anything is possible. It boils down to if you're a pessimist or an optimist."

"Which are you?"

"I'm like a pessimistic optimist," he says, and we share a laugh. "But I'm hopeful for them. It would be nice for the characters to get what they think they want, but maybe that isn't how things are supposed to go. This could be the end of their story, or it might be where it actually begins. But either way, I'd hope they'd remain friends, or at the minimum, exchange numbers and keep in touch."

"I feel like we're not just talking about the book." I point to the street sign up ahead. "I think this is it. Make a right here."

"Wait! This moment needs a soundtrack," he says and fumbles with his phone making a selection. I'm expecting something like "Jingle Bell Rock," but suddenly the car is flooded with ABBA's "Dancing Queen."

"Perfect."

We turn onto what is known as Candy Cane Lane and take in the ornate displays on house after house, one outdoing the next. The lights are beautiful. The homeowners have put so much time into this for no other reason than to share joy and make people smile. Jack looks at me and smiles then says softly, "You should know that when I leave in a few months, I'm not sure when I'm coming back."

I infer what he's saying without him having to say it. I mean— what did I expect? Still, my stomach sinks a little. "Well, then, I guess we're continuing our tradition of driving in cars, listening to ABBA, talking, visiting random attractions, and then going our separate ways."

"It is definitely shaping up to be our thing." He bobs his head and cracks a half smile.

"Along with really crappy timing."

"The crappiest."

We marvel at a house with an inflatable Santa the size of a whale. "So where should we go next?"

He strokes his beard thoughtfully. "Hmmm. I've always wanted to see the world's largest ball of twine in Cawker, Kansas."

"Twine? C'mon, we can do better than that."

"You have a better suggestion?"

"I don't know. I'm thinking Ostrichland could be cool. It's

not that far, and they have emus too. You can feed them. It looks kind of fun."

He laughs. "Okay, Ostrichland is officially on the list."

"We have a list?"

"I think we may have just started one. And we can...you know, keep adding to it as we think of more places."

I'm grinning ear to ear, imagining a list of adventures and a lifetime ahead in which to have them.

"So, where do we go from here?" I ask him.

"I don't know. Maybe we could start by exchanging numbers. And from there, we can let it be a surprise, like a gift our future selves get to unwrap." I smile, remembering saying those same words to him the last time we met.

He laces his fingers through mine, and we fall quiet after that, each of us just looking out the windows at the lights, blending our individual memories of the past with the ones we're building this very second.

He's right. We have time to figure it out as we go. Sometimes the best plan is having no plan.

ACKNOWLEDGMENTS

A week after my first book, *My Kind of Crazy*, came out, my father was diagnosed with esophageal cancer. I was due to turn in this book months later and suddenly found myself on an emotionally grueling yearlong journey navigating my father's heartbreaking illness, followed by another two processing the gravity of his passing. I completely shut down, and writing was the farthest thing from my mind, until ultimately, it became my way back. But I could never have gotten from here to there without the help, love, and guidance of some pretty phenomenal people.

First, thank you to my magnificent, hilarious, brilliant agent Leigh Feldman, for your patience, faith, wisdom, and guidance. I couldn't wish for a better wingwoman to help me navigate my career. I truly hit the jackpot.

Gratitude beyond measure to my incredible editor, Eliza Swift, whose vision and careful curation of these characters pushed me in all the best ways to find the beating heart of the story and bring it to another level. And to my publisher Dominique Raccah, who patiently and compassionately waited while I found my words, and for the continued gift of giving them a home. Over the top thank-yous to my production editor Cassie Gutman and my copyeditor

Manuela Velasco for making me look like I'm great at grammar and punctuation (and know my days of the week), and to Kelly Lawler, Nicole Hower, Helen Crawford-White, and Michelle Mayhall for that absolutely stunning cover, design, and illustrations! Additional thanks to marketing mavens Beth Oleniczak, Jackie Douglass, and Valerie Pierce, the fantastic sales team at Sourcebooks Fire, and to Sarah Kasman for reading those not-ready-for-prime-time drafts.

Thank you to my first editor, Annette Pollert-Morgan, who lovingly helped me grow this book in its early stages and has always remained a mentor and friend.

I could never have gotten through these last few years without the support and friendship from my writer tribe. Giant tackle hugs of love and appreciation to Demetra Brodsky, Gae Polisner, Lorianne Tibbetts, Nicole Maggi, Beth Navarro, Nadine Semerau, Romina Garber, Catherine Linka, Tracy Holczer, Misa Sugiura, Jeff Garvin, Jessica Brody, Gretchen McNeil, Courtney Saldana (my fave honorary member), too many to mention! And a special shout-out to all my amazing fellow LAYA writers, too many to mention, especially the Writer's Night Out crew!

Nothing but deep love for my friends that are like family to me and have always been there to cheerlead me on and lift me up in ways too numerous to mention: Susan Wolf and Marcus Ryle; Rachel and Todd Greenwald; Jill, Charlie, and Joey; and Chris Sheridan, Brittnee Bui, George Brooks, Jill Freeman, Alison Kinney (and Princess!), Ilene Keys Bobrowsky, Cori Henry, Debbie Blander, Julie Holliday, Teresa Rowen, Lisa Ross, Deb Sayer, Nancy Baca, Jenny Thullier, Julie Hallowell, Jacob Walker, Arun Burra, and especially my Witches of Westlake. My cup runneth over.

At the heart of everything is my amazing family, especially my incredible husband John, my rock, who has always pushed me to follow my dreams and given me the ability to make them come true. Thank you for making me laugh with your crazy songs, your Johnisms, your spontaneous dance parties, and most of all for being such a genuine, kindhearted, sushi-loving soul who keeps me grounded. On every level, this book would not exist if not for you. I lava you so!

Ethan and Katie, my finest work of all: may you always follow the path that feels true to your heart and know you are loved and supported in all you do.

Bonnie, Lily, Ben, Lee, Sasha, and John: thank you for all your positive energy, kindness, and always allowing me a soft place to land.

And Joy and Mark for the long-distance cheerleading and love.

To my beautiful mother, Sunny: I'm so grateful for your unwavering love and support and belief in me and my writing. I love you so much, and I am so proud of who you have become in the wake of such deep loss. You have inspired me these past few years beyond measure with your strength and resilience. You've taught me that it is what it is and that sometimes you just have to let it be, and sometimes you gotta change the app.

And last, but definitely not least, to my father, Jack. I love you and miss you every single day beyond comprehension. How I wish you could have been here to see this, but I felt you with me every moment, every word. Turns out you got a kid named after you after all.

ABOUT THE AUTHOR

Robin Reul is the author of *My Kind of Crazy* and *Where the Road Leads Us*. She has been writing stories since she was old enough to hold a pen. Born and raised in Los Angeles, she grew up on movie sets and worked for many years in the entertainment industry but ultimately decided to focus her attention on writing young adult novels. When's she's not busy making stuff up, she can be found in the wilds of LA suburbia drinking copious amounts of iced coffee, making her way through her TBR pile, and spending time with family and friends. Visit her website at robinreul.com and find her on Twitter, Instagram, and Facebook.